three
is a war
TANGLED LIES
PAM GODWIN

Copyright © 2017 by Pam Godwin

All rights reserved.

Cover Artist: Okay Creations
Interior Designer: Pam Godwin
Editor: Lesa Godwin, Godwin Proofing

This is a work of fiction. Names, characters, places, and incidents are the product of the author's imagination or are used fictitiously, and any resemblance to actual persons, living or dead, events, or locales is entirely coincidental.
No part of this book may be reproduced in any form, except for the inclusion of brief quotations in a review or article, without written permission from the author.

Visit www.pamgodwin.com

disclaimer

If you have not read books 1 and 2, STOP!

The books in the TANGLED LIES series are not stand-alones.
They must be read in order.
One is a Promise
Two is a Lie
Three is a War

epigraph

"Love does not begin and end the way we seem to think
it does.
Love is a battle.
Love is a war.
Love is a growing up."
James A. Baldwin

one

A heavy fog smothers my senses, trapping me in a netherworld between dreams and nightmares. Did I fall asleep? Am I awake? Why do I feel so uncomfortably warm and fuzzy?

I struggle to understand, my brain sluggish and not cooperating. Somewhere in the distance, the sound of a heartbeat whooshes a muffled rhythm.

My heartbeat?

Slowly, softly, my hearing clears. Then silence.

Something isn't right. I was outside just a second ago, freezing my tits off. Wasn't I in my car?

Think, Danni. Think.

I blink, and blink again. Why am I lying on my back staring at a ceiling I've never seen before?

Memories blur to the surface, each one spooling in

a drunken ribbon of confusion. The car wouldn't start. I climbed out to call a tow truck. Lost my balance. Ate the pavement. Then everything starts to warp—the buzzing in my ears, tunnel vision, disorientation. Shouldn't I be in pain from the fall?

I lift my hands toward my face, and my fingers contort in front of me, familiar yet strange. A piece of medical tape peeks around the base of my thumb, and I turn my wrist, following it to a white bandage on my palm.

Only one hand is wrapped. Did I catch myself on the driveway? With one arm?

I was holding a coffee cup.

As if a switch is flipped in my head, my senses snap online, launching me into a coherent state of realization.

Cole or Trace left coffee on my doorstep.

The car engine wouldn't turn over.

I fainted.

The coffee.

Oh my God, there was handwriting on the bottom of the cup.

It's not over.

What's not over? Cole's secret job? The revenge attempts against him? Whatever it is, I've been pulled into it.

A jolt of adrenaline spikes through me, energizing every muscle in my body. I lurch into a sitting position, swaying with wooziness.

Where am I?

The large bed beneath me sits across from an open doorway that leads to a dark hallway. Sheer drapes cover two perpendicular walls of the bedroom, filtering what

three is a war

appears to be full-length windows and a gray sky. If the sun is setting, I've been unconscious for hours.

Panic rises, chopping my gasps. Whose house is this? How did I get here?

I force myself to go still, listening.

Dead air.

It's so quiet the hairs lift on my nape, and every breath I take sounds like a hurricane. I need to get the hell out of here.

I need a weapon.

A round glass lamp sits on the side table. No clock or phone. But the massive bedroom reeks of wealth, from the opulent crown molding to the intricately carved wood-burning hearth.

My attention locks on the fireplace tools that hang on a stand. The wrought-iron poker looks heavy. And sharp enough to stab someone.

I shove a fleece blanket off my legs. I'm dressed in jeans, a sweater, and socks—everything I put on this morning. My knee-high cognac boots sit on the floor beside the bed.

No coat, which is where I stored my phone. *Fuck.*

Slipping off the bed, I yank on the boots and tiptoe toward the fireplace. Every step creaks the wood floors, shattering the stillness and chilling my spine in a cold sweat. I feel weak, unsteady, and slightly buzzed.

Someone delivered my favorite coffee to the back door of my house.

I was drugged.

It's the only explanation for my blackout and transport to…wherever this is. Neither Cole nor Trace would do this to me, but their enemies would. The sort of enemies who get their throats cut in my house and leave devastating photos in my car.

My heart rate explodes as I run the final few feet to the fireplace and snatch the poker. It won't stop a bullet, but it's better than nothing.

Cole and Trace would go ballistic if they knew someone touched me, let alone sedated and kidnapped me. Is that what this is? A kidnapping? I'm not tied up or beaten, and the bedroom door is open. But I didn't consent to this.

Full-body tremors lock my joints and quiver my chin. Why am I here?

Ransom?

Torture for information?

I lift my wrapped hand and peel off the bandage. A few minor scrapes redden my palm, nothing deep enough to warrant first-aid. If someone intends to harm me, why bother mending me at all?

None of this makes sense. I'm so out of my league and terrified it's crippling. I need to do something before they come in to check on me.

The curtained windows loom at my back, pulling me in that direction. Maybe there's an exterior door?

I step toward it, keeping an eye on the ominous hallway while fighting to silence the heaving of my breaths. Everything inside me wants to curl up and hide, but I keep moving until I reach the closest exterior wall.

Wrestling with the linen curtains, I find the seam, pull them open, and choke on a sharp inhale.

Gray leafless trees bristle like spines on hillsides that ripple toward the horizon. The woodland surrounds a calm inlet of water and a well-kept private dock. I've vacationed in southern Missouri often enough to recognize the vista of forest, high bluffs, waterways.

Given the position of the sun behind the lake in the distance, I must've been unconscious for four or five hours. Long enough to make a drive from St. Louis to the lower part of the state.

Someone carried and transported my limp body. Anything could've happened to me while I was dead to the world. My skin crawls, and I jump at the sound of an air vent clicking on.

The windows appear to slide open like doors along a track. When I pull on the handles, they don't budge. A keypad on the wall requires a code to open them. *Shit.*

I test the weight of the poker in my hand. If I swing it at the glass, it'll only jar my arm and alert whomever is here. I need to find another way out.

The 180-degree view gives me a decent layout of the back of the house—a massive one-story manor veneered in stone that wraps around several outdoor living spaces with walkways that lead into the woods. From the largest terrace, a bridge arches over a ravine, providing access to the covered dock on the lake.

I bet there's an enclosed slip at the dock. Maybe several. With boats. I've never operated any kind of watercraft, but I'll figure it out if it's a means to escape.

First, I need to leave this room, and the hallway is my only exit.

I feel like I'm going to throw up with every step toward the door. My heart is a booming drum, my insides frozen and trembling. At the threshold to the hall, I tighten my grip on the poker and strain my hearing.

The faint vibration of rock music thumps from somewhere at the other end of the house. It doesn't sound far away. More like the volume is set on low.

A knot of nerves strangles my throat as I creep along the hallway, following the random-sized pieces of slate that tile the floor. Some of the doors I pass are locked with keypads. Others are open, revealing more large bedrooms, each vacant and tidy, with the same natural hues and picturesque windows.

Whoever owns this place is wealthy and wouldn't need to capture a woman for ransom. Unless the payment for my release isn't related to money.

Trace could afford this property, but the modern design isn't his style. I can't picture him hanging out in a huge contemporary mansion in rustic-nowhere Missouri away from his work. Besides, if he wanted me here, he wouldn't drug me to make it happen.

Holding the poker out in front of me, I sneak around a corner and stop.

The corridor descends down a gradual slope of stairs that spill into a brightly-lit living room. Brown leather furniture occupies the center, and it isn't empty.

Someone's sitting on the couch.

I press my back against the wall and hold my breath. I can only make out a man's denim-clad legs, bent at the knees where he reclines. Did he see me? My heart hammers so loudly he can probably hear me freaking the fuck out.

The low rumble of a rock song drifts along the blond maple flooring and echoes through the soaring ceilings. The sound is coming from the TV on the wall beyond the sitting area. I know the melody—the dynamic vocals over electronic and heavy metal instrumentation. I squint at the song title on the bottom of the screen.

Go To War by Nothing More.

three is a war

A chill trickles down my spine. I've heard Cole play that song while working out. Maybe it's just a coincidence.

I tighten my grip on the poker and fix my attention on the man's legs. Frayed jeans, tanned bare feet, spread knees. I can't see the rest of him, but it looks like Cole.

That can't be right. Why would he be sitting here while I'm passed out and left alone in a strange house? Is he in trouble? Was he kidnapped, too?

With my back pressed to the wall, I gulp down my terror and edge forward on shaky legs. Every step down the long stairs requires stealth, vigilance, and a plan—none of which I possess. All I want to do is run back to the bedroom and hide under the bed.

When I reach the bottom stair, I see him.
Cole.

Stubble darkens his handsome profile, his brown hair tousled and physique seemingly stronger, bulkier, than the last time I saw him.

It's been five weeks.

My pulse slams into overdrive, and a sharp pain stabs my chest.

I kicked him out. Changed my number. Sold my house. I never thought I'd see him again.

And here he is.

He doesn't look at me, his attention transfixed on something I can't see. But I'm in his periphery. Experience tells me he's far more observant than he's letting on. He knows I'm here.

My stomach hardens as I watch him, waiting for a sign, a verbal cue, anything to clue me in on how to proceed.

Seconds pass like hours. My shoulders tighten, my heart rate reaching dangerous levels. Why isn't he speaking or moving? I need to know what he's looking at.

With the poker gripped in a clammy hand, I lean forward, stretching as far as possible while remaining hidden. When the width of the room comes into view, my heart slams to a stop.

Trace.

He stands behind a second couch, his arctic blue eyes and angry scowl trained on Cole. The sight of him in a t-shirt and dark denim jeans is arresting, but that isn't what holds my breath hostage.

He's aiming a handgun, finger on the trigger, directly at Cole.

"How are you feeling, baby?" Cole doesn't take his eyes off Trace.

I jerk my head back, and a sudden coldness hits my core. Cole's talking to me? Why is his tone so casual? Like he's not staring down the barrel of a gun. Like I wasn't drugged and kidnapped and dropped in the most fucked-up situation imaginable. What the fuck is going on?

"Danni." Trace cuts his eyes to me and returns to Cole. "Put down the poker and come sit down."

This isn't happening. They wouldn't have done this.

"Please tell me you're not responsible for drugging and kidnapping me." My voice is reedy, halting, disbelieving.

They continue to stare at each other in silence, with that damn gun hovering between them.

"Is anyone else here?" I grip the wall and scan the

three is a war

living room and open kitchen on the far end.

"Just the three of us." Cole stretches his arms across the back of the couch, making his chest a bigger target for Trace's bullet. "One big happy family."

I have so many questions, and my composure is eroding by the second. Fear from moments ago, grief from the past five weeks, the devastation of their betrayal, the utter shock and relief in seeing them both again—all of it churns into a cauldron of bubbling, maniacal emotions. My throat swells. My eyes burn, and the fireplace poker trembles so violently in my hand I can't hold onto it.

"Trace?" I set the poker on the stairs and take a cautious step forward, tears welling. "Did you do this? Did you kidnap us?"

It kills me to think he might've resorted to this level of madness, but he's holding a gun. I didn't even know he owned one.

He laughs, a cold cavernous sound. "Explain to me why you think I'm the bad guy."

I open my mouth to mention the weapon, but my assumption might be wrong. What if Cole kidnapped me and Trace showed up to save me?

That doesn't feel right, though. This entire situation is fucking with my head, but there's one thing I know for sure.

"You like to have the upper hand." I swallow, eyes on Trace. "When I left you, I took away your control over me. Is that what this is? Are you taking the control back?" I pause behind the chair that sits crosswise between them. "Please, put down the gun."

"Or shoot me already." With a humorless grin,

Cole softly sings along with the vocals of the song, taunting Trace with an arrogant lack of concern.

His beautiful voice is unnervingly distracting. Deep and seductive, he carries a humming tune, mouthing the aggressive lyrics about corrosion of trust, loss of security, and the total breakdown of love.

The song pretty much sums up the state of our ruined relationships. We circled an unsolvable problem, inadvertently tangling a web around us. Lies, jealousy, resentment, stubborn love, all of it spinning us into a vicious spiral. The more we struggled, the stickier and tighter the web became. So I walked away, gave up everything I loved, before it was too late to escape.

Or so I thought.

"I have more control than you know, Danni." Trace holds the gun steady, arm stretched and trained on Cole. "But that's not what this is about."

"You're holding Cole at gunpoint, and that has nothing to do with me?" I feel sick to my stomach with anxiety.

"We're just settling a disagreement." Trace scans my hunched, swaying stance. "Sit your ass down before you pass out."

"I'm not moving until you put away the gun."

"She's not impressed with your weapon, asshole." Cole smirks. "No wonder she left you."

"I left you, too," I whisper.

A dismal cloud darkens Cole's expression, and his hands clench on the back of the couch.

"Have you both lost your minds?" I stab a shaky finger between them, my voice rising to a teary shrill. "I quit this and moved on. I'm supposed to be on my way to a new life right now. A new life *without you*. So I'm

three is a war

struggling to understand why I'm here, knee-deep in your toxic, manipulative bullshit."

"How's that going for you?" Cole tilts his head, giving me the full brunt of his gaze.

"What?"

"Your life." His jaw sets. "Moving on. Without me."

It's only been five weeks, and I feel like a severed, broken sliver of the person I was. I've lost weight, lost energy, lost the will to do anything. The move to Florida is supposed to be a change of scenery, a way out of this miserable goddamn rut. But I'm not telling him any of that.

"Which one of you drugged me?" My throat scratches, my eyes gummy with hot tears.

Trace regards me for a moment, his brows pulling in and expression pained. Then he lowers the gun and releases the magazine into his hand.

"Do you have any idea how scared I was?" The muscles in my neck strain to the point of pain. "I woke alone, in a strange room, thinking the worst. I didn't know who took me, why I was here, or what would happen to me."

"I know my apology has no weight under the circumstances." Trace empties the chamber on the gun and sets the pieces on the sofa table before him. Then his blue eyes lift to mine. "But I'm sorry. We stepped out of your room to settle a dispute."

"It was a lapse in judgment." Cole bends forward, elbows on his knees, and regards me with shadows in his gaze. "We're both at fault. I'm sorry, too."

They're apologizing for leaving me unattended?

What about the whole damn kidnapping thing? Maybe it's the drugs, but I'm having a really hard time understanding what the living fuck is going on.

"Why did you do this?" I hug my waist, working to keep my blubbering emotions under control. "Why am I here?"

"You haven't danced since you left," Trace says softly.

I look away and grind my teeth. "You were watching me?"

"Always."

"My house is still bugged?"

My old house. The reminder that I sold it makes my chest hurt.

"I reinstalled the cameras the day I moved out." Cole studies me intently.

"It was all an illusion then." My voice rasps, thick with resentment. "I was never free of you." A hollow laugh bubbles up, choked by a sob. "You let me walk out of the penthouse that day, with every intention of monitoring me? That's so fucking ironic, because your cameras and listening devices and constant invasion of my privacy were big reasons why I left."

If they've been watching me, they know just how wretched I've been without them. I haven't been eating, dancing, or living. I haven't done anything but miss them with every goddamn pang in my chest.

How fucked up is that? To ache for not one but *two* men who lie and cheat and manipulate at every turn? Oh, and now I can add drugs and kidnapping to the list of reasons why I should be looking for a phone and reporting their asses to the authorities.

Is this Trace's estate? I don't even know where I

three is a war

am. "What is this place?"

Cole meets Trace's eyes and shifts his unblinking glare to me. "This is where we finish this."

two

"Finish what?" I gape at Cole, my pulse thrashing at the base of my throat. "No, never mind. I quit this shit five weeks ago, which means I'm done. It's over."

I whirl toward the front entry and take off at a sprint. Maybe there's a car outside or neighbors who can help me. Or maybe there's not. I just need to get the fuck out of here.

When I reach the door, I find it locked with another keypad.

"Let me out, dammit." I yank frantically on the handle, heaving with desperation. "You can't keep me here."

Their silence heats my blood, and I pivot to face them.

"Are you holding me hostage?" I glare at Trace's

irritatingly composed expression.

"We didn't kidnap you." Cole stands from the couch. "And we're not holding you here."

"You're a liar, Cole." I release the door and storm back toward them. "One of you drugged me and brought me here. Or was it both of you? Are you working together now?"

Trace scowls at Cole. Neither of them speak.

Two seconds ago, I walked in on a standoff with a gun. It's safe to assume that whatever arrangement they've cooked up is unstable at best.

I veer past them and check the patio doors. All locked with keypads. Circling the kitchen island, I search for another way out. "What was your disagreement about?"

"You've made some poor choices." Trace clasps his hands behind his back and follows me at a distance. "Specifically, your decision to move halfway across the country."

"It was the smartest decision I've made since I met you." I swing open a door in the kitchen, revealing a massive pantry. *Damn.* "Where's the garage?"

Open shelving on the kitchen's raw wood walls displays dishes and cookware. The floor plan is simple, airy, and bright, as if designed to pull visitors toward the exterior views of the lake and woodland.

There's another door beyond the built-in refrigerator, the wood frame blending with the maple cabinetry. I bet it leads to a garage.

"You're free to go." Cole prowls around the long kitchen island, standing opposite of Trace and corralling me in. "*After* I explain a few things and deliver your punishment."

three is a war

"Punishment?" My jaw drops, and my heart rate explodes. "Are you serious?"

Trace assumes an imposing stance, hands behind him, blocking my path to the garage door. His eyes flick between Cole and the gun on the table. "We haven't agreed on *who* is punishing her."

"*That* was the disagreement?" I stab my fingers through my hair, my voice pitching with disbelief. "You wanted to be the one to *punish* me, so you pulled a gun on Cole?"

"I want to be the only one putting a hand on you. *Ever.*"

"This is nuts." I try to dart around him, but he shifts with me, trapping me behind the island. I turn to Cole, who barricades the other end. I'll scratch and claw my way past them if I need to. "We're over. No more talking. No more punish—"

"You kicked me out of *our* house." Cole stalks closer, six feet away, three feet, every long stride forcing me backward toward Trace. "I haven't talked to you or touched you in weeks. Not cool, baby. Your ass is going to be so fucking red you won't be able to sit down for days."

"You cheated on me!" A sob rises up, shaking my shoulders. "I waited for you, mourned your death, while you were banging another woman!"

"Are you hearing this?" Cole glowers at Trace and thrusts a finger in my direction. "She just proved my fucking point. I win."

Trace's nostrils widen with a heavy inhale before he gives a slight nod. "Fine."

What the hell just happened? I swat a lock of hair

from my face, my vision blurring with tears. "You win what exactly?"

"*I* will be the one punishing you." Cole's eyes dance with ruthless fire. "And you'll love every minute of it."

"No, Cole." I ball my hands at my sides, my voice simmering with venom. "*You* will take your verbal masturbation and shove it up your cocky, lying, cheating ass!"

"There she is." Trace's scowl lifts at the corner.

"What does that mean?" I angrily swipe at the moisture on my cheek.

"You lost that feisty attitude over the past few months. I hoped this…action plan would inspire it to return."

"By *action plan* you mean knocking me unconscious and dragging me into the middle of nowhere?"

"Yes." Trace tilts his head, his towering frame deadly still.

"Move out of my way." I hold my fists at my sides.

"Danni—"

"I want to leave gently, gracefully. Give me that." I lower my tone. "Let. Me. Go."

"You don't get to go gentle." Cole leans in, his breath heating my neck. "Not when you have a reason to fight."

"Fight for what? Can you not see how hopeless this is?" I plaster my back against the cabinet, hemmed in and restless for space. "We're a tangled, damaged, unfortunate tragedy of love. I'm not fighting for that."

"You will." Trace steps to the side, opening a path to escape.

I take it, running toward the door at the edge of the

three is a war

kitchen and finding a three-car garage on the other side.

Cole's motorcycle, multiple ATVs, and a black Range Rover fill the stalls. I close the door, leaving them in the kitchen, and scour the garage for keys. Nothing. The SUV is the only vehicle that can get me back to civilization, and all the doors are locked. *Fuck.*

Maybe there are more cars in the driveway? I circle back and hit the button that lifts the garage doors. I'm surprised Cole and Trace haven't followed me. It's not a good sign. If there's a chance I can leave, I'm certain they'll prevent it. Doesn't stop me from racing into the blast of cold air outside of the garage.

The half-circle driveway is empty. My shoulders fall, and the frigid temperatures shiver through my bones. I don't have a coat or a phone. My stiletto boots are sexy as hell, but I won't last a mile in them.

I walk to the end of the black asphalt and pause at the narrow dirt road that winds into the woods. The estate sits on a dead end. No other houses. No rumble of traffic in the distance. Total isolation.

Dusk blankets the surrounding forest of leaf-less trees in a gray gloom, the sky growing darker by the minute. My only option is to go back inside, but my boots remain rooted to the pavement.

It's peaceful out here. Calming. Other than the sounds of squirrels rustling the undergrowth and the occasional chirrup of a bird, it's noiseless. Lifeless. Completely void of drama and trickery.

A cobblestone sidewalk leads away from the driveway and curves around the wing of the estate, the path illuminated by dim lights. I follow it, wishing I had my coat as the chilly breeze penetrates my sweater.

Gurgling, river-rock streams and mulched footpaths trail off in every direction, begging to be explored. Most lead into the woods. Others point the way to patios and exterior doors of the house.

I stick to the main walkway, which takes me to the rear terrace. The kitchen and living room are visible beyond the full-length windows, but I don't see Cole or Trace. They're probably watching me on hidden cameras, the fuckers.

From there, I cross the bridge that descends to the dock on the cove. The tree-lined shores wrap around calm dark water that stretches for miles. Several boat lights bob in the horizon, far outside of hearing range and not likely to venture near this inlet.

A metal gate bars entry to the covered dock. *Another keypad.* But when I pull the handle, the latch buzzes an electronic sound and opens. I look back at the house. Are they controlling it remotely?

Overhead bulbs light the way as I walk down the center between the boat slips. I pass a ski boat, fishing boat, pontoon, several jet skis—all buttoned up with heavy tarp. Even if I could unsnap the covers and find a key, where the hell would I go on a lake in the middle of January? It's off-season, and this part of the state is a ghost town.

I continue to the end of the dock, where it opens to the cove. Benches bolt to the uncovered section of the dock, facing the water. I lower onto one of the seats and wrap my arms around myself, shuddering against the cold.

The lake is so still it looks like black tar, enrobed by the shadows of skeletal trees. I bet the landscape is stunning in the warmer months.

three is a war

I glance over my shoulder at the stone-veneered lakefront estate. It has panoramic views from every room, lavishly set on acres of raw wilderness. The natural rock and wrought-iron terrace is beautifully landscaped with archway columns and discreet lighting. A private dock, six boat slips, no neighbors — it's a recluse's paradise.

If this is Trace's property, why didn't I know about it? Maybe it belongs to a friend? Maybe I should just head back inside and ask them. Cole said I was free to go after he talked to me and delivered my punishment.

My skin heats at the thought of him spanking me. I close my eyes, hating the way he still affects me. They both have so much power over my reactions. Too much. Even after the lies and the betrayal and the cheating, I want them.

This is why I can't be near them. I don't trust myself.

I don't trust my heart.

Leaving them went against my deepest instincts, and it hurts. It terrifies me. They make my pulse race and my head spin and stir things in me I'll never experience with another person.

My life began and ended with them. I might be able to physically move on, but I'm not kidding myself. I will never get over them.

While I had to stop the toxic cycle we were in, I never stopped loving them. The rare and beautiful thing I had with each of them was strangled by lies, gutted by broken promises, and infected with poisonous distrust.

I'm just as much to blame for its corruption. I hurt them with my indecisiveness. I held their hearts in my hands and forced them to bend painfully, unnaturally, to gain pieces of mine.

My weak, naive selfishness didn't solve a damn thing. I broke us, kiss by jealous kiss, breath by greedy breath.

What do I do now? Should I listen to what they have to say at the risk of being pulled into their lies? Or should I stay clear of them and get the hell back to St. Louis?

The sky darkens to a sooty black, and the cold air seeps in. I tug the sleeves of my sweater over my hands, stalling, waiting. It won't be long before they show up.

Just as I thought, less than a minute passes before footsteps sound on the dock. Except I only hear one set of treads. Probably Trace, since he's the one with the gun.

I don't turn to look as my visitor stops behind me and drapes a fleece blanket around my shoulders.

"Thank you." I burrow into the warmth, savoring the masculine scent that infuses the heavy material.

Strong, powerful legs fill my view—thick muscle beneath frayed jeans and heavy boots.

Cole.

He lowers onto the bench beside me, and the wood creaks under the weight.

"Did you steal Trace's gun?" I keep my eyes on the water, refusing to sink into the seductive pull of his.

"No." He stretches out a leg and reclines back. "He knows this conversation is between you and me."

I assume that means he's here to make excuses about his affair. "Where are we? Southern Missouri?"

"Yeah. Stone County." He flicks a finger at the lake. "That's—"

"Table Rock Lake. I know the area. We used to vacation here when I was a kid." I can't ignore the heat of

three is a war

his body so close to mine, so I scoot a few inches away. "Who owns the house?"

"I do."

"What?" My pulse kicks up. "How can you afford it?" Curiosity turns my head, and I plummet into his deep brown gaze. "Did your government job pay for it?"

"Not the government, but my skill set made me a wealthy man."

"I don't understand. You worked a minimum wage security job. I thought you needed money."

"That's an assumption *you* made."

"You never corrected me."

His jaw flexes. "There were side jobs over the years, as well as other means to collect assets."

"What other means? Or is that another secret you can't tell me?"

"No more secrets." He bends forward, forearms on his spread knees, and stares at the lake, seemingly gathering his thoughts.

His breath releases in white clouds, his black leather jacket unzipped and hanging open. Isn't he cold? I feel an aching need to share the blanket, but I don't move. He cheated on me, and the pain that would come with touching him and smelling his familiar scent would be my undoing.

I miss him. Goddammit, I fucking love him, and it's such a hopeless, miserable feeling. He's right here, close enough to hold tight and breathe in, yet the only thing we're capable of sharing is strained silence.

My lungs burn, surging all the bitterness from the past five weeks to the surface. "When did you sleep with her?"

He moves so fast my heart stops. In a heartbeat, he kneels before me with his hands braced on the bench on either side of my hips.

"*You* tell *me*." His eyes are as bare and smoky as the sky. "Look at me and tell me when I fucked that woman."

"I don't know! I tried to get that answer at the penthouse." My chin quivers. "I asked if it happened while we were together and you…you just glared at me." I lean back. "Like you're doing right now."

"Because you know the goddamn answer!" He slams a fist on the bench beside me, his enraged voice echoing across the lake. "Look at me. Look hard, Danni, and listen to your heart. Do you honestly believe I would cheat on you?"

The hurt in his eyes is tactile, his face lined and heartbroken. His inconsolable expression suggests weeks of suffering, sleepless nights, and soul-deep disappointment. I feel every tired crease and dark circle like a punch in the heart. As hard as I search, I don't find a trace of guilt or collusion. He just looks…wrecked.

A warm bud of hope blooms in my chest, followed instantly by the hard stab of shame. He stares at me like he's the one who's been betrayed. Like I'm the betrayer.

A flood of tears terrorizes my airway, and I gulp down the cry that tries to escape.

"In the five years I've known you—" I choke, devastated and nauseous. "You've been undeniably committed and loyal to me."

"That's right." He reads my eyes, waiting for me to continue.

"Goddammit, Cole. Why didn't you tell me?" My voice spikes with confusion and anger. "You could've

three is a war

explained it and told me—"

"I can't." He pushes off the bench and launches to his feet. "I can't prove it, and you know what? Fuck you, Danni, because I shouldn't have to."

I choke at the force of his rage and hunch deeper into the blanket.

Pacing to the edge of the dock, he speaks quietly with his back to me. "You *know* me. You fucking know I'd rather cut myself open than so much as look at another woman." He shoves his hands in the pockets of his jacket, gazing out at the dark lake. "It kills me that you so quickly believed the worst in me."

"I didn't want to believe it." My spine snaps straight, bristling with defensiveness. "But the last few months left me feeling so damn naive I stopped trusting my instincts. When I saw the photos, the proof was right there in black and white, and you said nothing."

"It *was* nothing!" he bellows and spins to face me. "It was another lifetime, another place, a mistake I made before I met you." His expression falls, his voice broken. "I would never cheat on you. Not for the job. Not even to save my own life."

The sincerity in his words molds around my heart and constricts it mercilessly. Another sob crawls up, and I cover my mouth, muffling the horrible noise.

I judged and convicted him without thought or examination. His innocence is all over his face, his unblinking eyes, and the strength of his posture. It's been there all along.

We stare at each other through the shadows, separated by five feet and a bottomless well of regret. He fucked up by not communicating, and I made it a thousand times worse by giving up on him.

I thought I was doing the brave thing by dropping the hammer and running away. I thought it was the *right* thing. But as it turns out, I didn't just hurt myself. I hurt a man who has only ever protected and loved me.

I should've stayed at the penthouse that day and let him explain. It's the least I could've done after sleeping with his best friend and digging the blade of jealousy deeper and deeper.

Cole isn't a cheater. I am. Those are the truths I conveniently ignored to convince myself to walk away.

"What I did is unforgivable." I wipe the tears from my face and slow my breathing. "You must think I'm a hypocritical piece of shit."

"Don't—"

"Let me finish." I suck in a breath. "I took one look at those photos and used it as ammo to leave you. The woman, the dead body, the cameras—it was all excuses to avoid the decision I couldn't make. I couldn't choose between you, and those photos gave me the coward's way out."

"You're not a coward." He takes a step forward, his timbre soft and low. "You're an emotion, a passion. You run deep and wild, rise with the storm, and adjust with the wind. No matter what direction life takes you, you endure with remarkable strength."

An ugly, sobbing laugh tumbles past my lips. "I'm a reckless, unsorted disaster."

"If I wanted prudence and order, I'd hook up with a nun. I want *you*, Danni."

Warmth unfurls inside me. I didn't realize how badly I needed to hear that, even if I don't deserve the assurance.

three is a war

"I hurt you." The words tremble on my lips, thick with self-loathing.

He remains several paces away, doesn't reach out or close the distance. But I feel the mystical cohesion between us, the union of parts of the same soul. The comforting sound of his exhales opens my lungs, and the steady touch of his gaze expands my ribcage. I can finally breathe again.

How terribly foolish I was to walk away from everything I ever wanted, when I had it all standing right in front of me. "I'm so sorry."

"I'm not."

My eyebrows pull in. "What?"

"I'm not sorry for my actions. I disabled your car, drugged your coffee, and drove you three-hundred miles away from your home. I won't apologize for it. In fact, if you leave before I say what I need to say, I'll tie your ass up and drag you back by your hair."

Unbidden, my insides tingle and heat. "*You* are the reason I'm here? Not Trace?"

"It was his idea. I executed it."

I try to picture the logistics of transporting an unconscious woman across the state. "Did you drive separately or—?"

"I drove the Range Rover. He rode in the backseat with you."

My eyebrows rise. That's unexpected. Too bad I wasn't awake to experience the awkwardness of that four-hour drive. "Is the car yours, too?"

"Yes."

"A lakefront estate, a Range Rover, boats, ATVs…? I know you have secrets, but it feels like the life I shared with you was a big fat lie."

"I brought you here to explain. I'll tell you everything."

"How?" I wrap the blanket tighter around me. "I thought you couldn't tell me anything?"

"I'll explain that, too." With his hands in the pockets of his leather jacket, he steps closer and stops within arm's reach, gazing down at me. "We'll talk inside, where it's warm."

It's a trap. If I go back in that house, I'll stay. It's two against one, and they know how to control me. The dynamics of our personalities put me at a disadvantage. I'm passive by nature and don't stand a chance against their domineering, persuasive modes of operation.

"I don't know, Cole. I'm outnumbered." I meet his eyes. "Like a lamb among wolves."

He huffs an exasperated sound. "You really don't know, do you?"

I shake my head, not following.

"This is *your* world." He spreads his arms wide. "I just live in it. You own my heart, my every thought. You have the power to take whatever you want when you want it. You're fucking gorgeous, Danni. Compassionate and smart. Independent and cool as hell. A titan of feminine influence." His eyes glimmer, and he laughs. "It's impossible to not feel…completely possessed by you. And I'm not the only one."

He glances at the house, where Trace awaits our return.

"Why are you telling me this?" I shift uncomfortably.

"The ends to which we've gone…" He swipes a hand down his face. "We've shared you, fought each

three is a war

other for you, broken laws to keep you. We're both so eaten up in love with you there isn't anything we won't do."

He says *we* as if they've worked out some kind of truce, but I'm not buying it.

"Will you let me go?" I ask. "Right now?"

"No." He releases a slow breath. "Trace and I will be making the decisions going forward. But there's only one decision that really matters, and it's in your hands. Whatever you decide determines the rest of our lives. So let me ask you…" He cocks his head. "Who do you think has the most control here?"

A knot swells in my throat. "I do."

"You got it."

three

"What do you mean you'll be making the decisions going forward?" I rise from the bench, heart pounding.

Why am I getting worked up? It's not like I'll be sticking around long enough to be pulled into their plans.

Cole smirks and thrusts his chin in the direction of the house. "Come on."

Without waiting, he walks down the dock, headed toward the shore.

"I'm not staying." I trail after him, holding the blanket around my shoulders.

"Okay." With a wolfish grin, he opens the gate and holds it for me as I pass.

"I mean it. Cole. I'll listen to what you have to say. Then I'm leaving."

"Not without your punishment."

"You're *not* spanking me." I walk beside him on the bridge that leads to the house, quickening my gait to match his long-legged strides.

"Do you prefer a different punishment?" He regards me out of the corner of his eye. "Hot wax? A ball-gag and blindfold? Orgasm denial?"

"Where the hell did that come from?" I squint at him. "Are you into those things?"

"I'm into anything that involves you naked and willing."

My legs tremble, and I gulp down a breath. I'm not in the right mindset for this conversation, especially not with Trace's silhouette looming on the terrace up ahead.

He stands about thirty feet away, beneath a wrought-iron lamppost, wearing a black overcoat and an intense expression. His bearing is so striking and soul-shakingly commanding I lose my footing and trip over the stone steps to the patio.

Cole catches my arm and casts an irritated glare at Trace.

"How long have you owned this place?" I ease away from Cole's grip and concentrate on walking in the stiletto boots.

"Eight years."

He owned it the entire time I've known him and never mentioned it. My shoulders crumple as a fresh wave of hurt crashes through me.

"It was a safe house, Danni." He rests a hand on my arm, stopping me a few steps from Trace. "I let people in my profession stay here to recharge and regroup. I couldn't bring you here or tell you about it and risk you running into someone or something I couldn't explain." His gaze sweeps over the sprawling estate. "It

three is a war

has an armory, control room, office, workshop—"

"The locked doors."

"Yes. They'll remain locked, unless it becomes a sticking point for you. Just remember I'm retired from that life, and so is this property."

"I don't care about the rooms, but I'm curious…" I glance from Cole to Trace. "Did you guys spend time here together?"

"Yes." Trace opens the back door and motions for me to enter the house. "We used to stay here between missions. Before we knew you."

I'd be lying if I said I wasn't interested in their history together. The friendship they once had is so nebulous and mysterious. They don't have pictures together. They don't talk about it. I've only ever seen them at war with each other. It's hard to imagine what they were like as best friends.

We enter the house, and Cole veers toward the kitchen. Trace guides me to an overstuffed leather chair, with a firm hand on my lower back.

Fireplaces dominate both ends of the living room, crackling with the savory aroma of hickory. The driftwood-gray cathedral ceiling and monochromatic decor blurs the distinction between indoors and out, bringing the primary focus to the wall of windows between the hearths.

The view of the lake, illuminated by the moonlight, is so captivating I don't realize I stopped walking until Trace clears his throat.

"Take a seat." He removes the blanket from my shoulders and pats the back of the chair. Then he slides off his coat and sits on the couch across from me.

As I lower onto the seat, Cole returns with an inch-thick folder of papers.

"Look through this." He sets it on the coffee table before me and opens the flap. "They're congressional documents that have been made public."

He sits beside Trace on the couch, leaving a cushion of space between them. They don't acknowledge each other, but they share the same single focus. Neither appear to be troubled or on edge. I assume that means whatever I'm about to read is safe for consumption.

Rather than jumping in, I take a moment to absorb their reclined postures and soft expressions.

While Trace looks insanely handsome in dark denim and a white t-shirt, his casual attire does nothing to detract from the formidable aura that surrounds him. It's the way he watches me, those alluring pale eyes sharp with promise and commitment. He hasn't washed his hands of me. Not even close.

Cole rests an elbow on the arm of the couch and props an ankle on a knee. The leather jacket came off when he stepped inside, leaving a black Henley that drapes across his wide shoulders. The thin material clings to the ridges of muscle he packed on since the last time I saw him.

"It's unclassified information." Cole lifts his chin toward the folder. "Go ahead."

With a deep breath, I pull the stack of papers onto my lap. The document on top has a United States seal stamped in the header with a line scratched through the words *TOP SECRET* and *NOFORN*. There's other text stringed with it, but it's blocked out by a black box of ink. *Unclassified* is typed above it.

"What does NOFORN mean?" I meet Cole's eyes.

three is a war

"No foreign nationals."

On the front page, there are references to *Senate* and *Intelligence*, as well as a list of declassification dates that are four years old. I flip to the next page and scan what appears to be an executive summary about nuclear, chemical, and biological security.

The language is vague and confusing. Every other word is an acronym, and it redundantly discusses things like exercising the authorities and carrying out the responsibilities of the activity in sections *443* through *blah, blah, blah* of Reference *(a)* and *(c)*, etcetera and whatever. I turn the pages and find more of the same.

"Am I supposed to understand this?" I rub my forehead, squinting at the meaningless text.

"Keep reading." Cole strokes a thumb across his bottom lip, his posture laid back and gaze steady.

As I page through dozens of documents, the verbiage doesn't become any clearer. More acronyms. More section references. I know the words — *negotiations, funding, allocations, resources, initiatives* — but I feel like I need a secret decoder to understand the context.

"You're going to explain this, right?" I hold up a letter with bullet points from *A* to *R*, each citing other alphabetized sections. "The only part I understand is the signature at the bottom."

This one is signed by the Secretary of Defense.

Trace removes an ink pen from the drawer in the coffee table and hands it to Cole.

"Bring the documents here." Cole shifts, making room for me to slide by.

He wants me to sit between him and Trace. I'm not excited about that, mostly because my body is excited about it. My skin remembers the warm pressure of their hands. My lips crave their unique tastes. My inhales are starved for their addictive musky scents.

I miss the feel of Trace's fingers stroking my hair and collaring my throat. I long to hear Cole's dirty talk as he stretches and fills me. I want to kiss Trace's scowl and rub my face against Cole's whiskers. I need them with a yearning that can only end in more heartache.

What if this conversation exonerates their secrets and lies? That possibility scares me. I need a reason to be angry with them. I need them to *not* be perfect, to make irredeemable mistakes that will drive me away.

Because if all is forgiven, I'm back to square one, facing an impossible decision.

Gathering the documents, I slide around Cole and lower onto the couch between them. Cole bends over my lap, using my legs as a table while scribbling marks on the pages.

My gaze falls on the back of his head, the tousled strands of thick brown hair, and the clean-shaved hairline on his nape. I want to press my nose against the base of his neck and breathe in deeply. I want to run my fingers over his scalp, wrap my arms around his bulky biceps, and hug him with the ferocity of my longing.

A flush of heat spreads across my cheeks, and I look away, colliding with crystal blue eyes.

"What's he doing?" I swallow, knowing full well Trace was watching me fantasize about Cole.

"Your trust is broken, and we're going to fix that." Trace's scowl twitches into a thoughtful expression. "He'll show you as much as he can without breaking too many laws."

I pick at a seam on the leather cushion, both excited

three *is a war*

and nervous.

Trace scans my face and lingers on a lock of hair that partially obstructs my view. He lifts a hand to brush it back, but I beat him to it, tucking it behind my ear. If he touches me, I'm doomed.

This would be so much easier if I didn't remember the rush of pleasure those hands have given me. Every second I spent with him is a thread sewed through my heart, holding it together. Seeing him, being near him, stretches those seams, swelling, expanding, aching. If I crumble and beg for reconciliation, I'll only hurt him again. Both of them.

I shouldn't be here.

Leaving them was agonizing. I don't know how I'll walk away again.

"All right." Cole lifts his head and re-stacks the papers. "Take another look."

When he leans back, I parse through the documents. Every paper has the same two words circled in blue ink.

The activity.

Page after page, I reread the statements around every circle he made, struggling to make sense of them.

...financing the activity *installation*
...appointing a distinguished panel to examine the activity *during this period*
...testimony of members of the activity
...articulate the activity's *strategy to Congress*
...requested information from the activity *and other federal departments*

The activity…the activity…the activity… Those are the only two words he marked.

"I don't understand." I reach the bottom of the stack and return to the first page. "What's the activity?"

"Me." Cole tilts his head toward Trace. "Him."

"That's what you were called?" A sense of relief settles over me. I can finally put a label on the entity that caused me years of pain.

"Trace and I were part of a special unit that goes by many names. OGA, ISA, Optimized Talent, Gray Fox… Every time there's a classified spill, they change the designator. But in congressional documents, we're simply referred to as *the activity*."

"Will you get in trouble for telling me this?"

Cole shares a look with Trace, and something unspoken passes between them.

"We're making a judgment call." Trace bends forward and meets my eyes. "You're aware of the breach that resulted in stolen information."

"You mean the revenge mission against Cole?"

"Yes. The photos were delivered to you because someone hacked into Cole's records and gleaned your contact information."

"Is that person—?"

"The perpetrator is imprisoned. We'll come back to that." Cole lifts the folder from my lap and sets it on the coffee table. "As you know, I can't share details about my job, but the problem is you've seen things."

"The pictures of the dead body." *In my house.* I shiver.

"That's right." Cole watches me carefully, his face inches from mine. "Trace and I decided it's better if you have the facts rather than no information at all, or worse,

three is a war

the wrong assumptions." He pulls in a breath. "The world we were part of isn't a place I want you anywhere near, and that's not going to change. You need to understand that your safety has always been my number one concern."

"And mine." Trace stares coldly at Cole.

Cole sets his jaw. "I'm going to share some details of my last mission. I can't tell you much about the operation itself, but I'll shed some light on the events that impacted you."

"Like your fake death?" My chest clenches.

"Yeah." He drags a hand through his hair and settles back on the couch. "Trace already told you I'm an operative."

"*Ex*-operative." I tug at the hem of my sweater. "I thought you were retired."

"Let me ask you something." Cole rubs his chin, studying me. "If you closed your dance company and pursued a new career, would you be an ex-dancer?"

"No." I jerk back my head. "I'll always be a dancer. It's who I am."

"Same principle applies here. Retirement doesn't change my DNA or mental make-up."

Beneath the dimples and soft brown eyes lives the muscle and heart of a soldier. A man who thrives on adrenaline and mystery.

And he gave it up for me.

Then I left him.

My heart thumps heavily, making a slow crawl to my stomach. "You miss it."

"Not as much as I miss you."

I close my eyes and press a hand to my mouth,

covering the quiver in my chin.

"What about you, Trace?" I whisper, peering at the quiet man beside me. "Do you miss it?"

"Sometimes." He grips my wrist, tugging my hand away from my face. "I miss the rush of a difficult mission and the invigoration that comes with success. But the past year hasn't been without its own challenges and thrills." His eyes glimmer. "You've given me the biggest fight of my life, and I'm prepared to do whatever it takes to win."

"We'll see about that." Cole scoffs.

I pinch the bridge of my nose. "So you're an operative and…?"

"I'm a deep undercover operative." Cole gives me a pointed look. "*Retired* from a clandestine group that's deployed all over the world."

"I suspected the undercover part." I lean back on the couch, letting his words soak in. "But I don't really know what it means. What does an undercover operative do?"

"Information gathering."

"Like what?" I imagine him stealing access codes or military secrets, but that's Hollywood shit.

"When the U.S. sends in the tip of the spear to some beach or undisclosed location, who do you think provides the information to the SEALs on where to land their ships or parachutes?"

"You?" The air whooshes from my lungs.

"It's a trite example, but yes. Sometimes we feed them the intelligence on where to drop and who to strike."

"The eyes and ears in the shadows," Trace murmurs.

three is a war

My imagination runs wild as I picture Trace sitting in a spartan control room, talking to Cole on high-tech communication devices. Of course, Cole would be dressed head to toe in black, maybe some black paint on his face and weapons concealed beneath his clothes as he runs across dangerous terrain in the dead of night. In the distance, bombs explode and bad guys die.

I shake my head. "It's nothing like what I'm imagining, is it?"

"It's not like the movies." He tucks my hair behind my ear, letting his touch linger on my neck.

My breath falters, and I lean away. "Did you do this undercover work behind enemy lines?"

He lowers his hand and stares across the room, his eyes losing focus. "The last mission embedded me deep within the enemy's ranks."

When he doesn't continue, I sneak a peek at Trace. His gaze is stark and fixed on the folder of papers.

Whatever happened on Cole's mission put into effect a series of events that changed the course of our lives. If Cole returned when he was supposed to, I wouldn't have fallen in love with Trace. I'd be happily married to Cole and oblivious. Maybe I would've met Trace down the line, but I wouldn't have seen him as anything other than Cole's best friend.

There would've been no Trace and me.

"When I was planted inside the inner circle of the target," Cole says quietly, "I used an assumed identity for the purposes of gaining trust and information. Nine months into the operation, my cover was blown."

"How?" My stomach turns to ice.

"I'll get to that." He clasps his hands together

between his knees. "When the leak occurred, I had to sever connections and find a place to hole up. I was running and hiding from the target I infiltrated, as well as the person who ratted me out. I couldn't contact you or Trace. Didn't know who was watching me. I couldn't risk anyone learning my true identity, where I lived, and who was important to me until the threat was neutralized."

"But someone learned you had a girlfriend." The bloody images of the dead man in my house flash through my head.

"Yes. That someone was one of our own, an operative like myself." Cole clenches his hands. "The traitor was the woman in the photos."

four

The naked woman in the photos didn't just blow Cole's cock. She blew his cover. *She* is the reason he disappeared for four years. An angry wave of heat flushes through me as my mind swims to fit the pieces together.

"The day those pictures were delivered, you said the woman was a defector." My legs bounce with the urge to pace, but I remain on the couch, wedged between Cole and Trace. "Was she with you on the last mission?"

"Yes." Cole scrubs a hand over the back of his head. "We were assigned together often, because we worked well together."

Given the variety of sexual positions in the photos, they fucked well together, too.

"You went on that mission…" My lungs slam together, choking my voice. "You left me, knowing you'd spend a year with a woman you had sex with?"

"I didn't have a choice!" Cole launches from the couch. "They say jump, and I fucking jump. That's how it works. I don't choose the missions or the team I'm working with."

I look to Trace for validation.

"It's true." Trace glowers back at me, his tone firm yet soft. "When I talked to him before he left, he was upset about being paired with her."

"I knew she'd be a problem." Cole paces through the room.

"Because you were involved?" I ask, resigned.

"We were never involved. When we were on assignments for months at a time, she scratched an itch. That's all it was."

"I have a feeling it was more than an itch to her." I drag my hands through my hair, emotionally drained. "What's her name?"

"It's classified."

"Did she make a move on you during the last mission?"

"Yes, and I turned her down." He pauses beside the coffee table, his face lined with frustration. "She doesn't like to be denied, but I made damn sure she understood I wasn't interested."

"Did you tell her about me? Is that why she sought revenge and sent the photos? She was jealous?"

"I didn't tell *anyone* about you." He lowers onto the couch beside me and stares at his hands.

I don't care about their history together. He has history with countless women. What freaks me out is this badass, secret-agent woman targeted *me*.

As the silence creeps by, I try to recall everything

three is a war

Cole and Trace said that day in the penthouse. Then I remember a comment that doesn't add up.

"The day I received the photos..." I turn to Trace. "Cole referred to this woman as a defector, and you said, *That was the mission?* like you were surprised. What did that mean?"

"When I saw the photos," Trace says, "I immediately recognized her. I used to work with her, too." He lifts his gaze to Cole and grimaces. "I used to sleep with her."

"Yes, you did." Cole laughs, as if it's a private joke between them.

"You both fucked her?" My eyes widen. "Is this a common thing for you guys? Sharing lovers?"

"No. Just her." Cole shrugs. "There are very few women in our profession, and guys like us don't trust easily, especially during an undercover operation. She was one of us."

"And she scratched an itch." My insides tighten. "Did you...do her together? At the same time?"

Cole makes a face. "Hell no."

I didn't think they were the double-teaming type. "So you just passed her back and forth?"

"I know where you're going with this, Danni." Cole shifts to look me directly in the eyes. "She is *not* you. Trace and I worked with her, had sex with her on occasion, and didn't give a fuck who else she was banging. Don't you dare compare a meaningless fling to what's going on here." He motions at the three of us. "It's not even in the same universe."

I want to argue there's nothing going on here, but that would be total bullshit.

45

"Moving back on topic…" Trace straightens beside me. "When I saw the woman in the photos, I knew she was the one who sent the envelope. Cole confirmed she was a defector, which clued me in on the purpose of his last mission. It isn't uncommon for him to go undercover to root out the source of a leak of classified information."

"In this case, the information was leaked to an enemy nation state." Cole clenches his teeth. "And the source of that leak turned out to be *her*."

"Hang on." My head pounds as I try to keep up. "You and this woman went undercover to find a traitor, and she was the traitor all along?"

"Yes," Cole hisses on a sharp breath. "By the time I caught on, she was already gone. Like I said, it was a goat fuck operation from the start. But Danni, you need to understand my handler was the only person who knew about you. I *never* mentioned you, not to her or anyone. So when I severed contact with you, I felt confident about your safety."

"How did you figure out she was a traitor?"

"Espionage is my job, baby. But it was also her job, and she was good at it. She knew I would catch her, and when I did, she was armed to protect herself."

"With a weapon?"

"With information. She hacked into my personal files at the agency, found you listed as my emergency contact, and learned everything she could about you." He drops his head in his hands, his expression creased with tension. "I fucked up. She was ambitious and power hungry and manipulative, and I trusted her. All those years, I should've been scrutinizing her every move."

"She passed the same rigorous investigation as the rest of us." Trace regards him, voice gentle. "It wasn't

three is a war

your fault. She fooled everyone."

"You say that, but you know damn well I failed."

"You didn't." Trace releases a sigh. "You're phenomenal at your job. The best. In the end, you saw what no one else did and brought her in."

I hold still, breathless, devouring the interaction. It's the most amicable conversation I've ever witnessed between them, and it spreads warmth around my heart.

Trace shifts his focus to me. "Cole didn't know she found out about you. He was off the grid, hunting her under the assumption that no one knew you existed. Meanwhile, she had your house wired with surveillance equipment, inside and out. That's when she sent the hitman and had the whole thing recorded on the cameras."

Shock strangles my windpipe. There were people in my house more than once? Where was I when the cameras were installed?

"She didn't know I was watching over you." Trace scowls. "And since I lost contact with Cole, I didn't know the circumstances around the threat. I just knew someone found out about you and they wanted you dead."

"Jesus." I slump against the back of the couch.

"When I finally caught her, she was ready for me." Cole grips my hand and laces our fingers together on my lap. "I'll never forget when she held up her phone and flashed the live video of that assassin walking into your house. I fucking lost it."

My insides shrivel with horror. "But Trace stopped him."

"I didn't know that," Cole says. "I didn't know where Trace was, if he was watching, or if you were home. She said she would call off the hitman, if I let her go."

I tense. "She could've been lying."

"Not about that." Trace catches my gaze, his expression cold. "She turned her back on her country to make some money. But she wouldn't have betrayed the honor code among us."

"He's right." Cole works his jaw, the movement vibrating with resentment. "I had a split-second decision to make. I could let her kill me and save your life. Or I could kill her and guarantee your death."

Talk about impossible choices. My chest hurts for him.

"I went with the third option." He strokes a thumb across my knuckles, his eyes dark and murky. "I initiated a struggle that made it look like I was trying to get away. As intended, it put enough space between us to force a gun fight. I had the obscurity of nightfall on my side, and there was a bridge with a sizable river beneath." He looks at me expectantly.

"You jumped?"

"I let her back me onto the edge of the bridge, knowing she'd shoot me like the soldier she was. Face to face. In the chest."

My heart stops, and my gaze darts to the front of his shirt.

"Bullet-resistant protective clothing. High-tech stuff." He presses a hand against his sternum. "The bullet broke the skin. Fractured a couple ribs. Left a godawful mark for months. But it didn't enter my body."

Holy shit. My breath leaves me, taking my voice with it.

"I hit the water." The cords in his neck go taut.

three is a war

"Then I swam up river, contacted my handler, and set the ball into motion."

"Cole Hartman had to die." As I echo the words he said the morning he returned, everything clicks into place. "You wanted her to think you were dead. But what about everyone else? The unit you're in? Your employers? Did they know?"

"No one knew I was alive except my handler. Since the threat was internal, even my classified records showed I was deceased. I know she was watching the agency and Trace. And *you*." His face falls. "She watched you grieve."

"You did the smartest thing you could've done." Trace tilts his head, eyes on Cole. "I'm not saying that because I benefited from your absence. Your actions ensured she left Danni alone."

"That's why you made me believe you were dead." My voice drops with understanding. "That's why you didn't come back." I stare at Cole's hand on my lap, aching to wrap my arms around him. "Trace said guys in your position don't marry or have attachments. I get it now. I was a weakness." Nausea rises, and I force my gaze to Cole. "I cost you the mission."

"You didn't cost me anything." He tightens his fingers around mine. "But the leverage she had over me cost me time. I couldn't come home until she was dead or in custody. It took me years to catch her again."

"How did you find her?"

"I can't say, Danni. I've already told you too much."

"He has an unparalleled skill set." Trace glances at Cole with something akin to pride in his voice. "That's all you need to know."

The gleam in Trace's eyes, his words, all of it melts through me. What I wouldn't give for them to be friends again.

"I will say…" Cole smirks. "The look on her face when she saw me years after she *killed* me almost made the whole thing worth it. *Almost.*"

I don't condone murder of any kind, but I wish the bitch was dead. "She's in prison now?"

"Sentenced a couple months ago. She'll never see daylight again."

"Why did she send the photos of Trace to me?"

Trace leans forward, pinning me with the command of his gaze. "She wanted to make sure you knew Cole's job put your life in danger."

"That," Cole says, "combined with the sex pictures, was supposed to be a driving wedge between us. Her last *fuck you.*"

It worked. I flipped the fuck out and left him. My heart sinks with regret.

"I'm not in danger anymore?" I'm stalling, delaying the conversation I know is coming.

"You're safe. It's over. But…" Cole gestures between us. "*We* are not over."

And there it is. I've been sitting between them for twenty minutes and suddenly, I feel too confined, anxious, *trapped.*

I surge from the couch, climb over Trace's long legs, and pace to the wall of windows. Heat blooms beneath my skin, and I press my forehead against the cool glass.

I left Cole because he cheated.

Except he didn't.

three is a war

I left Trace because he spied on me for years, knew I was in danger, and kept it a secret.

But he did it to protect me.

I left them because they broke my trust, and now they've told me everything. I have nothing to hold against them. Nothing to forgive. If anything, I'm the one who should be begging for forgiveness.

"How much of what you said tonight is classified information?" I watch their reflections in the window.

"Most of it." Trace stands and approaches my back.

"Punishable by time in prison?" My voice cracks.

"Yes." Cole remains on the couch, reclined back and seemingly at ease.

"I hope I never get interrogated. I'm the worst liar ever."

"It was worth the risk." Trace reaches my side and leans a shoulder against the glass. "You wouldn't have stayed without an explanation from us."

"You say that as if I've made up my mind. But we all know I'm as decisive as a squirrel in the path of a speeding car."

"You were pretty decisive," Cole says, with an angry growl, "when you stepped onto that elevator and out of my life."

Oh man, he's sore about that. With good reason. I've done nothing but make stupid choices over and over since he returned. And the most important decision of all is the one I continue to avoid.

"You and Cole are unemployed." Trace wets his lips. "I can run the casino from here. We have no distractions or priorities outside of this isolated corner of the world, nothing but the lake and woodland and sunshine until you're ready to move forward...with one of us. What are you unsure about?"

A thousand things, but I can't for the life of me remember any of them as I stare into the wintry blue of his assertive gaze. With his chin tipped down and his eyes fastened on mine, he's poised to persuade.

I pivot, resting my back to the windows and attention on Cole. "You quit the security job?"

"It interfered with more important things."

"Like drugging and kidnapping women?"

That's one of the reasons I can't stay here. What kind of person would I be if I let that behavior slide?

"What would you have done," Trace asks, "if one of us showed up at your door and invited you on a trip to the lake."

I would've looked through the peephole and not answered the door.

"It's called free will." I cross my arms over my chest. "You took that from me by bringing me here."

"You hated the secrets and omissions. We rectified that and will be completely open with you going forward." Trace wings up a brow. "If you tell me that doesn't change anything, I'll know you're lying."

It changes everything. That's the problem. They confided in me, explained their actions, and proved that everything they've done was with good cause.

The decision that's been looming over me for months returns like a cancer, harmful and un-treatable as it spreads through me, contaminating my heart and begging for a quick death.

"The decision to drug you," Trace says, "didn't come lightly. Had you been okay with losing me or showed any signs that you would truly be able to move

three is a war

on, I would've left you alone. I think Cole is with me on that."

"Yeah." Cole drops his head against the back of the couch.

"But you didn't," Trace says. "You stopped dancing. Stopped visiting the homeless shelter. Lost weight. Then you sold the one thing I thought you'd never let go."

My house. Sharp pain pricks the backs of my eyes. "The only reason you know all that is because you invaded my privacy. *Again.*"

"I don't regret that. Nor do I regret sedating you and bringing you here. But I *am* deeply sorry for the distress it caused you."

My chest hiccups with a choppy inhale.

"You're unhappy, Danni." Cole rises from the couch and prowls toward me. "And you'll be even more miserable in Florida."

"What makes you think I won't be miserable here?"

"I'm not saying it won't be hard." He stops beside me and rests his hands on his hips. "If you had to choose between us right now, could you?"

My heartbeat explodes, and I look away.

"I take that as a *no,*" Cole says softly.

"That's why I need to leave." Dread coils in my belly. "I can't do this again."

"You don't get to walk away," Trace says in a deep, unflinching voice.

"You're going to stick it out." Cole matches his tone. "You have a decision to make, and you're going to finish this. Because if you don't, if you forfeit your greatest chance at happiness, you'll regret it for the rest of your life."

I know he's right, but… "What you're suggesting is insane." I lean my head back against the window and stare at the ceiling. "We can't all stay under the same roof. We tried that the first week you came home, and it ended in a bloody brawl in the backyard."

"We worked some things out since then." Trace rests his fingertips in the pockets of his jeans.

"Like what?" I narrow my eyes.

"The only way we'll survive this is if we're honest and open with one another. No more secrets. No more sneaking around." Trace glowers at Cole. "No more fistfights."

"Only an hour ago, you were aiming a gun at Cole's chest."

"You're right. It was an unreasonable way to handle an argument. I guess you could say we're a work in progress."

With my back to the windows, they cage me in with the width of their shoulders while leaving a foot of breathing space between us. But that invisible space is tenuous and airless, waiting to be erased.

"We're going to try this again." Cole folds his arms across his chest. "And this time, we're doing it our way."

I love when they talk in terms of *we*, like they're a team. Using it in this context, however, implies I have no say in whatever they're planning. It makes me tense. "If you intend to team up against me—"

"Your way didn't work." Impatience seeps into Cole's voice. "When you were with one of us, the other one was left alone to stew and fester in jealousy."

My mind jumps to a threesome, triad, or whatever

three is a war

it's called when two men share a woman. Except they would never be okay with that, and I don't think I could handle it emotionally. On the surface, it sounds like a dream, but the reality wouldn't be good for *them*. Their happiness is more important than a sexual fantasy.

"What are you proposing?" I swallow.

"Not what you think." Trace pulls in a slow breath and releases it. "Look, Cole and I have gone through a range of emotions and expectations since he returned. In the beginning, jealousy drove most of our actions. Then came the rivalry. Suspicion. Bitterness. When you left, we reached a point of resoluteness."

"Meaning?" I hold my breath.

"We understand the stakes," Cole says. "I know he's not going to give up and vice-versa. And we know the ultimate decision is completely out of our hands. We're going to stay in this house, focus on you, and when arguments arise, we'll talk through it. *Together.*"

It sounds wonderfully ideal. *And unrealistic.* How can I spend time with one while the other one is present? They haven't mentioned sex, but it's a complexity we can't avoid. It'll start with meaningful glances and subtle gestures of affection. Then it'll build and invade until it refuses to be ignored. I tried the celibacy thing, the co-dating thing, the bed-hopping thing. I've resisted, surrendered, sneaked around, and run away. None of it worked. Because I'm right back where I started.

They're proposing that we stay here together, under the same roof, until I make a decision. The difference this time is better communication. I can get behind that, but it doesn't solve the problems we had before.

I suck at managing more than one relationship. It brings out the worst in me. I've never suffered from mental illness, but since Cole's return, I wonder if I've developed bipolar disorder. Narcissism. Maybe sex addiction. I guess it could be worse. Severely distressing events can breed all sorts of nutjobs — psychopaths, serial murders, scientologists. Bottom line is I'm not good at bouncing between them.

"What's putting that look on your face?" Trace captures me in a penetrating stare.

"All the reasons why your proposition won't work."

"Such as?"

Shifting toward him, I slide a hand down his chest while meeting Cole's eyes. "What would you do if I kissed him right now?"

"Nothing." Cole stands taller. "I won't like it, but it's better than the alternative."

"Which is?"

"You choosing Florida, a new life, and eventually another man who will never bring you the happiness you deserve."

I drop my hand and step around them, pacing toward the island in the kitchen. "Where's my phone and my car?"

"The phone is on the kitchen counter," Trace says. "Your car will be delivered tomorrow, along with the Maserati." He hardens his tone. "It's after ten o'clock. You're not going anywhere tonight."

"My parents expect me—"

"In two days. You're going to stay the night and think about everything we've told you. If you're still set on leaving tomorrow, you'll have your car."

three is a war

It's a logical argument. But he's always logical. And compelling. And impossibly gorgeous, studying me with those intelligent eyes.

This is a bad idea. The worst. Yet the next question is already falling out of my mouth. "Where would I sleep?"

"Follow me." Cole turns and heads toward the slight gradient of stairs that leads to the bedrooms.

Trace extends an arm, gesturing for me to walk ahead of him. I assume they have a guest room made up for me, but when I join Cole at the end of the hall, the room he unlocks with a passcode is not what I expected.

A massive king-sized bed sits in the windowed corner. Given the unmade bedsheets and picture frames cluttering the furniture, this isn't a guest room. I recognize the photos of me in the dance studio, Cole and me at my house, and Cole with my sister's family. There are others, however, I've never seen before. Like the photos of me at the casino.

The camera angles suggest they were taken with the surveillance equipment, and I'm surprised by the high quality of the zoomed-in images. There are some of Trace and me dining together at Bissara, mingling at the casino bar, and holding hands in the lobby.

I didn't know he was capturing and saving those images, but that's not what makes my pulse speed up. It's the sight of them intermixed with Cole's pictures. I recognize other things, too—Cole's sneakers on the floor by the bed, his watch on the side table, and the headboard that looks almost identical to the one he bought me years ago.

As Trace's scowling shadow follows me around the

room, I shift to look at him and Cole. "Whose bedroom is this?"

"It used to be mine." Cole leans against a chest of drawers and straightens a picture frame.

Trace watches me intently. "Now it's ours."

five

My mouth opens and closes, forming words that have no sound. *Breathe, dammit.* I can't tell them how insane they are if I'm hyperventilating.

I gulp, and gulp again, filling my lungs with air. "*Our* bedroom?"

"Yours. His." Trace clasps his hands behind him. "And mine."

"What?" I swing my head around, my skin heating as I take in the intimate space. "No, we can't—"

"It's just a room." Cole crosses his arms, frowning.

"A *bed*room with only one bed." I point needlessly at the mattress that now seems a lot smaller than it did a few seconds ago. "You need to explain whatever this is, because right now, I'm jumping to conclusions that aren't possible."

"Cole and I discussed multiple ways to approach this." Trace paces around me, rubbing his jaw. "If we all have separate bedrooms, one of us will come into your room at night without the other one knowing. Or maybe we won't, but we'll lie in our beds, wide-awake, worrying about it."

"You have all this high-tech security." I wave a hand at the keypad beside the door. "Just set something up that would trip an alarm and notify you when someone entered my room."

"We'd turn it into a competition." Cole's brown eyes glow beneath heavy brows. "We're trained to penetrate every security system ever designed."

I cross the large, open space and hold my arms out. "Then put three beds in here."

"And sleep like twelve-year-olds at summer camp?" Cole grimaces.

"Or we could behave like adults." Trace perches on the foot of the mattress. "And sleep in a bed that's plenty big enough, without making an issue out of it."

How do I not make an issue out of this? My stomach tightens with nerves. "The three of us in a room together is a ticking time bomb. All of us in the same bed after five weeks of being apart? That's a sure path to total disaster." I lower my voice. "I don't want either of you feeling uncomfortable."

"I don't know about you," Cole says to Trace, "but when I fall into that bed tonight, I'm going to sleep harder and deeper than I have in months."

"Same here." Trace's blue eyes bore into mine, like he's digging for a weak spot.

"I've slept like shit." Cole catches my gaze, his tone soft yet urgent. "I want to be next to you, smell your hair

three is a war

on my pillow, and hear the sound of your breaths while you sleep."

"We're trying to give you transparency and reestablish your confidence in us," Trace says. "No matter our failures and shortcomings, you *know* you can trust us to lie beside you while you sleep."

I want that. *So much.* But they're so jealous and possessive the idea feels strange and *forced*. It reeks of deception, like they're manipulating me into spending time with them. They're certainly not suggesting we share a bed because they *want* to.

But my gut tells me the simplest answer is the right one. They miss me as much as I miss them, and they can't fathom spending another night alone.

And poof goes my will to argue. And my reason. I think my nerves bit the dust, too.

This is the quintessence of love. It's what makes two friends-turned-enemies share a bed with a woman, even when there are plenty of other beds in the rest of the house.

As I wilt and cave, I hold onto my last thread of sensibility. "One night."

Cole's eyes gleam, and a twitch bounces Trace's scowl.

"The first hint of jealousy, and I'll find another room to sleep in." I can't believe I'm agreeing to this. "I need something to wear to bed."

Trace points at the closet across the room.

On my way there, I slip into the en suite bathroom. With the door locked, I empty my bladder and scrutinize the bottles on the built-in shelf in the shower. Shampoo, conditioner, body soap—all the brands I use. I flush the toilet, wash my hands, and peek in the cabinets. Makeup, hair products, everything I kept at Trace's penthouse.

When I exit the bathroom, the bedroom is empty, and the deep timbre of their voices echoes from the direction of the living room. I'm thankful they're giving me privacy, or at least the perception of it. God knows how many cameras are installed in this house?

In the walk-in closet, I find the wardrobe I left at Trace's place, including new clothes with the tags still attached. Given the impeccable organization — garments hung by color and season, drawers labeled, and shoes perfectly aligned on the racks — it's safe to assume Trace oversaw this part of the plan.

How long have they been plotting to bring me here? Did it start the moment I walked out of the penthouse? Is that why they let me go so easily? Or did my move to Florida push them over the edge? I guess it doesn't matter. I'm here now with no choice but to face the nerve-wracking decision of what to do next.

I can leave tomorrow and start over like I planned. Or I can stay.

If I stay, maybe it won't work out. But finding out if it does might be the most important thing I've ever done. My gut tells me I'm supposed to take this journey, with them, no matter how painful or scary. Maybe I should let my gut lead the way.

I change into fleece pajama pants and a plain cotton t-shirt. Then I pad out of the room and down the hall, the slate tiles warming my bare feet.

The floors are heated, and I bet the lake views from every room are stunning. The detailed craftsmanship, woodwork, and design throughout the estate is extravagant. And every square foot belongs to Cole. He

three is a war

never said he needed money and I understand why he couldn't tell me about this place, but the secrets still bug me.

I find them in the kitchen, pulling covered dishes and vegetables from the fridge. Moving seamlessly around each other, they seem completely at ease sharing the same space. Trace changed into gray lounge pants, and Cole wears black workout shorts. Both are bare-chested, beautifully sculpted, and… Fuck, I'm staring.

"You need to eat." Trace meets my eyes and smirks.

"I need a beer."

And a sanity check. Are they actually preparing a meal together?

If this is the *Twilight Zone*, I hope it isn't the case of *be careful what you wish for.* I used to watch the show with my dad and remember the episode about the man who wishes for power and wakes up as Hitler. Then there was the guy who creates a world populated with clones of himself, only to realize he hates himself. If I had a wish, it's to see Cole and Trace come to a truce. I want that so badly I'm tempted to stay just to encourage the synergy that's currently swirling around them.

Cole removes a Bud Light out of the fridge, pops the cap, and slides it across the counter to me.

"Thanks." I look over the spread of food—taco meat, hard shells, and all the fixings. "Did you have the ingredients delivered?"

Trace laughs, and the delicious sound liquefies my limbs.

"What's so funny?" I grip the counter for support and chug the beer.

"No one delivers out here." Cole says. "We're lucky to see the postman on a regular schedule."

"Where did the food come from?" I circle the island and grab a tomato and paring knife.

"There's a Walmart twenty minutes up the road." Cole hands me a cutting board and slides a tray of taco shells into the oven.

"Really? In the middle of nowhere Missouri?" I dice the tomato, smiling at the image of Cole pushing a cart in a superstore.

"Ninety percent of Americans live within fifteen miles of a Walmart." He opens another Bud Light and swallows a large gulp.

Trace grinds a block of cheese against a grater. "Did you know eight cents for every U.S. dollar is spent at Walmart?"

"No." I chuckle. "Are you looking to expand your empire and buy them out?"

"It's not for sale, and if it was, it would be way out of my price range."

We finish preparing the meal and eat at the island. I choose the seat on the end, so I can watch them together. When they're not ignoring each other, their conversations focus on fishing, casino business, and the upcoming baseball season. At some point, the lighthearted discussion switches to my favorite topic, and I spend the next ten minutes regaling them with Beyoncé trivia.

"Her song *Bootylicious* put that word in the Oxford English Dictionary." I finish off my second beer and switch to water.

"I'm calling bullshit on that one." Trace takes a sip of scotch from a crystal tumbler.

"Look it up." I flick a finger at his phone, where it sits beside his empty plate.

"What's the story behind her name?" Cole stacks our dishes and carries them to the sink.

"It came from her mother's maiden name." I stand to help him. "Celestine Ann 'Tina' Beyincé."

"Bootylicious." Trace reads from his phone, his expression perplexed. *"Of a woman…sexually attractive."* His gaze lifts, sliding all over me before meeting my eyes. "You were right."

I tremble beneath his imposing glare. "I'm never wrong when it comes to Beyoncé."

"Your entire face glows when you talk about her." Cole hands me a rinsed plate to put in the dishwasher, his grin dented with dimples. "Keep talking."

"She wrote *Crazy In Love* in two hours. With a hangover." I load the top rack while scraping my mind for more facts. "Her middle name is Giselle. She was on *Star Search* in 1993 at the age of twelve. She's allergic to perfume. I can go on and on, but I'd rather talk about you guys."

"We will never compare to Beyoncé," Trace says dryly, but I don't miss the playful flicker in his eyes as he approaches.

He nudges me out of the way and helps Cole finish the dishes.

I move to the far end of the island and wipe down the surface. It's crazy how similar they are in some things, like the whole dominating, hyper-alert, intimidating manner in which they control their environments. But they're so very different in other ways.

Cole rinses the dishes, completely unconcerned

about the water splattering everywhere. Trace immediately cleans it up, scowling at the other man. Cole drinks beer and rides a motorcycle. Trace drinks Scotch and wears suits. Cole lets his hair fall, messy and tumbled, right out of the shower and hopes for the best. Trace has a process, involving product and finger-raking until every strand is textured and styled to perfection. Cole smiles easily, and Trace doesn't smile at all. Cole reacts first and apologizes later. I'm lucky to get a reaction or an apology from Trace at all. But none of those things are important in the big picture.

What matters to me are traits they both possess. They'll dance with me when I ask, whenever, wherever. They'll hold me when I need it, tightly or tenderly. And they love me, even when I fuck up.

During the course of our relationships, however, there's been a crucial, missing element. *Honesty*. In that regard, I'm just as guilty.

The broken promises, the lies and secrets — all of it was grounds for war. Have we turned a corner? It's only been one night and a couple conversations, but I already sense a flutter of something I haven't felt in a long time.

Possibility.

I want to try. I owe it to myself, to them, to see where this goes.

Except I'm scared, and that horrible feeling makes me want to duck and run.

Fear is a handicap. It was invented to fill the weak spots in the soul, and heaven knows I'm riddled with weaknesses. But that's okay. I won't let it control my actions.

Fear is just a visitor, stopping by to remind me to be stronger.

three is a war

Because I have something important to fight for.

six

As I watch Cole and Trace finish the dishes, I replay everything they told me tonight and feel at peace with the choices they made. In fact, what occupies my mind the most is the breakdown of their friendship.

Trace told me once that they used to fight a lot. I suppose that's not uncommon. The ones you fight with the most are the people you love the deepest. But I'm dying to know just how deep their friendship ran.

"Can I ask you something?" I draw in a breath. "Both of you."

Cole starts the dishwasher and rests his hands on the counter. "Shoot."

Trace takes a seat beside me and gives me his full attention.

"The woman you were with, the traitor… When

you mentioned sleeping with her, I sensed there was a story there, something between the two of you. I know it's in the past. I'm just curious about your relationship before me."

"The woman was enamored with Cole." Trace drags a finger across his bottom lip. "She slept with me to get to him."

"I don't know if that's true." Cole huffs a laugh.

The hint of a smile touches Trace's mouth.

"That's what I'm talking about." I point at them. "There's a story there you're not telling me."

"You don't want to hear this." Cole opens the fridge and reaches for another beer. Then he changes his mind and grabs a bottled water instead. "It's meaningless."

"Now you have to tell me."

He braces a hand on the counter, his eyes cast downward and unblinking.

"She called out my name," Trace says without emotion, "during sex *with Cole.*"

"Oh." I grimace. "Ouch."

"Like I gave a shit." Cole scratches his whiskered cheek. "It was just an awkward way to find out my best friend was banging the same woman."

"Did you fight about it?" I try to keep my voice even, despite the jealousy thrashing inside me.

"No." Cole meets Trace's steady gaze. "I called him afterward, and we laughed about it." He pushes off the counter. "I need to hit the head."

He strides toward the bathroom off the kitchen. When the door shuts behind him, I lean a hip against the island, facing Trace.

"Did she prefer you over Cole?" I ask.

three is a war

"No." He swivels toward me on the stool and brackets my legs with his knees. "She was infatuated with Cole."

"Enough to send me photos of her having sex with him?" I rest a hand on the cloth napkin sitting on the counter and spin it around, fidgeting. "I'm sure she was pissed that he caught her and brought her in, but that last move with the pictures was an act of passion."

"You're probably right. But it's over, Danni. You'll never see her or hear from her again."

"Okay." I pull my hand back, and the napkin slips to the floor.

I crouch to pick it up, admiring the detail in the carved wood around the base of the island.

"While you're down there..." Trace rumbles in a casual tone.

I lift my head and my gaze falls on his groin a few inches away. My breath catches, and I pop to my feet, standing in the spread *V* of his thighs. "Was that a joke, Trace Savoy?"

"I would never joke about that." He touches a knuckle to my chin and ghosts his finger oh-so slowly to the hollow of my throat. "I missed you. Painfully. Your absence was a horrible way to remind me how much I love you."

"I missed you, too, and I'm the idiot who walked away."

"You're an idiot for thinking I'd let you go."

"Tell me what you really think." I let out a self-deprecating laugh.

"You're staying." His gaze illuminates with the infallible confidence he's known for. "Longer than one night."

"I don't want to make promises I can't keep." I step back. "Let me see how tonight goes."

"Everything that's happened, the good and the bad, has prepared you for this."

"For what?" I swallow.

"For the reason you're here."

My chest collapses beneath the gravity of his words, and the bathroom door opens.

Cole joins us at the island, glancing from Trace to me. "Heavy conversation?"

"Not yet." Trace studies me for a moment before turning to Cole. "We need to discuss the punishment."

My cheeks burn. I don't need to ask why I'm being punished. Cole didn't cheat on me. Trace saved my life, and I thanked them by kicking them out of my life. Being spanked for that won't be my finest moment. It'll hurt my pride, but my self-esteem could stand to be notched down a bit. After all, pride is the monster that stands between people in a relationship.

"She's tired." Cole rests his elbows on the counter. "It can wait until tomorrow."

They fall silent, watching me, watching each other. Our unspoken thoughts settle around us, creating a transition into the next step. We've eaten. We've talked. We've come to a temporary cease-fire. It's time for bed, and we're all thinking it.

"Have you changed your minds about the sleeping arrangements?" I shift my weight from one foot to the other.

"Nope." Cole finishes off his water and wanders toward the hallway.

Trace and I share a look and follow him.

three is a war

In the bedroom, Cole stretches out on one side of the mattress and flicks off the lamp, dimming the room to a single light.

Trace takes the other side, mirroring Cole's position, legs atop the tangled bedding and arms folded behind his head.

Three feet of empty mattress waits between them. Enough room for me to slide in without touching a muscled leg or sculpted hip.

I stand at the foot of the bed, nervous, excited, and most of all, relieved. I shouldn't want this. I shouldn't want to be here, knowing I'll hurt one or both of them in the end. Doesn't stop my heart from swelling in my chest at the sight of them waiting for me.

Cole's soft smile flips my stomach inside out. His gaze dips to my mouth, and the memory of his taste tingles my lips like a phantom kiss. I don't want to ever lose that feeling.

Trace looks like a half-dressed sex god, all laid out and ready to be devoured. Day-old stubble dusts his chiseled jawline, and his long fingers rest behind his head. If he crooks one of those fingers at me, I might forget we're going to bed *to sleep*.

No, that's not true. Despite everything that's happened, I don't want to do anything to jeopardize the contentment softening their expressions. I just want them to be happy.

Climbing in between them, I settle on my side and face Trace with my back to Cole. "Does this feel weird to you? Sleeping in a bed together?"

"We've shared smaller, far more uncomfortable spaces over the years." Trace rests a hand on his abs, drawing my attention to the corrugated ripples of muscle stretching his skin.

"Remember that night in the desert?" Cole's chuckle warms my spine. "Christ, it was cold as fuck."

"When were you in the desert together?" I ask.

"When we were both operatives." A smile sneaks into Trace's voice despite the ever-present scowl. "We were newbies on one of our first missions and barely knew each other. But we were so cold we spooned and shivered like pussies all night."

"Who was the big spoon?" I bite down on my grin.

"We're not talking about this." Cole groans.

That answers my question, though it's hard to imagine them cuddling in any position. "I wish I could've seen that. Specifically, the spooning part. Will you describe it? Like were you sharing a sleeping bag? Whose hands were where? What were you wear—?

"Enough, Danni." Trace sets his jaw. "If that's the outcome you're hoping for, you'll be sorely disappointed."

"I know that." I clench my hands at my sides. "But if the three of us could be together—"

"Not happening." Cole says firmly.

"Yeah, I figured." I blow out a wistful exhale. "A girl can dream."

"Why would you want that?" Trace's eyebrows gather. "Is one of us not enough for you?"

"No, God, that's not it at all. It's just…now that I've seen you two together without all the hostility, it makes it that much harder. Because if I stay here…" My voice breaks. "If I choose one of you, it'll ruin any progress you've made toward mending your friendship. How do I live with that?"

three is a war

"Danni, look at me." Cole lifts on an elbow, and when I roll to my back, his maple brown eyes lock onto mine. "What if we promise to remain friends after this, no matter what happens, no matter who you choose?"

"You can't keep that promise." My heart ricochets against my ribs. "There would be too much resentment."

"You don't know that." Trace lifts his eyes to me, hooded by thick lashes. "None of us knows what the future looks like."

"Trace and I have come a long way in the past five weeks," Cole says. "Other than the standoff earlier, which should've never involved a gun"—he shoots a glare at Trace—"we haven't had any major altercations. But I'll warn you. Even when we liked each other, we fought constantly."

"Because you're a stubborn prick," Trace says matter-of-factly.

"I'd tell you to go fuck yourself." Cole grunts. "But that would be cruel and unusual punishment."

"See?" Trace smirks. "We have it all worked out."

Maybe it's all the testosterone in the air, but I'm foggy on how it's *worked out*. "Two alphas in the same pack doesn't end well. It's usually a fight to the death."

"Which is why this arrangement has an expiration date." Trace releases a slow breath. "In the meantime, I'll keep Cole on a leash, and he'll…" His lips twitch, as if holding back an insult.

"Save your breath." Cole arches a brow. "You'll need it to blow up your girlfriend."

"What are you…?" My eyes widen. "You're talking about a sex doll?"

"It's the only action he's going to get for the next

six months."

"Whoa." My head spins. "Okay, I'm missing something. What happens in six months?"

"We put a time line on this arrangement." Trace rolls to his side to look at me.

"Why? So I'll make a decision by a certain date?" I sit up and scoot back to the headboard. "I haven't even decided if I'm staying."

"You're staying." Cole shifts to sit cross-legged, facing me. "Admit it, so we can move on."

"No." I cross my arms. "What's the six-month time line?"

"I put you at an unfair advantage before." Quiet, heavy, Cole's voice scratches in his throat. "You're so beautifully submissive, and I leveraged that, making it difficult for you to stick to your no-sex rule."

He seduced me, thoroughly and completely. But my actions are my own. I knew what I was doing and could've stopped it.

"This time, Trace and I are making the rules." Cole runs a finger over his eyebrow. "Decisions about sex are between him and me."

"What?" Fire ignites in my veins. "That's not—"

"I'm not finished." He leans closer. "We're staying here until summer—"

"But it's January! That's six…" My voice falls. "Months."

"Six months," Trace says. "We don't want a decision from you before that."

"That's crazy." I run a nail over my fleece pants, thinking. "What if I know before then?"

Wouldn't I know? Six months is a long time. Especially while living under the same roof with them.

three is a war

"If you know, we'll all know." Trace's eyes lose focus and clear just as quickly. "And that will be that."

"The point is there won't be any pressure." Cole tilts his head. "No pressure to decide. No pressure about sex."

"You're going to go six months without sex?" I look at them with disbelief.

"Trace has his inflatable friend." Cole shrugs.

"I bet your ass is jealous of the shit leaking out of your mouth." Trace grunts an abrasive sound. Then he turns to me and softens his tone. "With regard to intimacy, we're taking those decisions away from you."

"You can't—"

Trace moves so quickly I feel my air cut off before I see his hand wrap around my throat. I claw at his fingers, and he loosens them just enough to open my windpipe.

My breaths come fast and shallow. My skin heats beneath his ferocious gaze, and my heart hammers out of control.

The pressure of his hand doesn't make me fearful. It thrills me, arouses me, and he knows it.

Warmth trembles in my thighs, and a heavy ache swells between my legs, gathering, throbbing, and forcing a whimper past my lips.

Cole doesn't move beside me, his fist resting beneath his chin, his expression dark and unreadable.

"Nothing turns you on more," Trace breathes, leaning in, "than surrendering your power to another. You don't want the control. You want to be relieved of it. You crave the freedom it gives you. Shake your head if I'm wrong."

I don't move, my fingers curled around his wrist,

my breath lodged in my throat. He's right. I want to be owned, dominated, and pleasured by a man I trust. And I trust him when it comes to sex. Both of them. They know my limits, and they have the desire, experience, and skill to effectively master my body. It's one of the reasons sex with them is so damn good.

"Your face is flushed." Trace flexes his fingers against my neck and glances down. "Your nipples are swollen, and your heart is racing."

My gaze flies to Cole, and he stares back at me, his eyes pupil-black and half-mast.

"I'm making a point." Trace uses his grip to turn my head toward him. "Tell me what it is."

"If I stay…" My throat bobs against his hand. "All decisions regarding sex are between you and Cole."

"Tell me why."

"I prefer it that way." I wet my lips and whimper. "And it takes the pressure off me."

"Good girl." Trace releases my neck and touches his lips to my brow.

I melt beneath the warmth of his mouth and slide down on the mattress until I'm flat on my back.

Cole focuses on my hand where it rests between us. When I lift it toward him, he grips it, knotting our fingers together. Then he lowers his head to the pillow and stretches out on his side, facing me.

Trace turns off the light, blanketing the room in darkness. The bedding rustles as he slides a blanket over us.

While still holding onto Cole's hand, I reach my other toward Trace. His fingers find mine beneath the sheets and clutch tightly.

No one speaks. Not for the long minutes that

three is a war

follow.

I waver so uncontrollably between *I shouldn't be here* and *this is exactly where I'm supposed to be*, between resisting and surrendering, fleeing and fighting, that I doubt every thought in my head.

That's when it hits me. I'm not leaving. Because if I did, it would only prolong the inevitable. Since they know I won't be happy without them, they'll track me down and haul me back.

Why would they go through so much trouble? I'm just a woman. An average, pain-in-the-ass woman with a lot of flaws.

"Why are you doing this?" My voice drops to a whisper. "I'm not worth it."

"Since the moment I saw you…" Trace squeezes my fingers. "I haven't gone a day without thinking about you. No matter how much it hurts or how long it takes, I know that a lifetime with you is worth fighting for."

"I couldn't have said it better than that." Cole grunts a soft chuckle. "Fucking asshole."

I pull my arms to my chest, bringing their hands close and holding them there, against my heart. "I don't want to hurt you."

"Then don't leave," Trace says.

"What are we going to do for six months?" I ask.

"I'll show you tomorrow." Cole shifts closer and brushes a kiss against my shoulder. "Tell me you're staying."

"I'm staying." I let out a contented sigh.

I missed this. God, I missed them so much.

They're giving me a six-month reprieve from making a decision. That seems like an eternity to make them wait, but we tried it my way, and I messed everything up.

Things will be different this time.

While they're making the rules and controlling the arrangement, I'm going to fight.

Fight my doubts.

Fight my fears.

Fight my indecision.

I'll fight through the agony and do the hardest thing I'll ever have to do.

I'll choose which part of my heart I have to let go forever.

seven

I wake to a quiet room and sunshine warming my face. With a full body stretch, I rouse a little more, blinking, yawning, and *alone*.

The mattress on either side of me is cool to the touch. When I strain my ears, I'm met with silence. Where are they?

I sit up and spot my phone on Trace's pillow, next to a note scrawled in his elegant penmanship.

Passcode for all doors is the year your car was made.
Call your parents.

I grin at his bossiness and head to the bathroom, where I freshen up and brush my teeth. Then I grab the phone and leave the bedroom in search of coffee.

Down the hallway and through the living room, I pause at the kitchen island. The house is empty and still.

Unless Cole and Trace are in one of the locked rooms, they must be outside.

I find a pot of coffee waiting, prepare a cup, and step toward the windowed wall in the living room.

The stone terrace cascades toward the bridge and dock, the majestic scenery glowing in the early morning sun. In the distance, a few boats drift on the calm lake. Closer in, a heron soars over the water.

Something moves beneath the canopy of the dock. Shifting to the window closest to the bridge, I spot Cole and Trace walking around the ski boat. They're too far away to make out expressions, but it's easy to differentiate between Cole's broad build and Trace's height.

Cole tosses a bundle of rope to Trace, and they climb onto the boat. What are they up to?

Both are wearing jeans, heavy jackets, and sunglasses. I guess I should change clothes and make my way down there?

First, I need to call my parents.

Coffee in hand, I lower onto the couch in the living room and hit the speed dial for Florida.

Mom picks up on the second ring. "Good morning, darling."

"Hey, Mom."

"How's the drive going? Did you stay the night in Tennessee?"

"I'm still in Missouri." I sip the coffee, basking in the serene view beyond the windows. "I'm at Table Rock Lake. Cole owns a house here."

"You went back to him?" Hope whispers through her voice.

She hasn't met Trace, but she always liked Cole.

three is a war

Really, I think she'd like any man I date. She just wants me married and settled.

"Trace is here, too." *How am I going to explain this?* "They kind of bonded after I left."

"That sounds...complicated." Her tone shifts from thoughtful to worried. "What are you doing, Danni?"

"I don't know. I guess that's why I'm here. I need to figure it out."

"Does that mean you're not coming to Florida?"

"Can I get back to you on that?"

"Of course. Our home is always open to you." She sighs. "Just be careful, sweetheart. I know you're twenty-eight—"

"Almost twenty-nine."

"—and you think you know everything there is to know about the world. But you have a lot of growing up to do. Relationships are hard work. *Love* is hard work. Whether you choose Cole or Trace, make sure you pick the one you're willing to work the hardest for. Okay?"

"You work hard for Dad?" I grin.

"Oh, that man..." She groans. "Don't get me started."

I spend the next ten minutes answering her questions about the lake house and the surrounding property, going into detail about the landscaping. She loves that shit. Then I end the call and finish off the coffee while waiting for the phone to ring.

My mom and sister are tight. So tight they call each other about everything. Right now, I know my mom is updating Bree on the status of my life.

Five minutes later, my phone buzzes, flashing *Bree* on the caller ID. When I answer, I give her the same spiel

I gave Mom.

Her questions are more intrusive. *Why did you change your mind? How did you get there? Why didn't you tell me? Are you going to choose between them?*

I hate lying to her, so I keep my responses as truthful as possible. *I missed them. Cole drove me here. Just arrived last night. I'm here to finally make a decision.*

"You better keep me updated," she says.

"You have my number, Nosy Nancy. I love you."

"Love you, too"

We hang up, and I head back to the bedroom, change into the warmest clothes I find—jeans, fleece sweatshirt, UGG boots, and a thick Down coat with a faux-fur-lined hood. Slipping my phone into the coat pocket, I walk to the keypad for the bedroom's exterior door and enter *1974*—the Midget's birth year. It opens.

Bracing for the cold, I step outside and shut the door behind me. Surprisingly, the air is warmer than I expected. Not as warm as I would like, but there's no wind. No need for gloves or a scarf.

I follow the cobblestone path to the bridge, my boots scuffing along the wood planks. As I reach the dock, my pulse quickens. This feeling never gets old—the buzz in my belly, the anticipation of a lingering glance, and the consuming fixation on *what-ifs* and *could-be's*.

"Morning, baby." Cole stands in the ski boat a few feet away, his grin bright against the dark shadow of scruff on his face.

"Morning." I pause at the edge of the slip.

Behind him, Trace rummages through a storage compartment, grumbling about Cole's lack of organization.

"How'd you sleep?" Cole peers at me over the top

three is a war

of his aviator glasses.

"I don't remember." I return his smile. "That's a good thing. You?"

"Fantastic." His expression softens, and he leans over the railing and holds out a hand. "Come on."

I grip his fingers and let him haul me into the boat. "So this is yours?"

"Yep. Wanna put some hours on it?"

"Sure. Do I get to drive?"

"Not a chance." Trace stands, removes his sunglasses, and gives me a thorough once-over, lingering on my mouth. "You look gorgeous this morning."

"Thank you." I bite my lip, the flutter in my stomach showing no signs of fading. "Why can't I drive?"

"You don't know how." Cole moves behind the steering wheel. "But you have six months to learn."

Six months. I'm not sure how I feel about that time line. Maybe it's exactly what I need. Before I left, I wasted so much energy on beating myself up because I couldn't make a decision. It would be nice to just take one day at a time without worrying about making them wait.

Ten minutes later, Cole drives us out of the cove and into the open lake. The chilly air nips at my cheeks, but the sun is warm and energizing. Before the boat speeds up, I move to the front and stretch out on the curved bench seat. Trace sits beside me, his sunglasses back in place.

I open my mouth to ask if there are extra shades, but he's already removing a pair from his pocket. They look identical to the cat eye sunglasses I keep in my car.

"Thanks." I slide them on. "Did you steal these from me?"

"No." His teeth scrape his bottom lip. "I bought them because they reminded me of the first day we spent together."

The day he ran errands with me. He was so standoffish and rude when we met, but there was something compelling about him, something magnetic and so damn irresistible I tolerated his bullshit. In fact, I craved more of it. More of him.

"You kissed me that day," I whisper wistfully and peek behind me.

Cole doesn't seem to hear us over the wind and the motor. Aviator glasses conceal his eyes, his head turned slightly away as he steers us through the open water. Since there aren't many boats out, the lake is gentle and waveless.

Trace slides his fingers around mine, pulling my attention back to him. I hold his hand on my lap and trace his knuckles. The simple connection makes my chest feel lighter. The soft frown on his mouth heats my blood. And the caress of his gaze on my face makes me feel whole, more alive.

"Tell me a story." The wind swallows my voice.

He waves at Cole and shouts, "Find a spot to park."

Cole veers the boat into a quiet inlet enshrouded by trees and turns off the engine. The speakers in the boat crackle, and a second later, a punk rock song thumps on low volume.

Holding the remote to the stereo, Cole moves to the front and sits across from us. Beneath the heat of his stare, I squirm with the urge to put space between Trace and me. But Cole's jaw is relaxed, his posture reclined and easy. He seems oddly content.

three is a war

"What kind of story?" Trace hooks an arm around my back and toys with a tangled lock of my hair.

"I want to hear one about the two of you." I adjust the sunglass on my face. "Something outrageous. The more embarrassing the better."

Trace stretches his legs across the aisle and rests his feet on the bench seat beside Cole.

He's wearing boots? They look expensive, the brown leather smooth and scratch-free. Such a drastic departure from his spit-shined loafers.

"I have a story." The corner of Trace's lips twists. "We just finished an assignment, and I had to take our rental car through one of those automated carwashes."

Cole groans and pinches the bridge of his nose. "Of all the stories to tell…"

"This is a good one." Trace leans back, settling in. "Should I tell her why I needed to wash the car?"

"No," Cole says at the same time as I say, "Yes."

"Danni wins." Trace smirks at Cole before turning to me. "The prior night, we went out to celebrate the success of the mission. Cole celebrated a little too hard."

"Okay, for the record…" Cole leans forward. "We were in a place where I didn't speak the language and didn't know what I was drinking. Whatever they served me hit me sideways."

"He threw up all the way home with his head hanging out of the window." Trace grimaces. "Painted the side of the car in Technicolor."

"Gross." I laugh.

"Worse, I had to carry his heavy unconscious ass up three flights of stairs. So the next day, I made him go with me to the carwash, and that's when the damn car broke down."

"*In* the carwash?" I widen my eyes. "Were you stuck on those rail things that move the car forward?"

"Yes." Trace nods at Cole. "He decides to jump out and push."

"But there were water jets, right?" I shake my head, picturing him soaked to the bone and fuming mad.

"Yeah." Cole rubs a hand over his head. "My entire leg was in a cast, which by the way, isn't supposed to get wet."

I sober. "Why were you in a cast?"

"Just another day on the job." He winks at me.

"So Cole was out there in a cast," Trace says, "trying to push a car with a broken leg while the automated scrubbers slapped him in the face."

"Did you help him?" I arch a brow at Trace.

"Hell, no. I stayed in the car and waited for someone to shut off the water. You know, like a sane person." Trace rubs small circles on my hand. "But Cole has no patience. He lost his temper, stormed out, and hitchhiked back to the hotel."

"Not my proudest moment." Cole sighs.

Maybe not, but I thoroughly enjoyed the story. A few moments pass before another thought pops into my head. "Tell me about the coffee cup yesterday."

Trace stares out at the lake, his eyebrows pulling together. "The sedative was safe. No aftereffects. It's not something you'd find on the market, but we've used it many times on the job."

Interesting. "What about the writing on the bottom of the cup?"

He flicks his eyes to Cole. "What writing?"

"*It's not over.*" Cole shrugs. "That's what I wrote."

His soft brown eyes land on me. "I didn't expect you to see it."

"Then why write it?" I squint at him. "That message really fucked with my head. I was certain one of your enemies drugged me as part of a revenge mission that wasn't over."

"Shit, I'm sorry." He closes his eyes briefly. "I thought if you saw it, you would assume it came from Trace or me. I wanted to ease your mind, not freak you out."

"I never thought you guys would pull something like that, so I jumped to the worst-case scenario." I blow out a breath. "Doesn't matter. It's in the past. I was just curious."

Cole relaxes, his gaze drifting over the lake. "I've made a lot of mistakes with you, Danni. Given you more than enough reasons to leave." He meets my eyes. "But I have a new perspective now. Things will be different going forward."

"How so?" I ask.

"A couple of months ago, I wouldn't have been able to tolerate that." He nods at Trace's arm around my back. "When I returned home and found you with him, I sank into a miserable headspace full of doubts and insecurity about our future. Every second you spent with him felt like a threat. There were times I questioned if I deserved you, wondered if you'd be better off with him."

Trace's hand tightens around mine.

"And now?" My voice cracks.

"We belong together." Cole's gaze bores into mine, resolute and unshakable. "I'm more certain about that now than ever before. This…" He gestures to the three of us. "I see it as a journey of trials, like a training course to prepare me for all the obstacles you and I will encounter together in the future."

It's just like Cole to view our future together as a foregone conclusion. But the fact that he sees Trace merely as an obstacle to overcome is a little unsettling.

"This isn't the military." I frown. "You don't need a training course to be with me."

"There's always room for improvement." He glances at Trace, his expression expectant, as if seeking validation. "I'm making an effort to lock down my temper."

I've noticed. Granted, I've been here less than a day, but I haven't seen so much as a twitch of aggression from him. Not even when Trace held him at gunpoint.

"Before we brought you here," Trace says to me, "we had some heart to heart conversations."

"You did?" I know my eyes are bugging out of my head. "I can't figure out if you guys are working together or against each other."

"Both." Trace lifts his face to the sunshine and draws in a slow breath. "We dragged you to an isolated location without your consent and are forcing you to confront the decision you ran from. The least we can do is make the next few months tolerable, and that starts with how we engage with one another. There's a line between letting emotion control you"—he gives Cole a pointed look—"and suppressing it so completely it's assumed I feel nothing."

"I never assumed that, Trace." I chew on my lip. "You have me kind of worried, though, because I don't want either of you to change. Other than the lying and secrets…"

three is a war

"We're not changing," Cole says. "We're just going to be more open. Look, we can talk out our asses about being honest with one another, but that's something that will have to be proven over time."

Wow. They're serving up man-sized portions of maturity, and it's so weird to me. Especially after my mom said I have a lot of growing up to do. If Cole and Trace are taking strides toward civility, I need to up my game. *Growing up* isn't something I've ever strived for, but maybe Mom's right. I need to be responsible and accountable for my actions.

As another punk rock song bangs through the speakers, I hold my hand out to Cole, motioning for the stereo remote. "Let me see that."

"Nope."

With a dimpled grin, he taps on the remote's digital screen, and the melody changes to a song I know.

This Is What You Came For by Calvin Harris vibrates through me, tensing my muscles and accelerating my pulse. For the first time in weeks, I feel the overwhelming urge to dance. The feeling passes quickly, however, because the boat's too small and the audience is too close and intimate and watchful. I don't know what the protocol is for shaking my ass in this situation. A strange thought since I've never hesitated to groove when the impulse arises.

"You want to dance." Trace angles his chin down, peering at me over the glasses. "The quickening of your breaths gives you away."

I nod, gripping the seat as a wave from a passing boat rocks us in the water. "Not right now though."

"You don't want to dance in front of us." Cole

narrows his eyes.

"I guess…I don't know." I pull my hand from Trace's grip and shove it in the pocket of my coat. "I screwed up a lot. With both of you." My head lowers as I mumble, "I want to do the right thing."

"Explain what you're thinking." Trace hooks a knuckle beneath my chin, forcing my eyes up.

"Okay. Well…" I take a deep breath, looking at Trace. "I took advantage of your restraint. Meanwhile, I slept with Cole and didn't tell you." My face heats. "I know your plans are well-intended, and everything you've told me sounds reasonable. But I don't know how to maneuver through this without pissing one of you off or screwing up again."

"Be honest with us." Trace kisses the side of my head. "Like you're doing now."

"And follow your heart," Cole says. "Trust us to guide you through the rest of it."

"Okay." I clear my throat, uncertain.

"How about I give you a tour of the lake, show you all my fishing spots?" Cole stands. "Then we'll head back and fix lunch. There's something else I want to show you at the house."

Several hours later, after a heavy meal of steak and mashed potatoes, I shower and change into yoga pants and a soft shirt. Then I crash on the couch in the living room, my nose pink from the sun and my body exhausted from spending half the day on the water.

I don't know when I fell asleep, but I wake with a blanket wrapped around me and my cheek resting on a hard, denim-clad thigh.

Long legs stretch out before me, and bare feet rest on the coffee table beside a tumbler of scotch.

I roll to my back and stare up at Trace's arresting blue eyes. "How long was I asleep?"

"About an hour." He runs a hand through my hair, watching the movement of his fingers. "I could sit here forever with you like this."

I give him a sleepy smile, while my mind zeroes in on the bulge of his groin beneath my head. "Where's Cole?"

"He's locking up the boat and the dock."

Without warning, he yanks me up and positions me to sit sideways on his lap. His hands frame my face, and he leans his brow against mine, inhaling deeply.

"Nag Champa." His lips brush my cheek, hastening the patter of my heart. "My favorite smell."

He's close enough to kiss, and I'm afraid to move, afraid to breathe, afraid to close my eyes. I want to taste him. Saturate my senses with him. I want to delete the distance that doesn't belong between us.

"Trace." I rest my hands on his shoulders. "Tell me what to do."

"Be yourself."

His minty breath washes over me, stealing my train of thought. He's insanely potent. Not just his delectable scent. It's his intensity. The way he stares at me like nothing else exists. The subtle press of his fingers on my spine, reminding me he's in control. His unwavering focus on every twitch and blink, as if gleaning my thoughts through body cues.

But I'm reading his cues, too, and his unfaltering eye contact doesn't just tell me he wants to connect with me. That look in his eyes begs me to kiss him.

Sliding my hands to the thick column of his neck, I

part my lips and tip closer. Heart racing, skin tingling, I absorb the warmth of his exhale on my face and anticipate the feel of his mouth against mine. A hairbreadth away, he leans back.

His hand falls to the back of my head, and he guides my cheek to his chest.

My stomach hardens. But on the heels of disappointment is realization. This is what they meant when they said they would be controlling the intimacy between us. I can act on instinct and follow my heart, but when it comes to sex, they'll decide when and how far.

A sense of relief sweeps through me. Sex is the gray area. I don't want the responsibility of making rules around it and enforcing those rules. Even if that means I won't always get what I want.

"Trace?"

"Hm?" His deep voice reverberates in his chest.

"I'm sorry about Cole." I close my eyes. "Sleeping with him and not you wasn't a conscious choice or any kind of choice. It would've been you if—"

"You warned me it would happen, and I already told you I don't blame you." He grips my jaw and angles my head back to meet my eyes. "This is the last time we discuss it. Understand?"

"Yes."

He releases me, and I relax against his chest, burrowing into a snuggly closeness that rivals any kiss. Here, I can feel his heartbeat, smell the faint scent of cologne on his collar, and watch his pulse jumping along the vein in his throat.

And that's how Cole finds me when he steps inside a few minutes later.

My eyes lift, and my head follows, as if everything

three is a war

inside me is pulled toward his presence, as if my very soul knows its mate is near, and I need to go to him. That has to mean something, right? Do I feel the same way with Trace? Or am I fabricating signs that aren't really there?

Cole approaches the couch and holds out a hand to me. "I want to show you something."

"I should've let her kiss me." Trace unwraps his arms from around me and slides me off his lap.

I step back, glaring at him. Why would he say that? Is he trying to pick a fight?

To my surprise, Cole laughs and grabs my hand. "Lost your chance, pal."

"Pricks like you are the reason I drink." Trace lifts the scotch to his lips, smirking.

Cole laughs harder and turns toward the hallway, leading me in that direction.

"What just happened?" I glance over my shoulder and find Trace reclined on the couch, following me with his eyes.

He doesn't look upset or bothered. If anything, there's a calculating glimmer in his expression, and that confuses me as much as it concerns me.

"I know the way to your heart." Cole winks and guides me around the corner and out of view.

"Hang on." I pull my hand from his. "Is this a competition?"

He pauses in front of the first door in the hall and meets my gaze head-on. "This is a war, Danni."

My breath catches. "But you said—"

"We said no fighting," a colder voice tiptoes behind me.

I didn't even hear Trace follow. As I turn to face him, he's already at my side, holding his glass of scotch.

"No secrets," he says. "No brawls. No manipulations. But we both want the same thing." His gaze drifts down and up my body in an *I-own-you-you're-mine* way that trembles my legs. "And we both intend to win."

Everything's been so nonchalant today I feel sideswiped by this. But they warned me it wouldn't be easy, and even without the warning, I know better. This is Cole and Trace. They're not going to just sit back and let this play out on its own.

Does that change my resolve to stay and finish this? Definitely not. We're in this together.

"What's behind the door?" I ask.

"Enter your passcode." Cole points at the keypad, his expression indecipherable.

When I punch in the code, he opens the door.

My hand flies to my mouth as I gasp. I don't know what I expected, but polished wood floors, mirrored walls, and custom-built ballet bars wasn't it.

"When did you build this?" I take a hesitant step into a dance studio that's five times larger than my last one.

Cole lingers on the threshold and rests his hands in his pockets, his voice quiet. "I started the construction two years ago."

eight

"Two years ago?" I whirl toward Cole, my screech echoing through the dance studio. "How is that possible? You were on the run and—"

"Hiding." He steps into the room and approaches the wall of windows, staring out at the sunset glistening across the lake. "When my cover was blown, this is the first place I came. It was the safest place to regroup and plan a counterattack."

"Did you know he was in Missouri two years ago?" I ask Trace.

He leans against the wall in the hallway, his head tilted down, and a frown in his brow. "I recently found out about it."

I turn back to Cole. "You said you couldn't return to the States until you knew I was safe."

"The woman," he says, "the traitor, didn't know about this house. Nothing here connected me to you or St. Louis. That said, I didn't stay long. Others in my unit used to come here, and I didn't know who I could trust."

"How long were you here?"

"Three months."

"You severed contact with me, and for three months, you were only a few hours away?" My chest constricts as that sinks in. "You didn't check in on me during that time?"

"I couldn't risk it." His voice is so quiet, so thick with heartache it's difficult to hear him. "I stayed here longer than I should have." He glances around the room and returns to the view beyond the windows.

That's when it hits me. He was balls-deep in a mission, hiding from the enemy he infiltrated, and he stayed here to build me a dance studio.

A knot forms in my throat as I take in the space with new eyes. It's a beautiful, sun-drenched, open studio, at least a thousand square feet, with twelve-foot-tall seamless windows, stunning lake views, exposed brick walls, and hardwood floors. There's a lounge area with a leather couch, a built-in stereo system, and a dancing pole in the back corner. The ballet bars wrap the entire room, including the windowed wall. I could actually stretch on them while staring out over the lake, and I bet those windows reflect like mirrors when it's dark outside. *Incredible.*

"I started the remodeling two years ago," Cole says, "but I didn't finish it until five weeks ago."

"You came here when I…" I press a hand against my breastbone and lower my voice. "When I kicked you out?"

three is a war

"Yeah. I moved my belongings here." He nods at the door at the far end of the room. "There's a dressing room through there."

As I head that way, I catch Trace's eyes in the hall. He maintains a relaxed lean against the wall, an ankle crossed over the other, drinking his scotch. I'm still not used to seeing him in jeans and t-shirts, but he pulls off the casual look like everything else — with irresistible confidence and intimidation.

When I open the door to the dressing room, I'm once again stunned into breathlessness. Not only is it larger than the biggest room in my old house, it's stocked with every accessory a dancer could ever want. Ballroom dresses, dance shoes, leotards, tutus, glittery bras, belly dance costumes — the inventory is endless. A large vanity sits in the corner, facing full-length mirrors framed in globed lights.

My pulse thumps wildly as I run my fingers over taffeta, silk, and rhinestone beading. "How did you — ?"

"I bought out the floor room of a dance store in St. Louis," Cole says behind me.

This is too much. I accused him of cheating, kicked him out of my house, and he built me *another* dance studio.

Tears sneak up, surging through my throat, drenching my eyes, and choking my voice. "I don't deserve this."

"Fuck if you don't." He strides toward me and sweeps me up in a hug that lifts my feet off the floor. "I want to give you the world." He buries his face in my neck. "Dammit, Danni. Please don't cry."

"I can't help it." I half-sob, half-laugh, and wrap

my arms and legs around his muscled body. "Thank you so much, Cole."

Maybe he does know the way to my heart. Material possessions mean very little to me, but this is more than that. Dancing is my passion, my life, and he's given me the means to embrace that while I'm here.

"I can't believe you built this when I didn't even know the house existed." I lower my toes to the floor and crane my neck toward the doorway, unable to see Trace around the corner. "There was a chance I'd never come here."

"When I left for the last mission…" He touches my face, his thumb stroking across my cheek. "I knew it would be my last assignment. I had every intention of bringing you here after I retired."

I reach up and hold his handsome face in my hands, savoring the scratch of whiskers against my palms. Looking into his eyes, I tell him without words how grateful I am and how much I love him.

His expression softens, and his mouth parts. As his head dips lower, and lower, my pulse kicks up. He's going to kiss me, and I want that with an ache that burns through my veins.

But at the last second, he pulls back.

My breath rushes out. "That was cruel."

"You have no idea." His lips thin in a pained grimace, and he grips the back of his neck. "Go explore your dance studio before I fuck you against the sparkly…" He squints at a rack of sequined body tights. "Whatever those are."

I shake my head, smiling, and exit the dressing room.

Trace moved to the couch in the studio, his tumbler

three is a war

of scotch empty and sitting on the floor beside his bare feet.

"Well?" He curves up a brow. "Am I out of the running?"

"What do you think?"

"I think..." Cole trails behind me, eyes on Trace. "If you head to St. Louis right now, you'll be home before bedtime."

"You have the rest of your miserable life to be a dickhead." Trace stretches an arm across the back of the couch. "Why not take tonight off?"

Stifling my smile, I head toward the panel for the stereo. "I just want you guys to know that someone finds your insults entertaining. Not me. But someone."

The sound of their soft laughter releases my grin. I pull up the playlist on the digital screen beside the stereo.

"Christ, I missed you." Cole leans a shoulder against the wall beside me.

"I'll be here all night," I say with a shrug, "chilling on the corner of awesome and brilliant."

He watches me for a moment, flashing those adorable dimples. "What are you doing?"

"Checking out the music. Looks like you stole my playlist."

"I might've." He tilts his head. "Choose a song that inspires a red-hot burn."

"Why?" I drag out the word, infusing it with suspicion.

"I'm about to show your ass how hard I love it."

A tremble races through me. "You're going to punish me now?"

"One of the many services I offer." His eyes

glimmer.

Heaven help me, he's such a flirt, and I'm a total glutton for it. He has the ability to scramble my mind with a cocky smile and set my body on fire with a glance. I could spend days doing nothing but having sex with him in my head. The way he kisses my neck, bites my lips, holds me down, makes me moan, and doesn't stop until I'm boneless and replete—he's so damn good in bed I can come just from fantasizing about it. Sometimes I do.

But that's not why I'm here. While sex is crucial in a relationship, the indescribable way he uses his tongue can't be the basis for my decision.

I scroll through the song list and select *Talking Body* by Tove Lo. Then I step back and wait for instruction with a quiver of excitement in my belly.

"Danni." Trace shifts to the edge of the couch and points at the floor between his legs. "Come here."

"Are you—?" I stutter and look at Cole. "Is he…? I thought you were doing this?"

If Cole intends to spank me, he'll do it with my pants off. At least, that's how he always did it in the past. Maybe I'm jumping to conclusions and something else's going on here?

The only response Cole gives me is a chin lift in Trace's direction, wordlessly ordering me to cross the room.

I wipe my slick palms on my yoga pants and move my feet. When I reach Trace, I pause in the spread *V* of his legs and silence the impulse to hug my waist. Then I drag my gaze to his.

"Cross your arms together as high as you can behind you." He grips my thighs and pulls, forcing me to shuffle closer, until my shins touch the front of the couch.

three is a war

I fold my arms across my back and clutch my elbows. The uncomfortable position pushes my breasts out and shoulders back, magnifying my blooming nerves.

"Perfect." Cole steps behind me and gathers my hair, roping the waist-length strands over my shoulder and down my chest.

"Are you going to watch?" I ask Trace in a shaky voice.

"I'm going to restrain you."

The heat in my face rushes to my core, leaving a shiver in its wake. "Did you plan this? I mean, did you guys talk about how you would choreograph it?"

"We discussed the logistics." Trace's cool expression reveals nothing.

I don't believe for a minute that he's all right with this arrangement. I'd love to know how that conversation went. On second thought, maybe not, considering it ended with him pulling a gun on Cole.

"Since you're both going to be here…" My throat scratches, and I cough. "You're leaving my pants on, right?"

I'm held immobile by Trace's pale blue eyes, but it's Cole's hands on my hips that seize my breaths.

His thumbs hook beneath my waistband, and my shoulders tighten. Then he yanks my pants to the floor, taking my thong with them.

My lungs freeze up, and I lose my grip on my elbows behind me.

"Don't move your arms." Trace shoots me a flinty glare and lowers his gaze.

I tremble as he scrutinizes my naked body below the waist. Why do I suddenly feel so insecure? I'm a dancer, totally comfortable in my skin. But dammit, it's been weeks since I trimmed down there.

"I haven't shaved." I shift my weight, squirming with vulnerability. "I didn't know…I would've prepared…" *Stop rambling. Idiot.*

"You weren't expecting anyone to see you nude." Cole lifts my foot, then the other, sliding my pants off and tossing them away. "It validates what I already knew." He runs a hand along my leg. "In five weeks, you never tried to hook up with another man."

"No." *God, no.* I didn't even consider it.

"I prefer it like this." Trace stares at the blonde patch of hair between my legs. "I never understood why women want to infantilize their bodies."

"It's cleaner and more visually appealing."

"It's child-like. But this…" He bends forward and breathes in, slow and deep. "The hair traps your pheromones, which are odorless, detected subconsciously, and stimulate arousal."

Oh my God. I bet my face is crimson. If the floor opened up and swallowed me whole, I'd welcome the fast exit.

Cole steps around me and gives my pussy the same examination. Then he glares at Trace, and his hand flexes at his side, his chest rising and falling.

"Okay, show-and-tell time is over." I pivot away, dropping my arms.

"Hold still." Trace grabs my waist and turns me back. "Why are you uncomfortable? I've seen every inch of your body countless times, and it's safe to assume he has, too."

"Not at the same time." My neck tenses.

"What's making you nervous?" Cole touches my

three is a war

chin, nudging my gaze to him.

"I won't lie and say I don't enjoy…" My voice drops to a whisper. "The attention. But I'm concerned about how this is affecting you guys. You said you won't share, and if this makes you uneasy—"

"We're not sharing," Trace says.

"We're compromising." Cole crosses his arms over his chest.

"I guess I don't understand the difference." I tug on the hem of the shirt, stretching it toward my thighs.

"Stop fidgeting." Trace pries my fingers from the material.

The song streaming in the background comes to an end, and the sudden silence amplifies the heaving sound of my breaths.

I point at the stereo. "I'll go select another—"

"Arms up." Cole pins me with an unyielding glare.

I open my mouth to argue, but the words stick in my throat. I'm making this awkward because I don't want *them* to feel awkward. Except they don't seem distressed or troubled. I need to remember they're in control here, orchestrating every step. For reasons I can't figure out, they want to do this together.

With a steeling breath, I raise my arms.

nine

My insides coil with nervous energy as I stretch my arms over my head.

Cole yanks my shirt up and off. With a flick of his fingers, he unclasps my bra and takes that, too, leaving me completely nude and shaking all over.

"Straddle my lap." Trace leans back, sinking deeper into the couch. "And return your arms to the folded position behind you."

Cole shifts to the side, lashes hooded over warm, seductive eyes that make my blood burn.

With my arms locked together at my back, I slide onto Trace's lap, the stiff denim of his jeans brushing against the backs of my thighs. His legs are sprawled so wide I have to stretch out to straddle him, which I'm sure is the intent. It puts me fully on display with my bare ass in the air.

"Cole won the dispute over who gets to punish you," Trace says at my ear, raising goosebumps along my spine. "I wanted to be present while he administered it, but I don't relish the thought of watching him touch you." His gaze flicks over my shoulder, and his voice takes on a deadly edge. "In this position, he gets a phenomenal view of your ass and pussy."

"But Trace gets to see your beautiful face." Cole moves behind me, trailing fingertips over the curve of my backside. "He gets to watch every sexy little nuance in your expression as the burn releases chemicals in your brain and morphs into pleasure."

I'm still struggling to reconcile how they're okay with this, how Cole is tolerating my naked body spread out over Trace, and how Trace isn't knocking Cole's hand away as it slides down the crack of my ass.

I gasp as those fingers dip between my legs to trace the slit of my pussy.

Trace reaches behind me and grips my arms, pinning them tight against my back. His other hand wraps around my neck, holding my face in front of his. "Tell me why you're being punished."

"I gave up on both of you." My stomach bottoms out, and I choke on a ragged breath. "I should have stayed and fought for you."

He touches his brow to mine, his warm breath like an erotic kiss against my mouth. "I love you."

"I love y—"

A blazing sting shoots across my backside, the pain so razor-sharp I don't register the smacking sound of Cole's hand until it echoes through the room.

"Dammit!" I twist to glare at him over my

shoulder. "You could've warned me."

"That was your warning." He rears back his arm.

I return to Trace, teeth clenched, and brace for impact.

"Breathe, Danni." Trace holds my arms against my back and cups my face in his strong hand. "Deep breaths."

My lungs release as the next strike lands with a heavy smack. Fire spreads across my buttocks, permeates skin and muscle, and jars my bones. Fucking hell, it hurts, and he's just getting warmed up.

It doesn't take long for him to let loose. His breaths grow shallow, and fewer pauses come between the hits. The pain is all-consuming, stealing my air, watering my eyes, and blistering every nerve-ending in my lower body. But Trace holds me steady, in his hands, in the strength of his unflinching gaze.

I've been spanked by both of them more times than I can remember. Nothing compares to this…this dichotomy of staring into the eyes of one man while another pummels my backside. Every blow Cole delivers is meant to penetrate and arouse, and the panting sounds of Trace's breaths heighten the thrill. I already feel the pleasure gathering inside me, coiling, heating, and throbbing between my legs.

But I'm afraid to enjoy it. Terrified I'll crave what I can never have. My mind refuses to change course, however, my thoughts tunnel down a treacherous path that summons fantasies of Cole unzipping, pulling himself out, and ramming inside me while I writhe and buck on top of Trace's swollen cock.

The ruthless slaps of Cole's hand blur together in

an endless sea of velvet fire. Feverish flames melt through my body, intoxicating my blood and numbing my brain. I sag against Trace's chest, moaning helplessly and rocking my hips.

He tightens his grip on my neck, bringing my mouth an inch from his, teasing me with the sinful shape of his lips so close, so perfectly kissable. I know exactly how scrumptious he tastes, and the need to lick him rages inside me. I try to press closer, stretching my neck, reaching, needing, but he stops me, denying the kiss I want so badly.

I won't beg, won't make demands. I love the freedom in surrendering too much. Under their control, restrained by their will, I'm exactly where I belong.

Eventually, Cole's strikes transform into languid caresses, his hands roving hypnotically up and down my spine and over my backside.

It's heaven and hell, divine temptation and wretched torment. I'm naked and exposed between two virile, sexual, wickedly good-looking men—two men I love more than anything in the world, and I have no idea where this will lead.

It won't end in a tangled trio of panting, sweat-slick bodies. They've been very clear about not sharing. Doesn't stop the avalanche of hunger ripping through me in merciless waves. I'm insanely turned on, pulsing and soaked between my legs. And Cole knows it, *feels it*, as his fingers glide through my folds.

I gulp down a whimper, locked in the prismatic blue of Trace's eyes.

"Do you want to come?" His gaze dips to my mouth.

"Not if I'm the only one."

three is a war

"That's not up to you." He glances at Cole behind me.

I don't know if they're having one of those wordless conversations, but the instant Cole's fingers sink inside me, all rational thought evaporates.

His stroking, curling, diabolical touch spreads sparks of bliss across my skin, wrenching breathless noises from my throat. My arms ache to move from the unnatural position behind me, but Trace keeps them bound, my wrists clenched in his grip. I want to clutch his shoulders and pull him closer, but he gives me something better.

Ducking his head, he captures my mouth in a plundering kiss. His tongue swoops past my lips and slides against mine, licking, owning, and making me crazy with need. The onslaught of pleasure crashes through me, igniting every cell in my body and liquefying my bones. I groan against Trace's mouth and grind against Cole's hand, overstimulated, overwhelmed, and overflooded with emotion and desire.

Cole must be kneeling behind me, because I feel the warm brush of his lips on my backside, then his teeth, and holy shit, he's burying his mouth between my legs.

Trace devours my moans, his chest heaving and hands digging into my arms, holding me immobile. He kisses me until my tongue no longer knows how to move and my lungs only work because they have to. I squeeze my knees around his hips, glorying in the indefinable sensation of being pinned down, pleasured, and dominated by multiple mouths.

The rush toward climax swells through me, spasming along my inner walls and locking up my lungs.

I'm right there, rising, cresting, adrift in the passion of their lips, their tongues, and the erotic resonance of their groans.

Cole circles a finger around my clit and plunges his tongue wickedly, deeply inside me, spiraling me headlong into release. Starry bursts of light scatter my vision as I moan and pant and come undone. Cole grunts with me, the guttural sound vibrating against my pussy and prolonging the orgasm.

When my mouth falls slack against Trace's lips, he trails a path of kisses across my cheek to my ear. "So damn beautiful."

How can he say that? I don't know how he can be kind to me at all after I just came on another man's mouth.

"We need to talk about this." I pull on my arms, lethargic and deliciously twitchy as my breathing slows to normal.

Trace releases my wrists, letting me slide off his lap to sit beside him.

"You think too much." Cole grins, still kneeling on the floor.

At some point, he removed his shirt, and his chest glistens with perspiration. He lowers his gaze to the swollen length trapped behind his zipper, and a pained expression kills his smile.

I steal a peek at Trace's groin—also hard as a rock.

With a jab of guilt, I shift to the edge of the couch, aggravating the burn on my backside. "It's my turn to—"

"No," they say in unison.

I glance down at my naked body. Should I push the issue and try to seduce them? Or should I cover myself and forget about it?

three is a war

"I can..." I lower my voice, nervous. "I want to pleasure you. I can do it separately. In different rooms."

With an agonized growl, Cole stands and paces away, scrubbing a hand through his hair.

Trace drops his head on the back of the couch and closes his eyes.

"I'm making it worse, aren't I?" I whisper.

Without opening his eyes, he blindly reaches for my hand. "Your car was delivered while you were taking a nap."

"I don't care about the car. You're changing the subject."

Cole's amused huff draws my attention across the room. He faces the windows, bent slightly forward with his hands on the ballet bar, smiling at me.

"What?" I ask.

"Yesterday, you cared about the car."

"Yesterday, I wasn't staying." I stand and grab his shirt off the floor.

"Don't get dressed. I need to rub ointment into your sore backside." He glances at the outline of his erection. "In a minute."

"I'll just put the shirt on." I pull it over my head, and the hem falls midway down my thighs.

Trace doesn't move on the couch, his lashes low, expression sleepy, but I feel those heavy-lidded eyes watching me. Cole stares out at the darkening sky, his posture bent and stiff, his hands clenched around the bar. Each of them is battling desire in his own way, and I feel like a greedy tease, standing here half-dressed and glowing with a post-orgasm flush.

"Do you guys feel weird about what just

happened?"

"It's fine, Danni," Trace murmurs. "Let it go."

I make an irritated sound. "All that talk about being open and honest—"

"What do you want to know?" Cole straightens and rests his fingertips in his pockets.

"I feel like we're playing by rules, but I don't know what the rules are."

"We're not playing," Trace says.

"Maybe you should."

"What do you mean?" Cole tips his head, brows furrowed.

I walk to the stereo, scroll through the songs, and cue up one. When the soothing guitar chords lead into *Lovesong* by Adele, I step aimlessly through the room, gently swaying with the husky vocals.

"Music is the soul of life." I meet Trace's gaze and turn to Cole. "You sing to it, cry to it, dance, love, laugh… You *play* it."

I approach the dance pole and grip it high above my head, circling, humming, and smiling as they follow me with their eyes, seemingly mesmerized.

"Sixty…seventy years from now…" I tilt my face to the rafters, weighing my words. "I want to look back on my life and know that I played it like a song, that I felt it so deeply it gave me chills, and that I savored every vibrating moment—the tragic moments, the blissful moments. I don't want to miss a second of it. So I say play it in excess, live it up, surfeit yourself on every drop of pleasure. There can never be too many songs or too much dancing. Life *should be* playful—enjoyed and appreciated to the fullest." I suddenly realize I'm rocking my hips, subconsciously seduced by the music. With a

three is a war

laugh, I shake my head. "You must think I'm crazy, rattling on and dancing around with a blistered ass."

"You're *you*." Cole lowers his head, smiling to himself. "Flawless and addictive in every way."

Trace leans forward and clasps his hands together between his knees. "*You* are the soul of life."

My cheeks warm, and my chest rises with a happy sigh. "Are we playing by rules?"

"Loosely." Trace licks his lips. "Cole and I have guidelines that will bend and evolve as we go. We've intentionally kept these from you, because we don't want to limit you."

"How do I follow the rules if I don't know what they are?"

"You don't," Cole says. "We know the boundaries and will keep you safely within them."

I chew the inside of my cheek. "I have concerns."

"Such as?"

"Sex."

"One-track mind." He smirks.

"Only because it's the part I screwed up last time." I peer at Trace. "I feel like I shouldn't touch either of you or express my feelings affectionately. I don't want you guys feeling uneasy—"

"I'll make this very clear." Trace's bright blue eyes latch onto mine. "In a polyamorous arrangement, you can cheat on the rules, but not on each other. From your perspective, the only rule is honesty. We *want* you to act on your feelings."

"Okay, but we're not polyamorous."

"Cole and I aren't, but you are. You love more than one person, have multiple relationships, and everyone

115

involved is aware and tolerant of what's going on."

As I absorb his words, I loathe myself even more. "Then we'll just avoid sex and skip the whole poly—"

"Poly isn't defined by sex." Cole releases a heavy sigh. "As long as you're romantically committed to both of us and no one else, this is where we're at."

"It's temporary." I close my eyes, breathe in, and stare at the floor. "Is that why you're consenting to this? With your time line and rules and hope for a monogamous relationship at the end, you're crazy enough to believe this is all worth it?"

"Yes." Trace scowls at me.

"*You* are worth it," Cole says firmly and gentles his tone. "Are we good?"

"I think so."

"Head to the bedroom. I'll be there in a minute."

I narrow my eyes. What are they going to discuss without me here?

Suspicious and reluctant, I exit the dance studio and head down the hall toward the bedroom, slapping my bare feet on the tiles with deliberate loudness. Before I reach the doorway, I turn back, tip-toeing as quietly as possible.

When I arrive at the dance room, I press my back against the wall, remaining out of view.

"Because you fucking kissed her," Cole whispers angrily. "Don't look at me like that. Your goddamn tongue was down her throat."

"I'm not the only one who put my mouth on her," Trace says in a cool tone.

Jesus, I'm gone two seconds and they're already fighting?

"Yeah, well, I followed the plan," Cole says, "so get

three is a war

off my back."

A heavy exhale breathes from the room, followed by a tense silence. I strain my ears, listening for footsteps, whispering, something.

"Danni!" Cole barks, making me jump. "Get your ass to the bedroom."

"Fuck that." I storm into the studio and anchor my hands on my hips. "I thought we were done with secrets."

"I thought we were done sneaking around." Cole lifts a brow.

"I wasn't… Okay, maybe I was sneaking." Something tells me he expected me to do exactly that. "Why are you fighting behind my back?"

"We're not fighting." Trace reclines on the couch.

"We're communicating." Cole prowls toward me.

I back up, but not fast enough. He grips my thighs, tosses me over his shoulder, and carries me out of the room.

Down the hall and into the master bedroom, we go. I try not to feel him up, but he's shirtless and ripped and… I press my nose to his shoulder blade. Fuck, he smells so damn good. *Like home.*

He drops me on the bed. "Roll over."

I close my eyes and relax into the bedding, pretending to ignore him just for the fun of it.

"Danni," he growls.

"He thinks his bossiness is hot," I mumble, peeking an eye open. "And maybe it is, but dammit, you can't let him order you around all the time."

"Are you talking to yourself?" A grin pulls on the corner of his mouth.

"When I need brilliant advice, I consult an expert."

A smile cracks his face—all dimples and straight teeth and glittering brown eyes. Then he launches, his bare chest hard against mine, his hands in my hair, and a knee wedged between my legs.

"You shatter me," he breathes against my lips.

I hum with contentment. "We can fall apart together."

He gives me a searching look, expression raw with hope and hunger and something else—the mystery of chemistry, the irrefutable bond that glues us together. It's a look that shares a kiss and steals the breath without so much as a touch of lips. A look that teems with the desire to leap, to fall, to give in and go under.

He doesn't make us suffer, leaning his face closer and covering my mouth with aching softness. His lips slide lovingly, worshipfully, against mine. His fingers tighten against my scalp, and his breathing sprints into labored panting. He parts my mouth with his tongue, searching, sipping. The best part is the feel of his smile right before he plunges deeply and kisses the hell out of me.

We go wild, seething with heat and passion and surrender. I writhe beneath him, grazing fingernails across his biceps, relearning the silken feel of his skin, and relishing the steely flex of the muscle as he clenches me tightly against him.

He tastes exactly the way I remember, like sunshine on the tailwind of a thunderstorm. His whiskers scratch my cheeks. The heavy weight of his body presses me exquisitely into the mattress, and his devilish tongue annihilates my senses.

The way he kisses me gets me every time, his lips

three is a war

so full of desire it feels like a first kiss, a reckless kiss, a *forgot-my-own-name* kiss, all rolled up into a perfect alignment of ridiculous happiness.

And yet, as intoxicating as it is, I'm conscious of the man I left in the other room.

The instant I think of Trace, I open my eyes and collide with the crystal blue of his. He stands beside the bed with his hands behind him, head angled down and deep lines of displeasure bracketing his scowl.

I pull my mouth away, fighting for air and drowning in shame.

"Go away," Cole says to Trace and kisses along my neck.

I try to push him off, but he's stubbornly immovable. Panic sets in, speeding up my pulse. I don't want to upset Trace or cause a fight. At the same time, I don't want to rebuff Cole's affection and hurt him.

"You're not doing anything wrong, Danni." Trace's gaze flicks to Cole and narrows dangerously.

"Cole." I cradle his face and lean back, meeting his eyes. "If Trace is uncomfortable, I'm uncomfortable."

He releases a heavy breath and drops his head on my shoulder. I run a hand through his hair, watching Trace watch me. Cole is smart enough to know if the roles were reversed, if he were the one standing on the outside, he wouldn't like it.

Reluctantly, he climbs off the bed, avoiding Trace's stare. Then he stalks across the room and disappears inside the bathroom.

Trace removes his shirt and jeans and climbs into bed wearing only boxer briefs.

"What are you doing?" I glare at him, scooting

toward the edge of the mattress. "It's too early to go to bed."

He reaches over and pulls me across his chest, positioning me face down on top of him.

"Relax." Lifting the shirt, he bares my backside to the cool air.

"It's hard to relax when I don't know what's going on." As the words leave my mouth, my body betrays me, softening happily against his.

Cole returns with a tube of ointment, and his face hardens as he takes in my position. Then he blinks away the tension and kneels on the bed beside me.

"I'll be honest." He rubs a dollop of cold cream into the sore flesh across my buttocks. "This isn't easy."

I move to roll off Trace, but he wraps his arms around my back, preventing escape.

"Not being able to touch you the way I want…" Cole runs a finger along my butt crack. "Seeing the way you look at him, splitting my time with you over the next six months—none of this is easy." He caps the ointment and sets it aside, lowering his voice. "But it's worth it."

My chest constricts, and I reach a hand toward him. He grips my fingers and stretches on the bed beside me, resting on his side with his head on the pillow.

Beneath me, Trace doesn't move, his eyes closed and lips curved downward. As the silence drags on, they seem content to just lie here without talking. But not me. Silence makes me analyze, and over-analyze, and it won't be long before I start belaboring everything we've already discussed.

I stroke my thumb across Cole's knuckles. "I hate when it goes quiet and my brain is like, 'Hey, you should say something annoying just to fill the void.' But I've

three is a war

already said all the annoying things I want to say today."

"I'll never tire of listening to you talk." Trace peeks at me from beneath hooded eyelids.

"I was going to suggest we watch a movie." Cole rolls to his back. "According to you, there's only one movie in existence, and you know all the lines. So you can talk until your voice is raw."

His suggestion makes me want to jump up and down with excitement, except he knows all the lines, too, and Trace doesn't. Is that why he suggested it? To one-up Trace? My stomach sinks. For the first time in my life, I don't feel like watching *Dirty Dancing*.

"Don't freak out," I say, trying not to freak out, "but what do you think about choosing a different movie? What do you guys want to watch?"

"I feel like that's a trick question," Cole says.

Trace studies me with tapered eyes.

"We're here to grow and learn and figure out the future, right?" I stretch over him and snatch the remote off the night stand. "I can't do that unless I expand my horizons." I set the device on his chest and settle on the bed between them. "Might as well start with a new movie genre."

As Trace powers on the TV and surfs through the channels, I grip his free hand, still holding tight to Cole's in my other.

If being with one or the other is a choice, when did I decide to love them both?

I didn't.

Love happened twice, and I have no regrets, even if the situation feels impossible, even if the looming decision makes me believe I will never survive it. As much as I fear the future, it isn't going away until it shows me what I need to do.

I fell in love with two men and lost myself.

I'll stay in love with one and find myself again.

ten

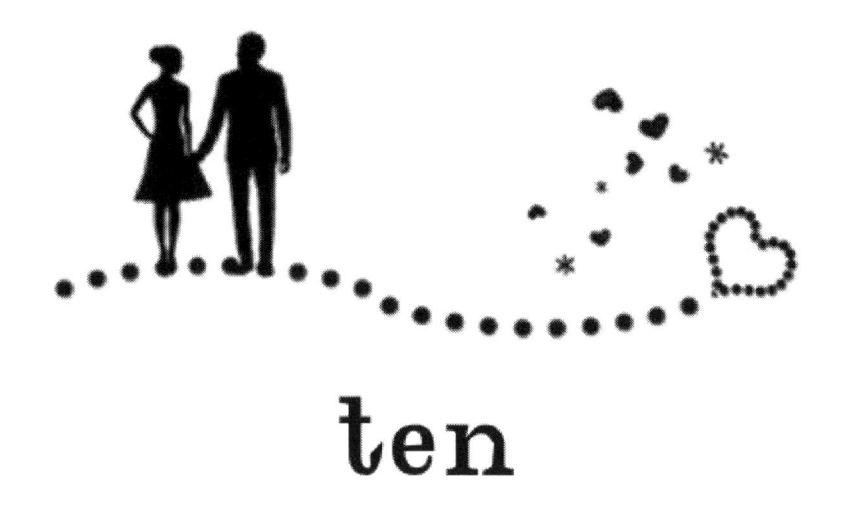

I wake the next morning to find Trace staring down at me, shirtless, hair tousled, and blue eyes illuminated by the sunlight crashing rudely through the windows.

I groan. *Too early. Need sleep.*

Cole's side of the bed is empty. Maybe it's later than I thought. I peek at the clock on the nightstand.

6:57 AM. Seriously? Why can't mornings happen after noon?

"Word of advice." I roll over and bury my face in the pillow. "If you're waking me, it better involve morning sex, coffee, or Beyoncé. Preferably all three."

Trace yanks the pillow out from beneath me and flips me onto my back.

His dominant energy precedes him. He doesn't even need to open his mouth to communicate his intention of controlling every breath I take today. His gorgeous face and steady glare kick my heart against my ribcage. Add to that, the memory of yesterday's punishment, of his drugging kiss swirling with his bold masculine taste, and I could be coaxed out of bed. Or rather, *into* bed.

"Morning." He smiles a barely-there smile that shines with more intensity than anyone should be capable of at this hour.

"You know what rhymes with *morning*?" I stretch, yawning. "*Fuck off.*"

He lifts a mug from the nightstand and brings it to his lips, sipping with a smirk.

Coffee! I lurch to my knees, reaching for his cup. He lets me have it, but a glance at the pitch-black contents has me passing it back with a grimace.

"You should know," I say grumpily, "I totally judge you on the way you take your coffee, you un-creamy freakshow."

"Someone left the bag of whiners open this morning." He drinks the coffee, eyes dancing.

"You opened it," I huff, "with your lack of creamer and flirty eyes and… Wait. You just made another joke."

"Get up." He stands and strides toward the closet, his crisp khaki slacks hanging deliciously low. "Your *creamy* coffee is waiting in the kitchen, princess. We have things to do."

I tilt my head, watching him slide on a starched collared shirt. "Where are we going?"

"Walmart." His fingers move deftly over the buttons. "We need groceries."

An hour later, I sit in the front seat of Cole's Range Rover as Trace drives along the winding road through

three is a war

the woods. Cole took the boat out to go fishing this morning, and I've yet to see him.

Slurping coffee from a travel mug, I watch Trace out of the corner of my eye. "Did Cole make himself scarce for a reason?"

"We're dividing up our time with you."

"Care to enlighten me on the schedule?"

"No." He adjusts the heat controls, directing those captivating eyes at the road.

"Why not?"

"Because you'll obsess over it." He scratches his clean-shaved jaw, his gaze straight ahead. "I only want you obsessing about one thing."

I don't need him to draw a picture. He wants me thinking of him and nothing else. I want that for him, too, and I hate myself for not being able to give it to him.

"Why are you putting yourself through this?" I stare at the windshield, voice quiet. "There are so many other ways to go about it, including not bothering with me at all."

"If I don't *bother* with you," he says in a biting tone, "I shouldn't bother pursuing anything in life." His nostrils flare, and his hand clenches on the steering wheel. "Or maybe my heart is too stubborn for the kind of woman who thinks her lover shouldn't fight for her."

Oh, for Christ's sake, I didn't mean to piss him off. "That's not what I'm saying."

"Then do a better job of explaining yourself."

Heat flushes my face. "You're the type of man who doesn't wait around for a woman to make decisions about your future. I'm just wondering why you're not demanding I kick Cole to the curb. Or why you haven't thrown me in your car, driven me back to your penthouse, and made the decision for me."

"I refuse to force your hand on this." His eyes, cold and hard, shift to me before returning to the road. "I'm patient, Danni. When you choose me, I want the realization clawing at your insides without coercion or doubt or the pressure of time. I want your heart to beat for me and only me, not because I command it, but because we're meant to be."

He wants pure, undeniable love. He deserves that and so much more.

An ache tightens my chest. "I'm afraid one day you'll realize I wasn't worth it."

"I'm afraid one day you'll ask me to leave."

A vehement denial jumps to the tip of my tongue, but I trap it there. I can't make promises I don't know how to keep.

I used to think forever was the only thing I wanted. Then I met Trace, and my heart filled with tiny moments, each one worth so much more than the whole of a lifetime.

But how can I cherish every moment written with his touch while my veins continue to burn for Cole?

I don't care if they orchestrated this arrangement. It feels like cheating, and the gravity of that is heavy enough to crush my bones. I can't drag this out for six months. My sanity won't survive it.

As if Trace senses my tension, he reaches over the console and rests a hand on my thigh. The heat of his palm penetrates my leggings, warming me, comforting me, until the anxiousness fades away.

"Tell me something about you." I lace our fingers together. "A truth you never share with anyone."

three is a war

He slows the SUV at a cross street, the first one I've seen in the fifteen minutes we've been on the road. Veering right, he enters a small town, lined with run-down stores, a gas station, and lo and behold, a Walmart.

Without acknowledging my question, he motors toward the parking lot filled with a dozen or so cars. He parks toward the back of the lot, turns off the engine, and faces me.

"You know my parents died in a car accident." He stares at our hands, where they intertwine on my lap.

"You said their deaths changed your perspective on life."

"Yes. They were killed because of my job."

"What?" I whisper as a chill spreads through me. "Why didn't you tell me?"

"I can't change what happened." His eyes lift to mine, stark and unblinking. "And I can't share the details."

"I'm so sorry, Trace." I cup his face, stroking my fingers through his soft blond hair.

"Don't be sorry. If it hadn't happened, I'd still be married to that job."

I nod, mind racing. Were his parents killed by an enemy nation state? Or by a traitor like the woman who threatened my life? The specifics are irrelevant. It's what happened after that makes my throat swell.

"That's why you agreed to watch over me when Cole left." I rest my fingers on the sharp angles of his face.

"I didn't want the same thing to happen to you." He caresses my cheek, my jaw, my lips, the kiss of his touch jump-starting my heart.

"Cole knows how your parents died?"

"He's one of the very few."

"He knew and still asked you to protect me?" I drop my arm and ball my hand on my lap. "I kind of hate him a little for that."

"Why?" His brows pull together.

"What if I died on your watch, Trace? You already lost your parents because of that job. I'm sorry, but that was selfish of him to put you in that position."

He makes a noise that resembles a laugh and swipes a hand over his mouth. "I should just let you continue thinking that."

"What do you mean?" I squint at him.

"Danni, he did me a favor." He leans back and gazes at the cars glinting in the sun-soaked parking lot. "My parents' murder wasn't my fault, but I accepted that job knowing full well it put everyone I loved at risk. After they died, I carried the guilt for years." He pulls in a deep breath. "Cole placed you in my charge because he knew I would do anything to prevent that from happening again. He also knew if I committed to a year of protecting you—"

"Four years."

"Right." He smirks. "After four years of protecting you, he hoped I might find atonement for the mistakes I made with my parents."

"Did you…did it ease the guilt?"

"Yes," he says hesitantly. "Until I asked you to marry me." He releases a humorless laugh. "Falling in love with my best friend's fiancé introduced a whole new level of guilt."

I angle toward him and rest my forehead against his. "Do you regret it?"

three is a war

"Never," he says fiercely, his breath whispering against my mouth.

"You didn't just save my life." I press closer, brushing our lips together. "You *gave* me life when I had nothing left to live for. Thank you."

His hand catches the back of my neck, and he slams his mouth against mine, swallowing my gasp and chasing my tongue. He kisses me with a fire that could burn forever, weaving its heat into my skin and melting our souls into one.

Every organ, muscle, and molecule in my body strains to be part of him instead of me. The need to be closer, to nuzzle up against his heart is a physical ache. I don't know how I existed without him. I'm certain I won't be able to again.

He wraps his arms around me, holding me as if he can't fathom letting me go, not now, not at the end of the road, not ever. I clutch him just as hard, falling fast and deep into the trance of his kiss, drunk on his love and high on my own. He can bleed my veins, drain me dry, and hold my desires in captivity. There's no limit to what I would give him.

Except the other half of my heart.

I can't give up Cole. Not easily. Not without losing the very essence of my soul.

Trace breaks the kiss, his lips swollen and damp as he searches my eyes. "You're thinking about him."

My breath catches, and my heart shrivels with shame.

"You don't have to say it." He brushes my hair from my face. "You look at me and see one of two choices. I look at you and see absoluteness. But we have time. Someday, we'll look beyond the question marks and just see us."

"I love you." I lean in for another kiss, desperate to hold onto to the connection.

But he shifts away and climbs out of the car. Circling the front bumper, he opens my door and grips my hand. "Ready for Walmart?"

"On a scale of *maybe* to *definitely*…" I slide out and shut the door, the air cool yet tolerable without a coat. "I'm going with *never*."

He locks the car with the keyless remote and leads me across the lot, holding my hand. "It has a certain appeal."

"Like what?"

"It's the only place you can get a prescription filled, an eye exam, a bag of popcorn, and an oil change, all while watching a real-life episode of *What Not To Wear*."

"Speaking of what not to wear…" I take in his white button-up and tailored khakis and feel lightheaded at how damn arresting he looks. "You're a little overdressed, aren't you? You're going to cause some serious whiplash in there."

"I won't be the one turning heads." He stops abruptly in the middle of the parking lot, yanking me to a halt. "Wanna play?"

"Always." I grin. "What did you have in mind?"

"A bet." He looks at me expectantly.

My eyes widen.

"Don't look so surprised." He gives me a smoldering once-over. "I'm in the business of gambling."

"Okay, I'll bite. What are the stakes?"

"You'll get propositioned first, and when that happens, I get to do whatever I want to do to you."

three is a war

I glance down at my black leggings, knee-high boots, and slouchy sweater. Not a lot of sexy going on here. Besides, he gets to do anything he wants regardless of a bet, so what do I have to lose?

"And if you get hit-on first?" I ask. "Do I get to do whatever I want to you?"

"Sure." His eyes laugh, arrogant and breathtaking. "Deal."

I want every hard, long inch of him in my mouth. Just thinking about it awakens a throb between my legs.

We step into the store, and he grabs a cart. I intend to scope out the female shoppers in anticipation of their blatant staring, but I can't peel my eyes away from Trace Savoy pushing a squeaky Walmart cart. The belly laugh that follows can't be helped, either, and before I know it, I'm doubled over, covering my mouth to muffle my cackling.

He pauses a few paces ahead of me and glances back, not amused. His dark scowl and rigid jawline only makes me laugh harder.

I reach for the phone in my back pocket and fire up the camera. Bree will appreciate how priceless this is. Hell, Cole probably will, too.

As I lift the phone to snap a picture, it vanishes from my hand.

He slips it in his pocket and gives me a hard smack on the ass, making me yelp.

I glance around at men and women of every age spilling out of the aisles to watch the show.

"There's more of that coming when I win the bet." Trace grips the cart and strolls toward the grocery section, like he didn't just spank me in the entrance of

Walmart.

We fill the cart with produce, dairy, and whatever. He has a list—one he typed out on his phone. Who does that?

Every time I toss a package in, he stops and rearranges the basket. Evidently, there are rules for stacking shit in a cart. Something about organizing the way the groceries are bagged and put away, yadda, yadda… He lost me at *organizing*.

Twenty minutes into our shopping spree, it occurs to me that no one here would ever hit on him. Oh, the women are definitely looking—teen girls, mothers with screaming kids, and blue-haired grannies. They stumble and stare, necks craning and mouths gaping, like they can't come to terms with the sight of a gorgeous Viking god pushing a cart down the cereal aisle.

I get it. He stands out in such a shocking way I find myself gawking right along with them.

But they don't approach, not even when I trail at a distance and pretend we're not together. I should've known. As recklessly impulsive as I am, I'm not sure I'd have the balls to initiate a conversation with such an intimidatingly beautiful man.

The bet is a total bust. So I wander off to check out the music section while he heads toward the auto department to get lawn mower oil.

I don't make it two steps down the pop music aisle before a passing employee stops in his tracks and flashes me a toothy smile.

Don't come this way. Don't come this way.

He prowls straight toward me, eyes fixed on mine. *Ugh.*

I turn on my heel and hurry down the aisle. But he

catches me in the next row over.

Short black hair, lean build, he's probably early-twenties. Too young to grow a beard or comprehend the danger lurking nearby in the form of a possessive, scowly male.

"Do you need help finding something?" His gaze makes an audacious journey over my body. "I'm at your service."

"Nope. All good here. Thanks." I pivot away.

He sidles around me and strokes a thumb across his bottom lip, grinning. "You're so fine I had to come over and tell you. You must be new in town."

"Yeah, so I'm going to sit this one out." I duck around him.

He chases. "What's your name?"

"Not interested."

"Give me a chance." He races past me and steps into my path. "Let's go out tonight."

"Let's not and stick with that story."

"Oh, come on. Don't be like that."

Blatant verbal disinterest apparently doesn't work with this guy.

"I have a confession." I arrange my face into pained embarrassment. "I have a raging yeast infection going on. With all the itchiness and discharge, I just can't tonight."

"Tomorrow night then." He searches my eyes, not a flinch in his expression. "Seven o'clock. Where should I pick you up?"

I have to hand it to him. He's smart enough to see through the lie and persistent to boot.

"Look, you seem like a nice guy…" I glance at his

Walmart name tag. "*Max. I'm sure you'll go far in life*" — *and I really hope he stays there* — "so you should probably run along and get going on that."

I'm really not judging him for working at Walmart. At least he has a job. Can't say the same for myself.

But he's earning major creeper points every second he stands here, eying me up and down.

His perusal freezes on something over my shoulder. Given his backward shuffle and paling complexion, it doesn't take a brainiac to know Trace is standing behind me.

"I'll…uh…" Max continues his retreat out of the aisle. "Catch you next time."

I wait until he vanishes around the corner before turning toward Trace.

My breath hitches. Damn, he looks murderous. Sharp blade-like eyes, deep-set scowl, shoulders back, and hands behind him, he stands a few feet away, glaring like a giant with a gym-honed physique. It's no wonder he's so confident. His towering stature allows him to stare down anyone who crosses his path. Including me.

"Stop scowling at me." I breeze past him. "I had that under control."

"Sounds like we should swing by the medicine aisle." With long-legged strides, he easily catches up. "Pick up something for your itchy problem."

"How on earth did you hear that?" I reach the cart, where he left it sitting in the main walkway, and lean on the handle. "Were you eavesdropping one aisle over? Or did you bug me?"

"I'm aware of my surroundings. This way." He crooks a finger and leads me toward the back of the store.

"I thought we were finished?"

three is a war

"I won the bet."

"Nobody likes a gloater. And it was hardly fair with that *don't-talk-to-me* scowl you wear."

"Nobody likes a poor loser. Leave the cart there." He gestures toward a corridor in the rear of the store.

I park the cart. "What are you—?"

He grabs my arm and walks me forcibly down the hall toward the bathrooms.

"Wait." I yank on his grip and lower my voice to a whisper. "We are *not* getting dirty in a Walmart bathroom."

Pulling me to a stop, he glares at an employee who skitters by. The poor woman casts her gaze to the floor and hurries out of the corridor.

"I don't want a scene," he says at my ear, "but I'll carry you if I have to."

"You can keep your threats to yourself." I relax in his hold. "I don't need them."

With a hand on my bicep, he guides me to the bathrooms at the end of the hall. The door to the women's room is locked, so he pulls me into the men's single-stall bathroom and locks us inside. Then his crystal blue eyes knife in my direction.

His demeanor shifts from intense to ravenously intense as he stalks toward me. I back up, heart fluttering and stomach swarming with nerves.

"I know you won the bet, but I need to understand the rules." I circle him as he circles me, and we move together in a vibrating dance of sexual tension. "Are you going to fuck me? Is that allowed?" I'm desperate for it, clenching and trembling from the inside out. But… "I'm not going to sneak behind Cole's back."

"I'll honor the guidelines Cole and I set." He prowls around me, drifting closer with each step. "You're more than welcome to tell him all about it when we get back."

My chest collapses. "I don't want to hurt his feelings."

He pauses behind me and runs his fingers through my hair, sending a shiver down my spine. "Cole understands the principles of love."

I'm not sure *I* understand. "What are the principles of love?"

"Pain." He squeezes his hand in my hair, yanking on the roots. "Risk. Self-destruction."

"Ow." I clasp his wrist, stumbling in my attempt to loosen his grip. "What about effort? Sacrifice? Trust? Kindness?"

"Do you want kindness right now, darling?"

I laugh at the endearment. "I wouldn't mind keeping some of my hair."

He releases me. "Turn around. Hands on the wall."

And there it is, the brutally beautiful command of a man whom I love to the ends of self-destruction. His dominance repeatedly draws me back to him, the strength of our love fused into two bodies that ache to align the way we're supposed to.

But my heart is divided.

If this is a war, Trace and Cole aren't the enemies. I am.

I'm the betrayer who loves them both. The persecutor who will rip us apart. The executioner who will snuff the light that burns so brightly between us.

Sex isn't the solution, but it's too late to have a conscience. I'm already committed, flattening my palms

three is a war

against the wall.

I don't want to control this. I need Trace to do it, whatever it is.

Punish me. Wreck me.
Tear down my ruins.
Excavate me from my sins.
Hurt me. Spank me. Set me on fire.
Make me burn.

eleven

A storm rampages inside me as I hold my hands against the wall in the Walmart bathroom. Desire battles guilt, one as poisonous as the other, robbing the strength from my legs and scorching my lungs.

But at the center of the turmoil is a calming presence. Trace stands behind me, silent, steady, compelling me to relax simply by placing a hand on my lower back.

"Are you still sore from yesterday?" His deep timbre curls around me, low and hypnotic.

My glutes are tender to the touch, but I'm a dancer. Sore muscles are a way of life.

"Answer me." He slams a hand against my backside, prickling sharp pain beneath my leggings.

I swallow a yelp. "Yes. I'm sore."

"Whatever's going on in your head stops now." He spanks me again, softer this time, but the impact still lifts me on my toes.

"You can't order me to stop thinking."

"No, but I can redden your ass until you stop feeling guilty about wanting this."

How does he do that? It's like he sees inside my head and interprets my thoughts better than I can.

"Now…" He molds his hands to my hips. "Tell me what you want."

"I want to burn."

He presses against my back, letting me feel the steel of his chest.

"Do you want to burn here?" He grips my backside with both hands. "Or here?" His hand slides around my waist and cups me between the legs.

"Whichever pleases you."

"Goddamn, you're perfect." He tightens his fingers against my pussy before stepping back and removing his touch completely.

His breaths grow louder, sharper, as he crouches behind me. I can't see him, but I don't dare peek. God help me, I love being at his mercy.

Lifting the hem of my sweater, he tucks it under my bra strap to hold it in place. The anticipation is too much. My fingers curl against the tiled wall, and my pulse roars in my ears.

With teasing fingers, he traces my spine and shifts closer to brush his lips against my tailbone. Then he yanks down my leggings and panties and bites the flesh of my butt the instant it's exposed.

I whimper and lock my knees, attempting to stay upright against the sharp sting. The leggings around my

three is a war

boots limit the movement of my feet, but the strong hand on my hip supports me as he pulls my exposed backside closer to his face. Pressing a palm on my back, he forces me to bend at the waist.

My hands slip down the wall as I lower my head, my breasts shifting in the cups of my bra, dragging my nipples against the itchy lace.

His labored breathing echoes through the small space, but the glide of his fingers is oh-so controlled. His hands are everywhere, methodically positioning my hips where he wants them, slowly caressing up and down my legs, and petting between my thighs.

Taste me, Trace. Fuck me with your wicked tongue.

He hears my unspoken plea and falls upon my pussy, burying his face, groaning, and licking with vigor. My mouth drops open on a gasp, and I snap it shut, stifling the cry in my throat.

I don't know if the bathroom door is thin or if there's a line waiting outside. I don't care. His lips feel too good pressed against me, kissing and sucking, warm and wet. I push against the wall, rocking against his tongue, seeking pressure, friction, desperate to come.

He licks me from bottom to top and plunges deep. Then his fingers are there, circling my opening and sinking inside. He thrusts in and out, grunting, panting, fucking me with his touch, his tongue, and the force of his need.

I gasp and tremble as the pleasure crests inside me, but he teases me, gives me just enough to hold me at the edge. Lips sliding, tongue curling, and fingers strumming, he plays my body like an instrument. My heart dances to the crescendo of his breaths. Electricity shoots through my veins, hot and wet and charged with emotion. The sensations are incredible, dizzying, overpowering. I think I might die.

I drop my chin to my chest, my head too heavy to hold up. Stretching the restraint of the leggings around my ankles, I shift my feet wider and roll my hips, grinding against his mouth, needing him, wanting this, silently begging him to keep going.

He clamps an arm around my waist, rubs a finger around my clit, and closes those sinful lips over my pussy, sucking viciously. My muscles spasm. My mind shatters, and my body detonates. His guttural groan reverberates through me, crashing waves of pleasure from my core to my limbs. *Holyfuckholyfuck.* I arch my back, and my mouth hangs open in a silent scream.

As the peak of orgasm tapers off and shudders into breathy repletion, he nibbles his way up my spine, panting and hungry. I shift to straighten from the wall, but the hand on my back holds me in the bent position.

"Don't move," he rasps, his voice whiskey and smoke.

The sound of his zipper shivers the air, followed by the whisper of rustling clothes. I peer over my shoulder just as he releases his hard, swollen cock and slides a hand over the length, once, twice… He kicks his hips, driving faster, harder, thrusting into the grip of his fist.

I want to turn around, but he clutches my hip, fingers shaking, mouth parted, gorgeously lost in an urgent race to completion.

"You make me so fucking hard." He doesn't ram inside me, yet he can't seem to slow down. "Nothing is more tempting than the sight of your ass perched in the air."

three is a war

Intensely focused on my nude backside, he chases his release, stroking himself, grunting, tensing...

"Danni, fuck. I'm fucking coming." His head falls back, and he groans to the ceiling as a warm spray of wetness covers my back and trickles into the crack of my butt.

My God, he's beautiful when he lets go. His entire expression softens. His pupils dilate. His shoulders loosen, and his eyes glow with swirling blue wonder. He looks younger, happier, and fuck if that doesn't put a teary smile on my face.

He tucks himself away as he catches his breath. Then he turns his attention to my back. Instead of wiping off the come, he rubs it in, spreading it like lotion across every exposed inch.

"You kinky bastard." I laugh as a finger digs into a ticklish spot on my ribs. "I'm going to smell like sex."

"No." He moves to the sink and washes his hands. "You're going to smell like *me*."

Marking his territory. With a blissful sigh, I pull my clothes back in place.

"Now that we got that out of the way..." He dries his hands and prowls toward me.

Holy shit, now what? He has that look—the scowling, smoldering, intense glare that suggests our liaison in the Walmart bathroom isn't over. I feel like I know this man down to the pith of his bones, yet there are moments like this when I'm utterly stupefied by the beauty of his mysterious frown. He holds me hostage with a glance, owns me with a crook of his finger, and intimidates me with his uncanny ability to keep me guessing.

Three paces away…two paces…he crowds me with his soaring frame, buries a hand in my hair, and crashes his mouth against mine. His kiss is strong and demanding, skipping the slide of lips and diving straight to teeth and tongue. I taste myself on him. It's dirty and intimate and makes me so damn hot.

A knock sounds on the door, and Trace tears his mouth away.

"Get lost!" He returns to my lips, the hand in my hair wrenching my head back as his other cups my breast with firm pressure.

He walks me backward until I bump against the wall. Clutching the backs of my thighs, he lifts me until we're eye-level.

With an arm around my waist and his fingers tangled in my hair, he forces my mouth back to his. Teeth grazing, tongues rubbing, the kiss is frenzied, humming with the sounds of our moans and shallow panting.

I wrap my arms and legs around him, rocking on instinct. He's hard between my thighs and positioned perfectly to slide right in.

Except we're both wearing clothes.

I pull at his shirt, deliriously needy.

"Slow down." He laughs against my mouth and pries my fingers from his collar.

"When do I get to taste your cock again?"

"When I decide." He kisses across my jaw and nips at my neck. "I intend to tease you for a long time."

"Sadist."

He bites the skin on my throat, hard enough to leave a mark. Then his mouth returns to mine, softer this time. Our lips glide together in a gentle motion, tongues meeting, releasing, repeating. Shared breaths, eyes closed, we kiss with the same love and hold each other with the same reluctance to pull away.

"There isn't a word in the English language," he says against my mouth, "that accurately describes what you mean to me."

"We don't need words, Trace." I frame his face in my hands and rest my gaze in the sanctuary of his. "This is all we need."

In the span of a wistful moment, it's just Trace and me and the unified beat of our hearts.

Until another knock rattles the door.

"Time's up," I whisper.

His face falls drastically, and his fingers dig into my back. Does he think I meant time's up forever?

"Trace, I didn't mean—"

"I know." He grabs my hand, gives my sweater and leggings a quick once-over, and opens the door.

Of all the people to find standing in the hallway, there's Max, the employee who doesn't understand the word *no*. He steps back, eyes wide, as Trace leads me out of the men's bathroom.

"Are the walls sound-proof?" I grin over my shoulder at Max, walking quickly to match Trace's long gait.

"Um...not really." Max rubs the back of his head.

"Oh good. See you around."

Trace grabs our cart of groceries, and we make our way to the front of the store. He's quiet to the checkout line, quiet on the drive home, and quiet still when he parks in the garage and stares straight ahead.

"What's wrong?" I unlatch the seatbelt and lean toward him.

"Nothing."

"You've been giving me one-word answers since we left the store."

He unbuckles his seatbelt and drops a quick kiss on my lips. "I'm just mentally preparing myself."

"For what?"

The door to the kitchen opens, and Cole steps into the garage. Trace glares at him through the windshield.

That's what Trace was preparing for—Cole, this arrangement, and the inevitability of watching another man make my heart race. My chest constricts.

"There will come a day when…" He grips my chin and growls against my lips. "I'll show no restraint."

twelve

As the last of the groceries are put away, Trace gets a call and strolls toward the rear of the house, arguing with whomever is on the other line about regulations on new gaming machines. With the phone at his ear, he steps outside, leaving me alone in the kitchen with Cole.

"How was fishing this morning?" I dig around in the fridge, avoiding Cole's eyes.

"Peaceful."

I keep my back to him, as if the row of fruit-flavored yogurt requires my attention when all I'm really thinking about is Trace's growled-out promise in the car.

If he showed restraint in the Walmart bathroom... *Sweet lord.* My skin tingles with his possessive marks, from the imprint of his teeth on my neck to his come rubbed into my back. He took me thoroughly and aggressively, and we didn't even have sex. The memory alone makes my muscles clench low in my body. I ache to put my mouth on him, to hold the weight of his cock—"

"How far did he go?" Cole glares at me from his perch on the stool at the kitchen island.

"Excuse me?" My neck goes stiff, and my tongue feels thick in my mouth.

"I won't repeat myself." His hands rest on the counter, cupped around a beer bottle.

There's no tension in his posture or expression, but something dark and restless churns in his brown eyes.

I close the fridge and stand on the opposite side of the island, facing him with lead in my stomach. The urge to glance at Trace's silhouette beyond the windows claws at me, but I keep my gaze on Cole. "What are you talking about?"

He jerks forward, his eyes thrashing. "You know exactly what I'm talking about."

"How far did Trace go?" My hackles rise defensively. "Are we talking in terms of first base, second base...? Maybe we should put on pajamas and braid each other's hair while I tell you all about it."

"Do *not* fuck with me!" he roars, crashing a fist onto the counter. "Understood?"

"Do *not* yell at me," I say in a low harsh voice and lift my chin. "Am *I* under-fucking-stood?"

He flattens his mouth in a line, staring at me blankly. Then he blinks, and a surprised sound heaves past his lips, an almost laugh thick with frustration.

Outside, Trace moves in my periphery. I meet his icy eyes through the windowed door. He's still on the phone, his mouth moving rapidly as he reaches for the door handle. I give him a sharp shake of my head, and he

three is a war

lowers his arm.

"You got your backbone back, baby." Cole rubs his hand over his face and drops his elbows on the counter, smirking to himself. "It's hot as fuck when you stand up to me."

The tightness in my neck loosens. If Cole were a dance, he'd be the Tango. It's moody, volatile, and thrums with passion. It gets angry, goes ballistic, and the choreography makes a dramatic display of feelings, severe expressions, and snapping arm gestures. Then it reconciles, composes itself, and dims the lights. Cue the romance, the seduction, and the slide of a hand over fishnet stockings. Hearts beating, bodies in a close embrace, it burns and consumes and never lets go. That's Cole in a complex nutshell.

I glance at the tall, refined figure on the back terrace and smile inwardly. There's no dance more stately, elegant, or alluring than the iconic Waltz. The footwork is timeless and controlled, augmented by proud posturing as it travels deliberately, gracefully, to the ends of the world. It's a legendary fairy tale, a well-dressed prince, and a palace glittering with promises. Trace is a beautiful Waltz.

Turning my attention back to Cole, I find his head lowered and sedate eyes fixed on his beer bottle, with a grim twist to his mouth.

My insides clamp with realization. He loses his temper when he's hurting. And he's hurting because of me.

I approach him hesitantly, noting the subtle twitch in his whiskered cheek. I search for something to say, and all thoughts lead to Trace and our stolen moment in the bathroom. That's what this is about.

When I step close enough, he reaches for me, pulling me between his legs with my back to the island.

"If you don't tell me what happened with him," he says quietly, staring at his hand on my waist, "he will tell me. That's the deal."

"What deal? Are you talking about the rules?"

"Yes." He rests his brow against my breastbone.

"You won't tell me the rules, because you don't want me dwelling on them. But you know what? I'm dwelling on them *because* you're keeping them from me."

He releases a defeated breath. "It's really quite simple. My actions set the limits for his and vice-versa. If I kiss you, he can kiss you. If he touches you here…" He cups me in between the legs and lowers his hand. "I can touch you there."

A chill ripples through me. That's why they were arguing about kissing me yesterday.

My knee-jerk reaction is to scream, *Have you lost your ever-loving mind?* But if I compartmentalize my emotions and look at it from their perspectives, it's not a bad approach. If Trace would've fucked me in the bathroom, it would've given Cole the green light to do the same. Trace doesn't want that, so he jerked off instead.

By controlling themselves, they're controlling each other. That's a whole lot more effective than my sad attempt at setting rules. But there's something I don't understand.

"What about the six-month time line?" I ask.

"We agreed to no sex while you're in limbo." His brow furrows, expression pensive. "It was my idea. I want you out of his bed until you make a decision." He gives me a pointed look. "Until you choose me, at which point you'll never fuck him again."

A swallow sticks in my throat. I don't blame him. Whoever I choose will carry the memory of seeing me with his best friend. How can either of them live with that?

"The problem is," Cole says, "I don't think I'll last six months."

No shit. I run my hands through his tousled hair, untangling the thick strands on top. "I need to just make a decision and end—"

"No." He tightens his grip on my waist. "You're not going to rush this."

"Why not? Dragging it out doesn't help…"

Then it dawns on me. They're not ready for this to end. They put off these confident vibes, speaking in terms of *when*, not *if*, but deep down, neither one is certain he'll be chosen.

"You're prolonging this." My gaze drifts to Trace on the terrace. "Because you're afraid."

"Yeah, I'm afraid." Cole straightens, eyes flinty. "I'm afraid you're going to flip a fucking coin and let luck decide. Right now, you don't have a clue who you want, and until you know, this is how it's going to be."

A ragged inhale shudders my chest. "I hate this."

"I love you." He trails his fingers across my cheek and tucks my hair behind my ear.

"Love you, too."

He grips my legs between the spread of his and looks me in the eye. "How far did he go?"

I cringe, curling in on myself.

"Danni." He touches my chin, lifting it. "As long as

you're honest with me, I'll never resent you for being with him."

Honesty is good. I nod to myself, gathering courage and searching for the right words.

"We—" My voice creaks, and I try again. "We didn't go any farther than you and I went yesterday."

I can tell he's trying to keep a composed expression, but the skin around his eyes is so tight he looks like he's seconds from exploding.

"Did you come?" He works his jaw and stills it.

I turn my face away as tears sneak up.

"That was answer enough." There's no judgment in his tone as he circles his arms around me, pulling my chest to his. "Did it happen in the Range Rover?"

"The bathroom at Walmart," I whisper.

He growls deep in his chest. "Classy."

"You'd rather I fool around in your car and disrespect you?"

"No." His hand absently strokes my back. "Did he come?"

My shoulders fall forward, and my heart hammers in my chest. "I know you prefer to hear these details from me instead of him, and I'm trying to be open about it. But it makes me feel cheap, Cole. Like the intimacy I share with him doesn't mean anything."

"If it didn't mean anything, we wouldn't be here." He caresses my back, affectionately, compassionately. "Trace can tell me the rest."

"No, I can do this. I just need—"

The back door opens, and Trace steps in, pocketing his phone. His gaze hones in on me, then Cole. Lips resting in a scowl, he strides toward us.

"You told her the rules." He glares at Cole,

three is a war

lowering onto the stool beside us.

"She wouldn't leave it alone." Cole pulls me closer in the *V* of his legs and says under his breath, "Pain in the ass."

"I don't like to be kept in the dark." I pinch his bicep, where it bulges in the short-sleeve of his shirt.

"Did he make you tell him what we did together?" Trace watches me closely.

"Yeah." My face heats. "We were just discussing it."

"I haven't heard everything." Cole rubs his thumb against my hipbone. "It makes her uncomfortable."

"I'll finish the conversation." Trace lifts his eyes to me. "You can go—"

"Don't treat me like I'm made of glass." I cross my arms.

"You didn't sign up for this." Trace slants toward me, expression grave. "We put you in a terrible position. You didn't choose to love both of us. But you stuck it out, tried to make it right. You didn't ask to be lied to, deceived, drugged, kidnapped, and wrenched back and forth. But you're still here, stronger and feistier than ever." He shifts back and rests a finger beneath his chin. "We *know* you're not made of glass."

"There's titanium in your veins," Cole murmurs, staring at my lips.

Says the man with arms of steel. I let my hand fall down the curve of his bicep and rest back against the island.

"My point is," Trace says, "Cole and I created this mess, and I refuse to distress you any more than we already have." He thrusts his chin in the direction of the hallway. "Go dance, Danni. It's been too damn long."

He's right. Five weeks ago, I thought I lost the most important dance of my life. *My first dance.* The music died inside me, because a broken heart has no rhythm. But it's beating again. I have them back for however long it lasts, and I want to dance for that. I want to dance the way I used to dance *for them.*

I move to leave then feel compelled to linger a moment longer. Sliding a hand against the back of Cole's head, I reach for Trace and clasp his nape. With a physical connection to both of them, I touch my lips to Cole's forehead and repeat the kiss with Trace.

I'm reluctant to let go. I just want to hold them, keep them close, for always. But that's not how this ends, and I need to get that through my thick head.

Dropping my hands, I step back, warming beneath the heat of Cole's brown eyes and shivering in the depths of Trace's arctic blues. The skip of my pulse propels my feet, and I make my way through the living room and up the sloping stairs. When I turn the corner in the hall, I stop and hold my breath.

A long silence. Then Trace's wooden voice. "I came on her, not *in* her. No part of her touched my cock…"

I tiptoe away, hating how clinical and unfeeling his words sound. But I get it. He isn't trying to evoke arousal. He wants to make sure Cole doesn't cross any of the boundaries he's very clearly spelling out.

In the dance studio, I slip into the dressing room and change into spandex shorts and a halter top. After a thorough stretch routine, I move to the stereo and spend an eternity scrolling through the endless list of songs. *Too happy. Too slow. Not enough attitude. Wrong mood.* Then a song I've never danced to rolls by, and I pause on it.

three is a war

Back to Black by Amy Winehouse. Beyoncé covered this song, but that's not why it resonates with me. It's about a twisted love triangle, somewhat downtrodden, but full of grit and spirit. I push play and pace to the center of the room.

The piano riff kicks off with an arrangement of drums, tambourine, and loads of reverb. As the nasally vocals echo in the room, the melody sifts through my ears and finds its way directly to the heart of me.

My spine elongates. My core tightens. My blood hums.

And I begin to dance.

thirteen

Aside from eating, sleeping, and showering, I haven't stopped dancing for four days. My muscles are brutally sore. Blisters cover the soles of my feet, and I'm pretty sure I pulled a hamstring. But my God, I found my groove again.

I haven't even thought about choreography or footwork. I don't have to create belly dance routines for a job or practice for an upcoming performance. I'm simply dancing for the sake of moving to music I love.

I feel liberated. Meditative. Entranced.

It's like driving a car to a destination I've gone to a thousand times. I don't have to think about where to turn or when to shift, because I know how to get there and what to do. My subconscious takes over, freeing up my conscious mind to entertain things, such as contemplating the curves of Trace's scowl, anticipating the next appearance of Cole's dimples, and deciding which mouth I want to lick more.

As I dance deep in thought, there are no distractions. No responsibilities. Just the music and the movements and this fluid hypnotic state where I burrow in, dig deeper, down to my foundation, to the very essence of me. And that's where I look for him. The one. The choice. The marrow of my soul.

Sometimes, I think I see him.

I think I know.

But he's shrouded by doubts and denials and…fear, because holy fuck, I'm scared. I torture myself by imagining the abhorrent moment when I rip out part of my heart and hand it back to the man who gave it to me.

So I keep dancing, changing up the songs and styles to fit my moods. Today, it's hip-hop. Laid back and playful, sexy and soulful, the electronic beats make it impossible to sit still.

As *Wait* by Ying Yang Twins streams through the speakers, I face the wall of windows, my cheeks warm from exertion and the glow of the midday sun.

Boom-ba-snap-boom. Boom. Snap. I jerk my hips. *Boom-ba-snap-boom. Boom. Snap.* My body writhes, punctuating the kick drum with sharp thrusts.

I feel the pattern, the accent of sound, the pulsing vibes. The energy owns me as I plant my feet wide and shake it for all I'm worth. My hands slide over my body. My shoulders roll, and my hair swings around me. I pop my hips and bend my knees, taking it down, low to the floor. My abs undulate. My ass flexes. And I pause.

I sense him before I spot his reflection in the

three is a war

window.

Rising to my full height, I turn around.

"Don't stop." Cole prowls toward me, barefoot, shirtless, the fly of his jeans left unbuttoned, and his hair a damp, sexy mess.

"Did you just get out of the shower?" I sway my hips, slow and steady beneath his perusal.

"Yep." He circles me, his hooded gaze touching every inch of my body, from my flirty smile and sports bra to my tiny dance shorts and bare legs. "I went for a run."

He and Trace run every day, making use of the trails on the wooded property. Sometimes, they run together.

I glance at the closed door. This is the first time one of them stepped in here since the day they punished me.

Cole follows my gaze. "Trace is holed up in the office on work calls all day."

"He said you would be dividing up your time with me. Is that what this is?"

"Yes. I wanted you to have a few days to yourself." He looks around the studio with pride in his eyes. "How's the space working out?"

"I love it, Cole." A gushy grin lifts my cheeks. "I don't ever want to leave."

"I like the sound of that."

The song ends, and the recognizable beats of *Yeah* by Usher pumps through the room. Seized by the tempo, I move on instinct. Hips, torso, arms—my body knows the catchy rhythm and loves it.

An impish smile steals over Cole's mouth.

I step backward, bouncing and swinging my arms

overhead. "What?"

"I'm going to smack that."

"This?" I slide a hand over my rear as I dip to the floor and slide back up.

"Yeah."

"Come get me." I reverse through the room, jumping to the electronic beats and popping my movements.

He chases, his expression so intensely hungry it makes me feel giddy, alive, and wildly turned on. When he catches me by the windows, he spins me toward the ballet bar. Then he moves in, syncs our hips, and grinds with the music.

His bare chest burns against my back, his mouth hot on my neck, and his hands roam everywhere. Bodies pressed tightly together, we move as one, rocking, grabbing, and panting. It's the sound of our breaths that really gets me going. His is labored and shallow, telling me he wants me as badly as I want him.

Perspiration slicks his skin as his chiseled physique bunches and plays around me. He's hard, so damn long and swollen pressed against me, and I can't stop thinking about that unfastened button. And the zipper that needs tugging. And the underwear I know he's not wearing.

His body is made for sex, and he dances like he's mating. Hips thrusting, hands squeezing flesh, he leads, and I follow. He pulls, and I give. Then I break away, spinning around him in teasing circles.

He watches me like a predator, his eyes drunk on desire, and his kiss-shaped mouth beckoning. Utterly possessed by him, I drift closer with fire in my belly. He snatches me by the waist, aligns our bodies chest to chest, and rolls our hips. Then he crushes his mouth against

three is a war

mine.

We kiss for a moment that carries on forever, in an airless space, dancing as one body, skin sliding, limbs entangled, and hearts wild.

God, I love his lips. Our story was born there, on his dimpled smile. Every kiss we share validates what we knew the day we met. He's my first love as I am his. We're a constellation of fate, love spiraling to death to lies to love, and despite it all, we continue to spin with stars in our eyes.

We dance through several songs, kissing and grinding until my lungs burn and my mouth goes numb. I feel like more than flesh and bone when I'm in his arms, like I'm one half of something momentous. Like I'm an elemental part of something so rare and untouchable only a few people in the world ever experience it.

"I want to learn the dance you choreographed." He nuzzles my neck and spans his hands over my backside.

"Which dance?"

"The one I should've learned four years ago."

Our first dance.

The dance that never happened.

My heart trips as I envision a dream I thought I'd buried with his ashes.

A marriage to my first love.

A wedding dance.

With Cole.

As warm, gooey hope flutters through in my veins, another emotion knocks inside me, crashing everything to a halt.

Fear.

As much as I love the idea—the ballroom, white

dress, tuxedo, wedding rings, and our smiles as we twirl through the room—all my happiness shatters when fear shoves its way in, that jealous whore.

Cole hurt me in the past, and he could do it again. I'm so attached to this dance, and teaching him the steps could deepen my attachment to him. What if he knows that and this is just a ploy to outmaneuver Trace? What if I teach him and give the dance to Trace in the end? I can't do that to Cole.

I open my mouth to tell him…what? I don't know.

He cradles my face in his hands and looks at me like I'm a coin at the bottom of a well. A flickering candle on a cake. A star shooting across the sky. I'm his wish, and he is mine.

"Lie to me, Danni. Tell me we're not made of the same destiny."

"I can't." I blink, heart stammering. "I won't lie."

Over the span of four years, we leapt and soared. We fell and crashed. Then we brushed ourselves off and jumped again. We're not a phenomenon of chance. We're meant to be, and fate always finds its way.

I lean my brow against his, hugging the broad slopes of his shoulders. "When do you want to start learning the steps?"

A smile lights up his whole face, popping those dimples and painting his brown eyes with an eager glow. He lifts me from the floor and carries me to the couch, kissing me as he lowers me to my back.

I crane my neck to the look at the door. "What about—?"

"Trace wouldn't dare come in, and there are no cameras in here." He nibbles my lips. "No more spying."

Kneeling over me, he deepens the kiss with fevered

licks. His hand slides over my neck, through my hair, down the length of my body, and pulls on the sports bra impatiently, aggressively. I help him work off the top, and his mouth falls upon my nipple, tongue flicking and curling around the bud.

"Swear to God…" He moves to my shorts, yanking them down my legs while holding my gaze. "I'm not stopping until your pussy's sore and the walls in this room know my name."

My legs tremble, and I glance down at the bulge straining his zipper. "Are you always hard?"

"Yes." He tosses my shorts and climbs up my body. "Because you're always goddamn sexy." He molds his hands around my breasts. "Ninety-nine percent of the time, I'm fucking the hell out of you in my head."

"And the other one-percent?"

"I'm blowing my load in my hand."

"Cole," I moan, wriggling beneath his sweeping caresses. "I love when you get all poetic. You and your dirty mouth."

"My dirty mouth is a sucker for the romantic stuff." He grazes his teeth across my breast. "Like eating your pussy and lapping up your come."

He shoves a hand between my legs, using his muscular forearm to spread me wider. With a knee on the couch beside me, he plays with my wetness, opening me, spreading my heat, and plunging his fingers deep inside.

My back arches, and my knees fall open as he thrusts and teases with wicked skill. I bury my hands in his hair, whimpering and rocking my hips. I want. I need. Christ, I don't know the difference when his long fingers are stroking inside me.

He worships my peaked nipples with hot, wet lips and slides back up, face to face. I sprawl my hand across his scratchy cheek, and he kisses me like we're the last of our kind, like we're an extinct species in a loveless world.

Then he leaves my mouth, trailing kisses down my breastbone, across my abs, tickling his whiskers against my skin. His lips are the greedy kind, the kind that possess, devour, and plunder every part of my body they touch.

Dipping his head, he groans against my pussy. "So tight and sweet." He sinks his teeth into my tender flesh. "I want to break this pretty pink cunt."

"Have at it." I gyrate beneath him, high on lust.

He flashes a wolfish grin and lowers his face between my legs. Then he eats me like it's the last time he'll ever eat, kissing, sucking, and rolling his tongue around my piercing. He plunges deep and licks every drop of wetness. I tighten my fingers in his hair and wrap my legs around his neck, groaning, holding on, and making it last as long as possible.

Sliding a hand up my body, he cups my breast and tweaks the nipple. The insides of my thighs become stubble-burned, and my inner muscles build in the spasmodic contractions.

His eyes lift to mine, and he presses his lips harder against me, pushing me closer, faster along the rising tide of pleasure.

"Cole!" I jerk against his mouth and tug at his hair, writhing on the couch as everything inside me surrenders. "I'm coming. Don't stop. Don't stop."

He sucks and nuzzles until my moans wane and my body goes slack.

I'm still trying to catch my breath when he crawls

three is a war

between my legs. The sound of his zipper speeds up my pulse as his fingers trace my soaked, overstimulated lower lips. Then it's not his fingers. It's the fat, plump head of his hardness. He slides it through my wetness, circling my clit and making me squirm.

For a second, I think he's going to slam it in. But instead, he pulls back and straddles my hips.

His jeans gather beneath his ass and stretch across his sculpted thighs. No underwear, of course. The length of him juts from the open fly—thick and veiny and jerking for release.

"I give you permission to choke me with that." I peer at him from beneath my lashes.

He groans and wraps a hand around his cock. "You know that look you get when you're being sweet and innocent? Me neither."

Then he bows over me, braces his weight on an arm beside my head, and proceeds to stroke himself off.

His eyes connect with mine, his pupils blown and lips parted erotically. He's so worked up he won't last long. Too bad, because I could watch him like this for hours.

He's a wall of muscle, not an ounce of fat on those chiseled bumps and valleys. His golden skin is smooth as silk with a dusting of hair on his chest and forearms. He's a man's man, a rough-and-tumble, sexual beast of a man, and if I told him right now that I'll be his and only his, he'd fuck my lights out.

"Danni." His strokes accelerate, and the rock of his hips stumble into an erratic tempo. "I'm going to fucking come all over your gorgeous tits." His chin drops, but he doesn't move his eyes from mine. "Fuck. Oh, fuck, baby.

I'm there."

I grip his denim-clad thighs, digging my nails in as he spurts milky white ropes of come across my chest.

Panting and spent, he collapses on top of me. Then he rolls us until he lies on his back. His possessive lips find mine, and he kisses me adoringly while grabbing my ass aggressively.

I sprawl across his chest and lick inside his mouth, relishing the taste of him. "I love the smell of my pussy on your lips.

"I love the feel of my come on your tits."

"I love being sticky with you."

"I love being with you. Period." He clenches his hand on my butt and throws us into a kiss that erases the world around us.

It goes from rough to slow, from sexy to profound, and every notion in between. That's what I get with Cole—the extremes, the middle ground, and all the perfect little moments in between.

He's the song stuck in my head, the one that makes me dance until I'm knotted up in heartstrings.

If he's my choice, if this is my decision, it doesn't come in a bang of fireworks. It's a whisper in the back of my mind—a faint, tiny voice reminding me what I knew the moment I met him.

He's my first and last love. It's him. He has to be the choice.

But what if I'm wrong?

At the very least, it's something, a feeling to explore and try out.

I have to be sure.

fourteen

I spend the next two months trying to determine if my future is my past, if my first love will be my last. Mentally, I've made a decision. But my heart hasn't clued in yet.

Damn my flaky heart.

And damn Trace. He's the reason I'm all twisted up and turned inside out.

When I'm alone with Cole, I find a certain peace at the center of my flustered thoughts. We fish on his boat several times a week. We go shopping, jog on the trails, and prepare meals together. And we dance.

I taught him the steps I choreographed for our wedding reception song, *XO* by Beyoncé. When he twirls me through the room—his posture strong, footwork confident, and eyes glittering—fuck me, but I'm a fool for him. I love him with all the love that exists in the world.

Until I'm alone with Trace. He hasn't danced with me, but whenever I ask him what he wants to do, his answer is always the same.

I want to watch you dance.

And boy, does he watch. His impossible eyes hold me in bondage as I freestyle dance, pole dance, belly dance just for him. When we're not spending our one-on-one time in the studio, we're on the couch or in the bed, watching movies. The man is a cuddler. Not in a warm, fuzzy, *isn't-he-adorable* way. More like a *get-your-ass-over-here, I'm-restraining-you-with-my-arms* way.

Today, the three of us are at an indoor shooting range a couple towns over. I shot a few of the guns Cole brought from his armory. Some bullets hit the paper target. Most curved around the paper and spit at the sloped berm on the back wall. I might've accidentally hit the target in the next lane over, which sent Trace and Cole into an uproarious fit of laughter. Whatever. I tried and had fun doing it.

But not as much fun as watching them shoot lethal weapons.

Sitting on the bench behind them with plugs in my ears to muffle the gunfire, I have a glorious view of their backsides. They stand in their own lanes next to each other, sharing bullets, swapping guns, smiling, and seemingly having a good time.

I love to watch them interact. Cole grabs Trace's attention when he wants the other man to see a target he shot or when he has a technical question about a gun. Sometimes, Trace stops what he's doing just to observe Cole firing down the range.

But there's an undercurrent beneath the

three is a war

camaraderie. The competitive tension between them is thick. It's little things — the rigidness in their postures, the cutting looks between them, the glances back at me. Since I'm not planning for a zombie apocalypse, I don't care who's the better shot. But it matters to them.

This is a war, Danni.

I didn't have a good understanding of Cole's comment those first few days at the lake house. But after living with them for two months, I get it.

We're still sharing a bed at night, and they haven't crossed the sexual boundaries they set in the beginning. It's as if they're using the temptation of sex to undermine each other's steadfastness and determination to be the better man.

Blow jobs? They won't allow it. They seem to accept the fact that I'm engaging in cunnilingus with them both. But evidently, neither of them can stomach the idea of me putting my mouth on a cock that's not his own.

Or maybe something else is going on. Maybe they're playing a game to see which one can hold out the longest, as if it's some kind of determining factor in who I choose.

Is it? Would I have more respect for the one who didn't base a relationship on sex?

I think I would.

This isn't a war of fists or blood. It's a war of character and willpower, of psychology and heart. They're fighting each other on an emotional level, without words or physical force. While I sense the nuances of an ongoing battle, I wonder how much rivalry goes on that I'm not savvy enough to pick up on.

It's up to me to end this.

Trace told me at the start if I knew my decision, we would all know. *And that will be that.*

If I really want to over-analyze his words—which I have a propensity to do—does *know my decision* mean *know in my mind* or *know in my heart*? Because I think my mind knows, but I haven't discussed it with them. They're still carrying on like we'll be here, floating in limbo, for another four months.

Meanwhile, I'm trying to prepare myself for a quicker resolution, starting with subtle attempts to shut out Trace. Sometimes, I force myself to *not* respond to his affection. Sometimes, he notices and steals my breath with a brutal look. But he never says a word.

Can he read my thoughts? Or is he looking for deeper clues? Clues that tell him my heart belongs to another? If it's the latter, he'll be looking for a while. Maybe forever.

I think I've been spending too much time in my head. So much so I'm starting to annoy myself.

Rubbing my temples, I redirect my attention to the view before me.

They stand together, heads bowed, examining the chamber of a pistol Cole's holding.

Taller and leaner than Cole, Trace is polished masculinity in designer denim and a white collared shirt. He's probably the only man in history who wears starched clothes to a shooting range. Blond hair flawlessly styled, aristocratic features carved with a divine hand, his sophistication only makes him look deadlier with a gun.

Cole is raw, rugged power in ripped jeans and a black leather jacket. He's anarchy personified with his

three is a war

messy brown hair, sexy scruff, square jawline, and dark eyes that make me feel winded every time they shift in my direction.

"It's not the gun." Trace glares at him. "Your accuracy is shit. Retirement doesn't agree with you."

"Cool story, bro." Cole releases the slide with a metallic *clank*. "How about we get to the good part when you shut the fuck up?"

"The village called." Trace returns to his lane. "They want their idiot back."

My pulse accelerates as I flash back to the last time they involved a gun in a disagreement.

"Okay." I jump up and clap my hands. "Who wants to go for ice cream?"

"Is that what you want?" Cole softens his eyes, letting me know he'll give me anything I ask.

Almost anything.

I want the three of us to love and laugh and live happily ever after. *Together.* But it's a fool's dream.

"Want…need…" I grin. "The fine line between is ice cream."

fifteen

Three weeks later, Cole leads me through a buzzing dark nightclub called *The Angry Fly*. A thick haze from smoke machines clots the air, punctured by shards of neon light. All around me, college kids hop to the thumping music, bodies pressed together, grinding with sexual frisson and revving my heartbeat.

Trace broke away at the door to order us drinks. This isn't his scene. It's not mine, either. Not anymore. But as *Lose My Breath* by Destiny's Child vibrates the speakers, excitement builds inside me, twitching to let loose.

We drove forty minutes to get here. It's the closest venue with a dance floor and decent music. Springfield, Missouri is a college town, and evidently, this is the happening place. From multi-colored hair and piercings to barely-there miniskirts, young girls drip from the walls and bar stools.

The atmosphere conjures images of dirty cloakroom sex, the huge space crammed with frat boys smelling out pussy and bearded Millennials punching the air to the electronic beats. I might be the third oldest person here. Cole and Trace have me beat by a couple years.

I turned twenty-nine today.

A few weeks ago, I mentioned in passing that I wanted to rock out with them on a crowded dance floor. A couple hours ago, they surprised me with a new dress and a night on the town. If they dance with me, this will go down as the best birthday ever.

I run a hand along the black sheath minidress, loving the way it molds to my body. With strategic cutouts, it looks like it was attacked by an angry pair of scissors. My skin peeks through the wide slashes from chest to thighs, making undergarments a no-go. Paired with strappy stilettos, the outfit is sexy with an edge.

The looks sliding my way from eager college boys causes Cole to yank me against his side, crushing my shoulders under the heavy weight of his arm. I hug his waist, delighting in the flex of lean muscle as he guides us toward the dance floor.

One thing's for certain. He and Trace would never leave me by myself in this place. Not for a second. That means I don't have to worry about getting hit on. There isn't a guy here with balls big enough to approach me while my possessive sentinels are hovering.

The warm March weather made it possible to leave our jackets at home. Cole looks fashionably old-school and rebellious in his worn *Sex Pistols* t-shirt, faded jeans,

three is a war

and spiked hair. He's so irresistible my hands shake to touch every inch of his hard, carved body.

We reach the dance crowd, the writhing bodies rippling like waves in a vast ocean under the strobing lights. He tugs me in, but I pull back, scanning the bar.

"We should wait for Trace." I shout over the music.

Cole grips my chin and angles my face toward the far side of the dance floor.

Reclined on a bar stool, Trace lifts a glass of amber to his lickable lips. His elbow rests on a high-top table next to two unopened bottles of Bud Light. He wears dark fitted slacks with a tucked-in collared shirt that he left unbuttoned at the neck.

If there's any emotion in that delicious scowl, I don't see it. Expressionless, almost stern, he's so hard to read I have second thoughts about dancing.

Then he winks, and everything inside me melts. Fuck, he's sexy, and he damn well knows it. So does every woman in the bar.

Two brunettes start circling, creeping in from both sides, corralling him. When they reach him, their painted lips move. The glare he shoots at them widens their eyes. I almost feel bad for them as they turn heel and strut away.

"Come on." Cole raises his voice above the din. "Go get your sexy on."

I unglue my feet from the sticky floor and follow him into the sweaty chaos. When he slows at the center, I keep going, pulling on his hand and bouncing to the music. I came here with two men, and I want to see them both. So I head toward the far edge and stop a few feet from Trace.

My blond-haired Viking props a polished shoe on a knee and gives me a chin lift that commands me to dance.

I find the beat, mentally tapping out the count and clapping my hands on two. The movements start with my head and work their way down to my feet. A hair toss, shoulder pop, hip roll, and step together. I feel it, work it, and strip the last of my inhibitions beneath Trace's heated gaze.

Cole dances around me, keeping it clean as he warms me up. When it comes to a man dancing in a club, less is more, and he has that figured out. He puts his personality into it, infusing every move with swagger, but it's subtle. His hands go up, raising the roof. Then he buries it, snapping at his sides, snapping in front, and out again. Open, close, open, close... Every action is subdued, sensual, and undeniably confident. Damn, but he knows what he's doing.

Whenever he circles me, he puts a hand on my waist, keeping the connection. Then he steps closer, and I give him a flirty hip-check, laughing as he pops me on the ass.

Booty by J.Lo shakes the room, charging the air with seductive energy. I throw my hands up in a double-arm lasso, getting my whole body involved and spinning toward Trace. I crook a finger at him, mouthing, *Dance with me.*

The corner of his frown twists upward, but he doesn't move. *Stubborn man.* He can fight it if he likes, but I'm going to lure him in.

I turn around, find his blue eyes over my shoulder, and jam it out. That earns me a real smile, inspiring me to groove my way to the floor, low, lower. Then I slide back

three is a war

up.

And come face to face with Cole. Perspiration glistens his brow, his breaths labored and expression burning with hunger.

I shimmy up against him and do a little chest bump. He joins in, bumping me back in time with the music. Bump, bump, bump, we're caught in it. Contagious, suggestive, the bumps roll into waves that ripple down our bodies.

My hand falls to his shoulder, and his arms hang loosely at his sides and slightly behind him, giving me full access to his ripped physique. I oblige, drifting my other hand down his torso, tracing the grooves of muscle through the shirt, and lingering on the button of his fly.

He leans in, leans out, putting a sexy roll into it. With each slant forward and back, he grows closer, smoother, sliding up against me. Then we're grinding, feeling the same rhythm and motion, and dancing as one. *This* is where it's at. The sizzling burn. The fire and the thunder.

Our hips undulate together. Our eyes connect, and I'm buzzing, lost in the molten brown of his gaze. He doesn't just look at me. He eats me alive with his eyes. My pulse thrums. My blood pumps, hot and fast, beneath my skin. The rock of his pelvis controls the pace of my mine, and his hands wander, stroking my back, molding around my waist, and slipping down my bare thighs.

Then there are four hands. My gaze flies to Cole's, but I don't need to see his relaxed expression to know who's behind me. I'm intimately familiar with the touch of those fingers, the dominating pressure.

The scent of scotch warms my senses as Trace

slides up behind me, gripping my hips and taking control. He slows it down. Sets the pace. Pulls me closer. Grabs me a little tighter. And lets me feel his rhythm. *And his hardness.*

I shiver and tremble, my breaths growing faster. What are they doing to me?

Cole moves in, pressing his chest to mine and holding my face in his hands. His gaze is electric, sparking with blistering desire. As hard as I look, I don't see jealousy or frustration. His smile's too bright, too easy. But those dimples are deep pits of trouble. Doesn't matter that I'm with both of them tonight. He's going to tease me until I'm dripping, and it'll run down my legs because dammit, I'm not wearing panties.

He rocks against me, sandwiching my body between him and Trace. His tempo is faster than the hips crushed against my backside. Trace tightens his grip, tries to take back control. But Cole changes it up, drops it here, stops it right there, and returns to a slow grind.

They go back and forth, fighting for the lead in our erotic dance. Pushing and pulling. Slowing down and speeding up. Until a remarkable thing happens. Their rhythm syncs, and their hips grind in unison, as if connected. They stop fighting and work together, falling into the thrall of the sensual music.

I'm in heaven. Nothing is sexier than grooving between two gorgeous men who want me as much as I want them. Cole's smile. The press of Trace's hands. The heavy sounds of their breaths. The sexual way they move against me. I could do this forever.

Trace maintains the connection by leaning around me to see my face. I angle back, keeping my hips pinned between theirs and holding his gaze. We dance like that

three is a war

through several songs before taking a break to catch our breaths and drink our beers. Then we dance some more.

The longer I'm held between them, the bolder my hands become. Strong necks, chiseled pecs, muscled forearms, swollen cocks—I touch them everywhere, rubbing, caressing, stroking. I'm burning up, soaked between my legs, and shaking with the impossible need to jump them.

The blatant arousal vibrating through their bodies doesn't help. They seem to have forgotten each other, their mouths and hands aggressively focused on me.

When Cole's lips capture mine, I tense up and try to pull back. He grips my neck and deepens the kiss, chasing my tongue and going wild. Then Trace is there, wrenching my mouth from Cole and stealing his own kiss before Cole swoops back in. They pass me between them, over and over, controlled by a desire that grows greedier by the second.

We continue to dance, three souls spiraling in a private world of kissing, neck licking, lip biting, and ass grabbing. Whatever this is, it's reckless, carnal, *dangerous*. But we don't seem capable of stopping. It's too powerful, too deliciously tempting as it wraps around us and attempts to break every rule.

The energy between us crackles across my skin, turning the longing inside me into a physical necessity. I've never experienced sexual tension like this. It seethes and growls like an eight-hundred-pound gorilla, as it follows us off the dance floor and stays with us during the ride home.

Cole drives the Range Rover with Trace in the passenger seat. I squirm and tremble behind them, clenching my thighs together and seeking relief. The only remedy for what ails me is in the form of two tense men in the front seat.

Neither of them speak or make eye contact. The steering wheel creaks beneath Cole's grip, and I'm not sure Trace is breathing.

"Is it just me," I ask, "or is there a lot of tension in here?"

Silence. More tension. Then Cole's eyes find mine in the review mirror, his lips pinned.

"I call first dibs on the cold shower." I arch my brow.

He returns his attention to the road and tightens his grip on the wheel.

I need one of those hugs that turns into a primal bang against the wall. I want their hands on me, pulling my hair and wrenching my legs open. I want them to fuck me like they hate me.

It's physically painful to just sit here, staring at their rigid profiles and breathing in the testosterone saturating the confined space. By the time Cole pulls into the garage, my face is flushed and my thighs are drenched.

Leaping out of the SUV, I dart toward the interior door with thoughts of self-pleasure in a cold shower.

When I step into the kitchen, an arm catches my waist. My feet lose contact with the floor, and I'm tossed over a hard, broad shoulder.

"Cole!" I grip the back of his t-shirt and buck to get free. "What are you doing?"

He carries me through the living room, caressing a hand up the back of my thigh. With my head hanging upside down, I watch his boots fly up the stairs to the hall. Then his fingers sink between my legs, sliding through my wet heat and racing my pulse.

"Jesus, fuck," he whispers. "You're soaked."

I brace my hands on his back and lift, meeting ice blue eyes. "Trace?"

His scowl is deep, but I can't interpret its meaning. Cole's fingering my pussy right in front of him, and he's not stopping it. Instead, he slowly trails behind and unbuttons the cuffs on his shirt with methodical flicks of his fingers.

I narrow my eyes at him, and he narrows his right back. Something shifts there, in the crystalline depths. Something carnal. Tameless.

His expression darkens, and he quickens his gait. Then he strides past Cole and leads the way to the bedroom.

sixteen

I know things got out of hand on the dance floor. Wild and uncontrolled, we worked ourselves to a feverish pitch. As I hang upside down over Cole's shoulder, my fingers tingle with the need to touch. A fluttering ache persists in my chest, and there's another, more demanding heartbeat throbbing between my legs.

But Cole and Trace can't possibly intend to do anything about it. Not in the ways I fantasized during the ride home.

They don't share.

Cole carries me into the bedroom and drops me on the bed. I land on my back, and he follows me down. His expression is pure wanton lust, his hands like supercharged static as he pulls on my dress and hikes it up my hips.

I twist, seeking Trace, but he's already here, falling on me with ferocious caresses and a starving mouth.

"You're not—" I gasp at the sharp scrape of Cole's teeth against my butt. "We can't—"

Trace devours my words, plunging his tongue past my lips and swallowing my air.

I squirm and writhe between them, sawing my legs together, desperate to be fucked while struggling to slam on the brakes.

Cole works my dress over my chest, my head, and off, leaving me completely bare. Then his hands are everywhere, stroking my hips, my thighs, and between my legs while Trace kisses me breathless. Their hot mouths and impatient fingers flood me with warmth and loosen my knees. I want…

We can't do this. They'll resent me. They'll hate each other.

I try to break the kiss, but Trace presses closer, harder, tangling our tongues. I try to wriggle away, but I'm outmatched, overpowered.

Four hands.

Two mouths.

One of me.

Cole moves down my body, licking and nuzzling my hips as he caresses me from chest to toes. When Trace releases my lips to suckle my neck, I find my voice.

"Why are you doing this? You'll regret—"

Trace grips my throat in an iron fist. "Shut the fuck up."

His tone, the gravelly heat in his growl, I'm a slave to it.

I scratch at the collar of his hand, and he lightens the pressure just enough to allow breath.

three is a war

"Do something for me." Cole climbs over me, his fingers sliding over the fly of his jeans to free the button.

I whimper, flicking my gaze between him and Trace.

"Get out of your goddamn head and enjoy this." Cole yanks off his shirt and attacks my breast with tongue and teeth.

Trace releases my throat and moves to my chest, licking and sucking my other breast. My hands fly to their heads, holding them to me and pushing them away as my entire world comes undone in a crashing wave of need.

Enjoy this.

That isn't the problem. What freaks me out is the regret I'll see in their eyes tomorrow morning. There are so many conflicting thoughts pounding in my head, but I need to remember we're all adults. No one is here against his will. They're controlling this, and whether or not they thought through it, they're committed to it.

Inching down my body, Cole palms my ass, squeezes my thighs, and slides his hand between my legs, spreading the moisture. Trace tears off his shirt and returns to my mouth, kneading my breasts with strong fingers. Then he lifts on his knees, and I watch with ragged breaths as he unzips his pants and strips the last of the clothes from his body.

His erection jerks inches from my face, and my mouth waters with a rush of saliva. He's beautifully endowed, swollen and long with a flared head beading with pre-come.

Kneeling beside my head, he angles over me and rests the tip against my lips. I dart out my tongue, savoring his salty taste as Cole grips my thighs and hooks them around his shoulders. Then he lowers his head and buries his tongue, licking me aggressively.

"Fuck!" My back bows, and my heart slams out of control.

The instant my mouth opens on a choked gasp, Trace shoves in his cock.

OhmyGod, OhmyGod. This is happening.

I suck hungrily, slurping along his shaft and gripping the base in my fist. Then we're rocking, grinding, licking, and groping. They are muscle and flesh, passion and sin, flexing and burning beneath my greedy fingers. They surround me, consume me, twisting us into a tangle of sweaty limbs and shameless self-indulgence.

There are so many hands on my body I'm delirious beneath the sensations. I've never seen them this worked up, this desperate to fuck. They don't look at each other, yet somehow, they avoid each other's touches.

As I swallow and suck Trace's cock, Cole's head moves between my legs. He closes his eyes and groans, his jaw grinding against me and tongue plunging with wicked strokes.

Trace shoves a hand in my hair, gripping my head. Then he rolls to his back and takes me with him. I fall to my side, curled around Trace's leg with my cheek on his abs as he drives himself into my mouth.

My legs tangle around Cole's shoulders, and he repositions, running his hands up and down my thighs and lifting my ass toward his face. Restraining me in his unbending grip, he spreads me open and sinks his fingers deep inside.

I buck against the penetration, moaning around the

three is a war

cock in my mouth. Trace growls and reaches for my chest, pinching the ever-loving hell out of my nipple. With an anguished moan, I lick up and down his shaft. Suck hard on the head. Clamp a fist around him. Jerk him off. Make him grunt and grind against me.

The heaving of their breaths reverberates through the room. Their hands are rough and ruthless, their bodies hard and demanding. They can seduce my mind, make love to my flesh, and enslave my soul. I'm already theirs.

Affectionate fingers stroke through my hair, tangling and straightening. *Trace.* A nimble thumb finds my clit, circling and pinching without apology. *Cole.* Together, they surge a trail of tingles from my head to my toes, making me restless, fevered, and insanely turned on.

Cole leans up and removes his jeans. I watch him over my shoulder as he kneels behind me, his thick cock jutting from between powerful thighs, engorged and ready.

I meet his smoldering eyes and shiver. He's going to fuck me. Right now, while I'm sucking off Trace.

Trace lifts me, adjusting my body on hands and knees between his legs. Then he cradles my face and holds me with his gaze in the space of a breathless moment.

Seduction isn't a kiss or a touch. It's this. The mystery and intelligence in his eyes. The connection they reinforce. The intoxication of feeling the depth of his emotions. He undresses our skin and strips us down to our souls until we're bared to each other in every way, until his love fills my ribcage so completely it becomes the life force that pumps my heart.

Then he blinks, breaking the spell and lowering his attention to my lips.

"Open up, my tiny dancer." With an unyielding hand on my head, he guides my mouth onto his waiting cock.

Pressing past my lips, he sinks slowly, hot and heavy on my tongue. He pushes deep, deeper, and holds me on him as my throat relaxes around the invasion. I breathe through it, my thoughts drifting to Cole right before he cups my breast and squeezes the tight nipple. I groan for more and lift my ass, spreading wider in invitation.

On his knees behind me, he fits himself against my opening and rams, hard and mercilessly, inside me.

Goddamn, I feel that—the stretch, the savage burn. It's been months. Three months? Four? I don't even know, but it's been just as long for Cole. Longer for Trace. He hasn't come in me since the night before Cole returned from the grave.

Cole gives me a few seconds to adjust. I hover my mouth over Trace's cock, afraid I might bite him as I brace for the brutish way Cole fucks.

With a sharp exhale, Cole lets go, pounding deep, hammering hard, gripping my ass, smacking it, panting, and grunting something fierce. Trace sits up and shifts to his knees, mirroring Cole's position behind me. With a hand collaring my throat, he shoves himself into my mouth, thrusting slower than Cole but no less hard.

I suck him with everything I have while reaching up his chest toward his face. He clamps his fingers around mine, holding our hands against his heart.

Then they fuck me, tugging at my hair and pinning

three is a war

my body between the force of their need. It's depraved. Filthy. Perfect. Everything I imagined it would be.

Cole picks up the pace, holding tight to my hips as he stabs into me, over and over. Licking up and down Trace's length, I stare up into fathomless eyes and melt beneath their scorching heat.

"Be right back." Cole pulls out and leaves the bed.

I turn my neck to watch him prowl gloriously nude toward the bathroom, but Trace jerks me back and drags me up his chest.

"Show me how perfectly we fit together." His timbre scratches as he arranges my legs to straddle his hips.

I move without hesitation, positioning his cock and sliding down slowly, relishing every long inch. His mouth falls open, and his chin lifts, the cords in his neck stretching against his skin. I roll my hips, and he groans, eyes closed as pleasure sweeps across his expression. *Fucking gorgeous.*

Cole returns from the bathroom with a tube of lube and pauses beside the bed, watching Trace move inside me.

Nerves creep in, coiling my stomach. I can't imagine what it must be like for him, seeing his ex-best friend balls-deep in the woman he wants to spend his life with. I press a hand against Trace's hip, stalling his movements.

"Cole?" I sit up, and my inner muscles clench around Trace's cock. "We can stop. We don't have to—"

"Lie back down." Cole grips his erection and strokes from root to tip. "Ass in the air."

That's what the lube's for, of course. But is he

going to take me there while Trace is still inside me? We should have a conversation about this, but as Cole moves in behind me, he seems to be more interested in the conversation between his finger and my rear entrance.

His touch presses in, and I gulp down a breath, writhing on Trace.

"You're so fucking wet." Cole slides his thumb toward my pussy, gathering my arousal and smearing it over my anus. "I don't even need lube."

"Yes, you do." I glare at him over my shoulder and soften my voice. "I've never done this…" *Double-penetration.* My cheeks burn. I can't even say it out loud. "Have you?"

He shakes his head, eyes on the finger working past my ring of muscle. What else can he see down there? The base of Trace's cock stretching me open? His balls slapping against me?

"What about you?" I turn back to Trace.

"You're my first and last." He cradles my face with both hands, searching my eyes.

My chest squeezes. If I could have one wish, it would be to wake up tomorrow to the sound of their hearts beating happily against mine.

"Please, don't regret this." My breaths quicken as the lubed crown of Cole's cock nudges against me, seeking entry.

"I would never regret being inside of you," Trace says.

"Breathe, baby." Cole leans over my back and trails kisses up my spine, his voice gruff. "Push against me."

I let my lungs do what they're supposed to do and crane my neck to check out the positioning. Trace's legs are together behind me with Cole and me straddling his hips. They look comfortable…considering the circumstances. I turn back and press against Cole, without taking my eyes off Trace.

Pressure ignites a dull ache in my back opening, stretching and filling. Cole sinks deeper, his fingers biting against my hips. It doesn't take long before the sting ripples into languid pleasure.

Cole bears down with gentle, shallow strokes, shooting supernova tingles through my sensitive tissues. It feels so damn good it's almost too much. Too many sensations. Too much fullness.

Trace's eyes tell me he feels it, too. He brushes the hair from my face and feathers his fingers down my neck, rocking against me in a hypnotic rhythm.

They're inside me. Both of them. Physically. Emotionally. The mattress beneath me disintegrates and time ceases to exist. I only feel. Them, us, joined in a way I never thought would happen and may never happen again.

"How are you doing?" Cole brushes his lips against my back.

"I might die if you don't move faster."

I don't have to ask twice. He rolls into a swift grind, sliding his cock in and out and matching the rhythm of Trace's thrusts.

Trembling and boneless, I lean forward and rub my hands over the muscled physique beneath me. My hair falls around my face as I lick the grooved valley at the center of Trace's chest, kissing and nuzzling, awash in bliss.

Cole's scruffy whiskers and warm breaths caress my back as he fucks me slowly, teasingly, like he doesn't want to rush it.

Focusing my attention on Trace, I memorize the sharp angles of his clean-shaved face. Golden hair, straight nose, kissable scowl—he's irrationally beautiful with his soulful blue eyes studying me the way I study him.

"Are you good?" I pant breathlessly, gripping his shoulder against an onslaught of pleasure.

"Trying not to come." A muscle flexes in his cheek.

"You need to hurry, baby." Cole hooks an arm around my waist and yanks me to a sitting position.

With my back against Cole's chest and my legs spread around Trace's hips, my clit is exposed and throbbing. Trace presses a thumb against it, rubbing circles and applying precise, consistent pressure.

My head falls back on Cole's shoulder, his mouth at my ear, letting me feel every hot moaning gasp as he strokes his cock in and out of me. Then he grips my jaw and yanks my mouth to his. The kiss is hard, wild, and all-consuming. It's more than I can bear.

I plunge fast, breaking the kiss and screaming out. Powerful, violent, the orgasm cleaves through me, splitting me open and moving me in a profound state of oblivion. Stars blot my vision as they grind their hips, speed up the pace, and join me.

Panting breaths, groaning shouts, and fingers bruising my flesh, they come together, apart, whatever they may be. It's glorious. Unforgettable. A dream in the flesh.

I collapse on Trace's chest, light-headed and spent. Cole falls on his back beside me and drops a forearm across his eyes, breathing heavily past parted lips.

Trace cradles my cheek with a warm palm and

three is a war

strokes his thumb across my mouth. I kiss it, grasp his wrist, and hold on. I don't want this to end. I'm afraid of what comes next.

"I hope you didn't do this for me…for my birthday." I glance at Cole and return to Trace. "Did you plan this?"

"No." Trace untangles his hand from mine and rolls us to our sides. "It wasn't planned."

My head jerks back. Trace Savoy just engaged in an impulsive, unintentional threesome? How very free-spirited of him.

Cole shifts to the edge of the bed and grabs his shirt from the floor. With a hand on my shoulder, he pushes me to my back and uses the shirt to clean between my legs. He does the same with himself and tosses it. Not once does he glance at Trace. Maybe I'm imagining it, but the awkwardness is already creeping in.

"When we got home tonight, you both seemed to be on the same page." I rest my head on Cole's chest and hook a leg around Trace's thigh, desperate to keep us joined. "But you didn't talk about it beforehand?"

"Not exactly." Cole pets my hair, his breathing returning to normal.

"I made the decision in the car," Trace says in an icy tone, at odds with the soothing way he caresses my thigh.

"Same." Cole's hand tightens in my hair.

They didn't even look at each other in the car. Did they have a telepathic conversation? I have so many questions, but if I start interrogating them, this delicate peace between us will evaporate.

I lie still, absorbing the touch of fingers on my skin,

the rasps of sated breaths, and thrum of love beating between us, knowing I'll never find this with anyone but them.

Too soon, Trace lifts my leg off his, sits up, and captures my gaze.

"This was a one-time thing, Danni." His eyes turn to frozen glass. "It will never happen again."

My breath hitches, and my hackles bristle. "I didn't ask for it. In fact, when I opened my mouth, you told me to shut the fuck up."

"You didn't have to ask for it." He rises and strides toward the bathroom. "You *wanted* it."

"Don't do that to her," Cole shouts, launching off the bed. "This isn't her fault."

Trace closes the door behind him and locks it, freezing us out.

Fault. There can only be fault if a mistake was made.

The shower sounds behind the door, and my chest turns to ice. I cover a hand over my mouth to stifle the quiver in my chin. *Don't you fucking cry, Danni.* All the tears in the world won't fix this.

"How did this happen?" I ask, more to myself than to Cole.

"That?" He points at the bathroom door and returns to the bed. "I don't have time to list all his problems, but the one he suffers from the most begins with ass and ends with hole."

"I'm serious, Cole." It feels like my heart is sinking into my stomach.

Lying on his back, he pulls me into his arms and wraps the sheet around us. "Let it go."

"No." I snap my head up, glaring at him. "I can't

three is a war

just…just chuck this in the *fuck it* bucket. What we're doing to one another is heartbreaking."

He returns my stare for a long moment before releasing a sigh. "I'm pretty sure he thought I was going to break the rules tonight."

"Were you?"

"Yes." He looks at me with unflinching eyes. "He knew he wouldn't be able to stop me."

"If you can't beat them, join them," I mumble sadly.

"Or *control* them. He participated because he couldn't fathom me making love to you without his almighty hand involved."

I love Trace's almighty hand and his control, but not at the risk of hurting him. "Did he tell you this?"

"I know him, baby. Better than you do."

As I turn that over in my head, I kick myself for not being as perceptive as Cole. If I'd known Trace wasn't acting purely on passion, I would've stopped it from happening. Or at least *tried* to stop it. I have a hard time saying *no* to them when it comes to sex. It's just not in my DNA. I bend, yield, surrender, and they shine in the power it gives them. That's why we're so good together.

Braced on an elbow, I trace a finger along the ridges of his abs. "Did you want the threesome?"

"No." His muscles tense beneath my touch. "I had to block him out of my mind the entire time." He runs a hand down the length of my spine. "I agree with him on that point. I'll never do it again."

He doesn't say that he regrets it, but it's there in the creases around his mouth. It feels like a slap in the face.

Maybe I'm just emotionally and physically drained, but I can't hold the dam on my tears. They rise fast, spilling down my cheeks, but I keep the sounds trapped beneath rapid swallows.

"Why did you do it?" I whisper.

"Because I love you. I *want* you."

"I don't understand why you want anything to do with me. I'm a mess."

"I'll take you messy and crying and in love with another man." He hugs me against his chest and rests his lips on my head. "I'll take you anyway I can have you."

"That's just it. You shouldn't have to."

We fall quiet—a silence that brings everything into sharp focus. Seductive words, sexy dimples, arctic blue eyes, passion, and self-control… I fell in love with two men, went to war to keep them, and now it must end. Someone has to choose the break-up song and dance to the mournful melody, and that harrowing fate is meant for me.

I have to choose. Not in four months. I need to do it soon, within a week, and put us out of our misery. No more dragging my feet. No more waiting for some enlightening *aha!* moment. That's never going to come. I just need to reach in and tear out part of my heart and be done with it.

After a while, Trace emerges from the bathroom and returns to bed in a pair of boxer briefs. He slides in behind me, aligning his body along the length of mine with my chest against Cole's side and my head on his shoulder.

"Happy Birthday, Danni." Trace kisses my neck, telling me with his lips that he loves me.

And I silently cry.

seventeen

I wake to the sound of rain pelting the windows. A dreary morning. Cold mattress. No Cole. No Trace. Only the sick weight of dread pressing down on my chest.

Shower, clothes, coffee—I move through the motions, wretchedly numb.

Trace is locked away in the office, working. Cole left a note, letting me know he's fishing.

With a mug of creamy coffee in hand, I stand at the kitchen window and stare out at the freezing rain. Who goes fishing in this weather?

Someone who wants distance from an awkward situation.

It rains for the next three days.
Three.
It's an impossible number.

A cruel number.

Three is an emotional war.

Cole and Trace go out of their way to avoid each other. They live under the same roof, share the same bed, but they don't exchange a word or a glance. We don't talk about what happened. Every time I try, I'm shut down. So much for open communication.

When they're alone with me, however, they arrest me with their eyes and undress me with their words. Each man makes me feel loved in his own way. A tender touch, sultry suggestion, brush of lips... But the intimacy ends there.

I understand. The rules are wrecked, and the future is unclear. They want space to process or do whatever it is they need to do.

I'm giving them space, but they're crazy if they think we can go another four months like this.

While they spend the rainy days in separate parts of the house, I've been holed up in the dance studio. Well, not exactly *holed up*. I leave the door open and blare the music. I'm here, ready to listen when they're ready to talk.

I have some things of my own to say.

Gripping the ballet bar, I face the rain beyond the windows and sync my hips to the somber melody of *You Don't Know* by Katelyn Tarver.

Cole and Trace make me insanely happy. A lifetime with either of them is a fairy tale come true. No matter how much I compare and separate and weigh their differences, there's no wrong choice.

But Cole's the one I found first.

He set my soul on fire with a look and kissed me with lips infused with forever. There's a dance soldered

three is a war

to my bones choreographed for him and him alone.

Our chemistry is magnetic, undying, our history so deeply sown it can't be uprooted. We're soul mates, finding our way back together, over and over.

He has to be the choice, and the only way I'll know for sure is if I make it.

When the song ends, I walk to the stereo and play it again, swaying and humming to the painful lyrics while thinking about Trace.

I dance in mourning for the hurt I inflicted on him. I dance in longing for the love I share with him. I dance in fear for the words that will rip him away.

With my back to the door and my emotions running amok, I don't sense him approach. Not until his hand curls around my hip and his forehead rests against the back of my head.

Everything inside me starts to melt.

Don't give in, Danni. You must *do this.*

Against all instinct, I force myself to go cold, emotionally, mentally, pushing him away.

His hand slides down my thigh, tracing the hem of my spandex shorts. I tense up, and he notices, removing his touch.

My stomach shrivels, but I keep my voice even. "Do you want to talk…about the other night?"

"No." He prowls around me, hands behind his back, and ensnares me in his analyzing gaze.

Fitted black trousers and a crisp white button-up, his attire is as sophisticated as his composure. The way he scrutinizes me, the subtle sharpening of those incisive eyes, it's as if he already knows.

My resolve weakens, and I consider waiting until

tomorrow. Or the next day. But the longer I delay, the harder it will become. It's now. Right now. *Open your mouth, idiot.*

Shifting to the stereo, I power off the music. Then I turn back, standing taller, and fix my expression into one of bravery. "I want to talk—"

"I want you to remove your clothes and whatever is putting that fake look on your face."

Cold bones, hunched shoulders, hemorrhaging heart, I wither beneath his command. My brave mask gives way to rising tears, and I step back, clasping my throat and fighting down the anguish.

He glares at my trembling hand, my leaky eyes, and his entire demeanor changes. His arms fall slack at his sides. His scowl loses its intensity, and he shakes his head slowly, imperceptibly, as if in shock. Denial.

I wipe the wet misery from my cheeks and hug my waist. "Trace…"

He snaps straight, and his eyes bore into mine as his words echo in my mind.

If you know, we'll all know. And that will be that.

"Say it." Harsh and guttural, his voice cuts me to the quick.

My throat seals up, holding the confession captive.

I'm a heartless bitch if I choose Cole. I'm a heartless bitch if I choose Trace. I'm the queen of all bitches if I don't choose at all.

I made a decision. It's time to grow up. Declare it. *Fight for it.*

Pulling in a serrated breath, I release my lungs slowly. "I choose Cole."

He goes chillingly still, doesn't breathe, doesn't blink, his stark eyes locked on mine. He wants to argue.

three is a war

It's right there in the rigidness of his jaw. The impulse to demand a different answer is eating him up inside. But more than that, he wants what he cannot control.

I refuse to force your hand on this...I want your heart to beat for me and only me, not because I command it, but because we're meant to be.

I know the moment he accepts my choice. His throat bobs. His chest heaves, and he stumbles back.

The look of total devastation on his face tears me apart. His pain is scarring, like the sharp edge of a knife leaving its marks inside me.

He glances around the room like he's unsure where to go or what to do. Stunned, lost, he's beautiful, fractured perfection.

"Trace..." I approach him, dying a thousand deaths. "Say something."

He stabs a hand in his hair and spins toward the door. Then he walks out.

I run after him, chasing him down the hall and through the bedroom. I scan the rooms for Cole, but the house is quiet. He must still be down at the dock.

"Please, talk to me." I follow Trace into his closet.

He shrugs on a suit jacket, buttoning away his emotions behind expensive threads. His hands shake as he yanks random clothes off the hangers and shoves them into a leather bag.

"You're leaving?" My heart crashes into my shoes.

Of course, he's leaving. What else is he supposed to do?

He doesn't answer me, doesn't look my way as he continues to pack. I gulp down a sob, refusing to give it life. I'm hurting him irreparably. I don't deserve to cry.

"It can't end like this." I reach for his arm and think better of it. "We have to talk about it."

"It must end this way. A clean cut." He slides past me, bag in hand, and strides out of the bedroom.

I follow him into the living room. He grabs his keys from the kitchen island and heads toward the front door. His car is parked in the driveway, a twenty-second walk away. Twenty seconds is all we have left.

"Trace, stop!" The shrill in my voice announces my desperation. "Please. Wait."

The slowing of his gait lets me know he's considering. The pause of his feet at the door tells me he's analyzing the risks of hearing what I have to say.

He enters the code in the keypad, grips the door handle, and drops his arm. Then he turns and faces me.

My breath catches at the agony tightening his face. He stands twenty feet away, his eyes wet and drowning in heartache.

Tears lurk at the backs of my own eyes, but I hold them at bay.

Putting one foot in front of the other, I approach slowly and pause a few paces away. Then I let him read my expression, let him delve deep into my eyes as I tell him without words everything I need to say.

I will always, always love you, and I will never forget. I won't forget the taste of your scowl, the way it curved against my mouth when we kissed, our lips rough with passion. I won't forget how you watched over me and saved my life, how you gave me your love when I didn't believe in second chances. I won't forget the stage you erected for me, the heat of your eyes on my body in the beam of light, and the adoration in your voice when you talked about my dancing. I won't forget your bed in the penthouse, our bodies tumbled together, your hand,

three is a war

my throat, your jawline, my fingers, the caress of your brush through my hair, your orderliness, your control, your uncreamy coffee, the scent of scotch on your breath, the infinity pools of your eyes, and the depths of you, who showed me how to smile again.

A tear escapes, and I brush it off my cheek. "I'm so sorry."

"Don't apologize, Danni Angelo." His timbre is quiet, shaky. "I gave you my heart. It was always yours to break."

I shake my head rapidly, battling an impending meltdown. "I didn't want to—"

"Shhh." He looks down, squeezes his eyes shut. "It was always going to come down to a choice. I knew that, and I don't regret a single second."

The back door opens, and Cole walks in, yanking a beanie off his head, his leather jacket soaked from the rain. He glances up and spots us standing by the front entrance. Then his gaze zeroes in on the bag in Trace's hand.

He freezes, mouth parting before he lurches forward, headed this way.

Trace opens the door and turns to leave. Then he stops, spins back, and closes the distance between us. With a heavy hand on my neck, he pulls me against him and rests his lips against my forehead. I hear the shallow sound of his breaths, feel the thunder of his heart, and watch the pain shake through the length of his body.

He's not the first man I loved or the first love I lost. But his is the love that cuts the deepest and does the most damage. The loss is immeasurable. I'm bleeding internally and sobbing wretchedly, unable to silence the gasps.

Without a word, he releases me, strides out the door, and into the rain.

This is the moment, the one I dreaded since the day Cole returned. It hurts more than I could've ever imagined, like I'm hacking away vital parts of myself, breath by mangled breath.

Cole chases Trace outside and hovers behind him as he opens the door to the Maserati and tosses in the bag. Cole says something, his voice indiscernible in the pouring rain. Trace turns and faces him, expressionless, blinking away the heavy drops.

Cole's mouth moves faster, and his hands swipe through his hair, sweeping off the rain. More words. More blank stares from Trace. Then Cole drops his arms, lowers his head, and stares at the ground.

There's nothing he can say to alleviate the pain. I wish I could find comfort in knowing a broken heart can't break again. But it does. It breaks and breaks, and no matter how much destruction is done, it puts itself back together so it can break some more.

Cole speaks again, and whatever he says causes Trace's shoulders to hitch. Then Cole moves, wraps his arms around Trace and embraces him in a strong, heart-wrenching hug.

As Trace hugs him back, I fall apart. My legs buckle. My vision blurs, and a horrible keening sound rips from deep inside me. I stumble away from the door, doubling over and zigzagging toward the stairs.

My knees hit the first step, and I cry, gasping, shoulders shaking, nauseous, and inconsolable. Then I picture myself—my ugly, shattered reflection in the broken mirror at my old house. I can't go there again.

three is a war

I have to let him go.

And move on.

I'm not alone.

Flattening my hands on the stair, I breathe in, out, in, out. Then I rise to my feet and wipe the tear-soaked hair from my face.

The door closes behind me, and the squeak of Cole's boots sounds his approach. He stops at my back, drops his jacket on the floor, and grasps my upper arms with cold, wet hands.

"Did he leave?" I whisper, staring down the dark hall.

"Yes." He slides his touch along my arms and grips my hands. "How about a warm bath?"

I nod jerkily. "What did you say to him?"

"Danni…" He expels a breath. "You're hurting. I know I can't take that away, but I'm going to comfort you as much as I can." He lifts me into his arms, cradling me against his chest. "Bath first."

"Okay." I rest my head on his shoulder, my mind broken into a thousand aching thoughts.

He carries me through the house and into the master bathroom. There, he draws the bath and strips our clothes. When we settle in the hot water, I curl up on his lap and absorb his warmth.

"I'm not questioning my decision." I trace a finger across his collarbone. "But I'm going to need time."

"I'd question your humanity if you didn't grieve him, baby."

I place a kiss on his jaw that asks for patience. He trails a caress along my spine that offers strength.

He won the war, but what if all I can give him is a

body of broken parts? I'm not the woman he fell in love with five years ago. When he died, the life inside me burned so low it barely flickered. And now… I only see darkness.

It's hard to be strong when I know Trace is out there, in the rain, driving away from me, hurting, and alone.

"What did you say to him?" I ask quietly.

"I told him to call me, to talk to me, that I would be whatever he needed me to be."

"Friends?" Hope blooms in my chest.

"Yes. I reminded him of my promise to you. I'll work on that friendship."

"Thank you." I kiss his shoulder, his neck, and cup his whiskered face. "What did you say right before you hugged him?"

"You little voyeur." His soft exhale whispers across my lips. "I told him my biggest issue with him is that I care. I care about what happens to him."

My chest feels a little lighter. He'll be there for Trace. And I know, without question, he'll do the same for me.

His arms will hold me until the fractures heal.

His dimpled smile will breathe new life in me.

His love will toughen the pain into scar tissue.

It won't happen overnight, over a week, or even a month. But for the first time in a long time, we have forever.

eighteen

Two weeks later, I lift my face to the sun and stretch out my legs along the bench seat in Cole's boat. Sitting in the *V* of his thighs with my back against his chest, I absently play with the hem of his baggy swim shorts. The sadness hasn't waned. It feels duller, maybe, but it takes up just as much space inside me as the day Trace left.

When Cole died, I only had to deal with my own loss. Somehow that was easier than...*this*. I like to tell myself Trace is moving on just fine. He's stronger than me, after all. But I know better. He's alone in St. Louis, stuck with our memories and no shoulder to lean on.

I need to stop this. Channeling any kind of energy, time, or thought into Trace feels like I'm emotionally cheating on Cole. So I push away images of blue eyes and blond hair.

Cole anchored the boat in a quiet cove, out of view of the active part of the lake. It's just him and me and the sounds of lapping water.

I'm wearing bikini bottoms and a long sleeve shirt. It's a warm April day, but when I dipped a toe in the water earlier, the chill went straight to my bones.

In lieu of swimming, we decided to sunbathe. Not that he needs more color. He spends so much time outside his golden skin glows as bright as the sun.

"Tell me eleven things I don't already know." I twist around on his lap, facing him with my bent knees bracketing his sides. "Eleven things about anything."

"Eleven?"

"No more. No less." It's the same response I gave him the morning we met. If I can recreate that feeling, that playfulness that connected us so quickly, maybe it won't hurt so much to breathe.

"Your eyes remind me of storm clouds. Deep and gray. Always swirling. Threatening. Like thunder and lightning. Torrential downpours and puddles. I hated the rain. Until I met you."

My chest heaves with a hicupping inhale. "Cole..."

"I speak seven languages with excellent fluency. I once strangled a long-haired man with his ponytail. I won't drink from a straw while driving because I'm afraid it'll stab my throat on a sudden stop."

I gape at him. "Can we go back to the man with the—?"

"Trace called me this morning."

My heart crashes against my ribs, but I repress my excitement and keep my tone casual. "He did?"

"This isn't how we're going to do this." A muscle flexes in his jaw. "You will *not* hide your feelings from

three is a war

me."

He nudges me off his lap and stands. I straighten my spine, holding my breath. The tension in his posture tells me he's gearing up for a conversation, and I owe it to him to listen.

Bent over the steering wheel, he messes with the stereo. A moment later, the gentle texture of guitar chords stream through the speakers, the melody unfamiliar. Definitely not his usual punk rock noise.

"Do you know this song?" He moves to stand before me.

I shake my head. "What is it?"

"*Where's My Love* by SYML. I heard it the other day. Made me think of you."

It's hauntingly beautiful, full of longing. A plea for love gone astray.

He kneels between my legs, wedging his muscled frame in the small walkway. His hand lifts, cradling my face. "Trace called to see how you're doing."

"How is he?" I search his warm brown eyes.

"He's Trace. Cold and barren as ever. It's like having a conversation with Antarctica."

"What did you tell him?" My neck tenses. "About me?"

"Told him you turned into a nympho." His cheeks dent with dimples. "Can't get you off my dick."

I sigh. Cole and I haven't had sex since the night the three of us were together. Guilt has kept me away. It doesn't make sense, because I'm with Cole now…exclusively. Maybe I'm punishing myself, pushing away all means of enjoyment while Trace tries to start over alone.

"I know you miss him, and I don't like it." Cole trails his thumb across my cheekbone. "But you chose *me*. You chose me to be the one to pick up the pieces, to be the ear for your sadness, to be the arms to hold you up. Don't bury your pain, Danni. Give it to me."

My face falls, and I lean toward him, touching my lips to the corner of his. "I love you."

"I love you." He fits his hand inside of mine and presses something small and round against my palm.

I pull back and uncurl my fingers to see what he gave me.

My engagement ring.

I don't have to angle it to see the inscription. The words are written in the cracks of my heart.

One Promise ~ One Forever

My pulse accelerates, and my mouth dries. I don't know whether to laugh or cry. I wasn't sure I'd ever see this ring again.

He takes it from me and slides it on my finger. The wrong finger. "When you're ready, move it to your left hand. Then I'll know."

My brow furrows. I don't want to make any more decisions about love. I want him to put the ring on my finger and not give me a choice. I don't want to control this. I want to surrender to it.

"What?" His voice snaps, sharp and deep. "Why do you look pissed?"

"Are you unsure about us?" I lift my eyes to his. "Is that why you're not demanding I marry you immediately?"

His nostrils flare, and his jaw turns rock-hard as he climbs to his feet. Then he scoops me up and tosses me into the lake.

three is a war

I land with a shriek and plunge deep, swept under by the shocking cold. With wild kicks toward the surface, I come up with a gasp.

"Fuck!" I angrily punch the water. "You fucking prick!"

Oh my tits, it's cold. My joints freeze up as I paddle, swimming in a circle until I face the boat.

He stands on the edge, staring down at me, arms folded across his bare chest with a gleam in his eyes.

"I can't believe you did that." My teeth chatter.

He grins. "You need a man who will dunk your head in cold water and shut you the fuck up."

I pin my lips together, properly shut up. Because he's so very right.

"Come on." He crouches, extending his hand.

I kick my legs, reaching for him, and he pulls me out of the water like I weigh nothing. As I climb into the boat, the air chills my skin, prickling my body with goosebumps.

"We have to work at this relationship." He grips the hem of my wet shirt and yanks it over my head.

"Yeah." I shiver, soaked to the bone and frozen in the skimpy bikini.

"It's going to be hard." He unties the string on my back and removes my top.

I hug my nude chest, shoulders curled forward, and scan the isolated cove. My brain doesn't register his comment until I look down at the swollen bulge in his shorts. My breaths quicken as I trail my gaze over the cut indentions of his hips, the ripple of honed abs and pecs, and the sexiest lopsided grin I've ever seen.

"Those puns are only funny if you're a boy." I try

not to smile. "A twelve-year-old boy."

"Ask me how hard it's going to be."

We're definitely not talking about our relationship anymore. Not with that heated look in his eyes.

"How hard?" A shifting feeling stirs near my heart, trickling warmth through my body.

He grabs my hand and presses my palm against the steely length of his cock, trapped by his shorts.

A delicious shudder raises the hair on my arms and nape, and I clamp my fingers around him. He grunts a heavy breath and hooks his arms around my back, lifting, then lowering me to my back on the bench seat.

He kneels beside me, crowding in, a hand beneath my thigh, fingers feathering against the crotch of my bikini bottoms. His other arm slides behind my shoulders. Then he's kissing me, licking inside my mouth, and panting hungrily. The hand between my legs grows bolder, presses harder, anchoring me to the man I chose, the one I was always meant to marry.

I grind against his touch, melt into his kiss, and thaw from the inside out. My legs fall open. My nipples harden, exposed and needy. "I need you."

He smiles against my mouth and pulls the crotch of my bikini to the side, baring me. "Say it again."

"I need you, Cole." I moan as a finger enters me slowly, deeply.

His mouth doesn't leave mine as he pumps his hand and strokes me to orgasm. Then he removes the last of my clothes and kisses every inch of my body, caressing, teasing, worshiping—all while holding my gaze.

When he finally climbs between my legs, I bury my hands in his hair and stare into his hooded eyes. We

three is a war

make love like that. Pressed hard against each other. Hips moving languorously together. Connected on every level. Never looking away.

He has beautiful eyes. Wild and passionate. I see my future in them. Him and me.

As we peak together in groaning ecstasy, I wonder what he sees in mine.

nineteen

As the months pass and the seasons change, I remain fully committed to Cole and our future together. It isn't easy. *Love* isn't easy. We fight. We fuck. We argue about petty shit and slam doors. But we always make up.

I won't allow myself to long for Trace. Not even for a tiny tempting moment. It's been four months. He's running his empire in St. Louis and no doubt enthralling the panties off gorgeous women everywhere. Meanwhile, I'm slowly settling into the tranquility of lake life with a man whose patience amazes me endlessly. Cole has grown up so much in the past few months. Maybe I have, too.

It's a blissfully hot August night. The deafening buzz of cicadas sings from the surrounding woodland. The baked sky chars to a deep shade of black, and the wind whips my hair as Cole veers the motorcycle along the winding road toward home.

Home.

He talks about moving back to St. Louis, and I talk about opening a dance studio next to the Walmart near our little piece of lakefront heaven. My sister is the only reason I'd go back to the city. Trace is the reason I won't. If I ran into him, if I saw a hint of sadness creasing his handsome face… I can't. Maybe someday. But not yet.

I know Cole keeps in touch with him regularly. Though I've never overheard a phone conversation between them. I never ask. I can't flirt with the past. Happiness is forward, and that's where I'm headed.

My sister, on the other hand, loves to mention Trace during our weekly phone calls. Bree hasn't nosed around in his life, but she wants to. I threaten to disown her if she steps a foot into his casino. It's a hollow threat. I miss her terribly, even though I just saw her last month when she and her family spent a week with us.

Cole swerves into the driveway and parks the motorcycle in the garage.

I flatten my palms against his shoulder blades, rubbing circles across the sculpted terrain, his t-shirt damp from the humidity. I love to ride with him in the summer. Without the leather jacket, he's all muscle, flesh, and body heat.

We climb off the bike and remove our helmets, grinning at each other.

"What?" I smile wider.

"I'm still thinking about the man and the melons."

I roll my eyes. At the beginning of summer, I started volunteering at the local food pantry. Cole decided to go with me tonight to check it out. An hour

three is a war

after we arrived, a scruffy middle-aged man ambled in to collect his ration of donated groceries. When I handed him two small watermelons, he refused them and pointed at my breasts, saying, "I'd rather have the tiny ones. I bet they're sweeter."

To Cole's credit, he didn't lose his temper or swing a fist. He simply leaned toward the man and said calmly, "Take the watermelons and walk out the door."

The man grabbed his box of food and left without a backward glance.

"Are you tired?" Cole follows me into the kitchen.

"Nope."

"How about a naked swim in the lake?"

A grin pulls at my lips. Skinny-dipping with Cole has become one of my favorite activities.

"I'll get the beer." I turn toward the fridge.

As I pull out a six-pack, his phone buzzes. He removes it from his pocket and stares at the screen. And continues to stare.

"Who is it?" I approach him, craning my neck to see the caller ID.

Trace.

The enormous crack inside me stirs to life, quaking and bleeding with a vengeance. The strongest, steadiest hand can't sew it back together. The loss is too big, the ache too strong.

But I try. I stand terribly still and will my deepest longings back into the fissure.

Cole watches me closely, and the phone buzzes again.

"Don't ignore him," I whisper.

I tremble between *what used to be* and *what needs to*

be. If distress shows on my face, it's because I'm not masking it. I refuse to hide from Cole.

He studies me through another burst of buzzes before lifting the phone to his ear.

"Hey." He listens, eyes fixed on mine. "She's...she's doing good."

My chest collapses. Trace's concerned about me, still thinking of me. It's a torment so unbearable it's a physical pain inside.

"How are you?" Cole braces an arm on the kitchen island, scrutinizing my features. Then his head tilts at Trace's answer. "Really? That's great." He laughs. "No, I mean it. I told you it would all work out for the best. I'm happy for you."

My pulse hammers, and my mind swims. Trace is doing okay. Maybe even better than okay. Is his good news about the casino? A woman?

Another woman.

Something vile and nasty pinches in my stomach, but I don't let it take hold. I want him to move on. He must for the sake of his happiness. And I need to back away from this one-sided conversation for the sake of my sanity.

I hold up the six-pack of beer, snagging Cole's attention and pointing at the back door. At his nod, I head down to the dock. Every step into the dark isolation of the cove takes me closer to my thoughts. Blue-eyed, scowly, suit-clad thoughts.

I know from experience a broken heart doesn't mend in four months.

It doesn't mend until a cure comes along. Like *new love*.

Goddammit, I love him, and because of that, every

three is a war

cell in my body feels lighter at the prospect of his happiness. If I'm the only one hurting, I can live with that. It's so much easier knowing he's not in pain.

At the end of the dock, I remove the phone from my pocket and strip down to my panties. Then I guzzle half of a beer and select a song that fits my mood.

As *Honest* by The Chainsmokers strums through the silence, I slip into the warm inky water and swim. Kicking my legs, stroking my arms, I beg the water to wash Trace away.

But it doesn't work. He's with me, wired into my heart and declaring it home.

If I'm so in love with him, why didn't I choose him?

What if I *had* chosen him? Would I be sitting in St. Louis pining for Cole?

What the fuck is wrong with me? Why can't I be a normal woman who falls in love with a man and has a beautiful wedding and lots of babies and spends the rest of her life avoiding carbs and binging on TV shows? The end.

Never mind. That doesn't sound like my thing at all.

After a few laps in the cove, I swim to the dock, lift out of the water, and sit on the edge. The warm air kisses my nude flesh, and across the cove, a fish disturbs the motionless surface of the lake. It's so quiet here. The song ended a while ago, leaving thoughtful silence.

Until the sound of bare feet pads across the wooden decking behind me, growing louder, coming closer.

Cole pauses at my side, shirtless, dark hair tousled

from his raking fingers, and frayed jeans unbuttoned and low on his waist. He's pure sex appeal from head to toe, and he doesn't even have to try.

"What are you thinking about?" He crouches beside me.

I consider asking him about Trace, but do I really want to know about another woman? It's enough just knowing he's happy.

"Why am I so bad at love?" I ask.

"Why would you think that?" His eyebrows pull together. "If anything, you're very, very good at it."

"I'm being serious."

"So am I. People fall in and out of love every day. You don't. You fall in and no matter what is thrown at you—death, lies, fighting, uptight assholes…" His mouth twitches. "You never fall out of love. Once you're in, you're in for life."

"That's…" My chest shudders with an intake of nourishing air. "That's such an understanding way to look at it. Thank you."

"It's the truth, baby." He stands and holds out his hand. "Dance with me."

Those three words on kissable lips? Most decisive answer ever.

"Yes." I grip his strong fingers and climb to my feet. "Tango?"

"No." He lifts my phone from the nearby bench and swipes the screen.

As he returns it to the bench, *XO* by Beyoncé swirls softly, gently, around us.

Our wedding dance.

His gaze sweeps down my nude body, lingers on my panties, and lifts to my mouth. Then he holds me in

three is a war

his arms and rocks us to the beat, moving us along the edge of the dock. It doesn't take long to find the quick-quick-slow rhythm. We slide through Lambada Zouk steps with flowing body waves and sensual footwork, smiling, twirling, lost in the intimacy of eye contact. It's beautiful. It's everything.

Almost everything.

Something's missing.

I pull him tighter against me and continue moving through the routine. We've practiced the choreography so many times he's perfected it. He leads with confidence, his technique spot-on. He nails the hip movements, deep dips, fast turns, and upper-body torsions like a pro. But I don't feel the energy.

The energy that makes my heart beat.

Has it always been missing? I spent weeks teaching him this dance. How did I not notice? Maybe because I was distracted and oversexed trying to keep up with the desires of two men.

Maybe it's nothing. I'm just tired and in a mood.

I focus on dancing, on Cole's arms around me, on the sound of his breaths as he spins me across the dock. His knuckles graze my nipple. His lips brush my neck. His love is palpable, hungry, and undying.

But no amount of dancing or seduction will make my heart forget the other man it beats for.

It's like the universe is trying to tell me something.

I don't want to hear it.

I don't trust it.

So I ignore it.

I ignore it as we dance through three more songs. I ignore it when he lowers me to the decking and makes love to me.

I ignore it for the next three months.

Then one night, I find myself sitting alone at the kitchen island, spinning the engagement ring on my right hand. I told myself I'd move it to its proper place when I stopped hurting so much.

The ache hasn't ebbed. It's sprouted roots and grown fangs. Maybe if I move the ring, it'll go away.

With a deep breath, I slide it to my left hand.

Am I officially Cole's fiancé? I don't sense any of the warm, fuzzy feels that flooded me the last time we were engaged.

I feel guilty. Uncomfortable. *Deceitful.*

I'm wearing a token of Cole's love while staring at the front door, silently hoping Trace will walk in.

I need to talk to Cole. He's been nothing but understanding. I'll tell him what's on my mind, and maybe he'll tell me I'm over-analyzing. Maybe he'll tell me to shut the fuck up. Either way, we'll work through it. Together.

Assuming he's in the bedroom watching TV, I head in that direction, up the stairs and down the hall. And stop at the sound of music. It's not coming from the bedroom. It's closer.

The hallway has eight doors. Most of them remain locked. I've never tried to enter and invade that part of his past.

As I creep forward, following the morose melody, I focus on a door I've never opened. It's partially cracked, spilling light into the hall like an invitation. I approach it and slowly push.

The evocative lyrics of James Bay's *Let It Go* pours from the dimly-lit room. The back wall is covered with

three is a war

racks of guns. Little ones. Big ones. Guns that don't look like guns. My pulse kicks up. This must be the armory.

Rows of file cabinets, multiple desks with running laptops, tables stacked with goggles, vests, boots, belts, computer and camera equipment, and gear I don't recognize—all of it looks expensive and high-tech. Another table is dedicated just to cell phones. There must be dozens of burner phones, all plugged into a power strip that runs along the wall.

And hanging on a hook in the far corner is my wedding gown. It looks so out of place yet lovingly cared for. My chest squeezes.

I feel like I wandered into Cole's secret room of longings. I shouldn't be here. As I turn back, I spot him sitting on the floor by the door. I must've walked right past him.

He drapes his arms over bent knees and rests his head against the wall, staring up at me. His expression is as soul-searching as the music playing in the background.

"I thought you retired." I glance back at the charging phones and powered-on laptops. "What is this?"

"I *am* retired. I only come in here to check my messages." His gaze cuts to the table of phones. "I get a lot of job offers."

"Job offers?" I move toward him and sit against the wall at his side. "What kind of jobs?"

"The kind that paid for this house."

There were side jobs over the years, as well as other means to collect assets.

I struggle to swallow.

"The dangerous kind," he says woodenly, "that

send me out of the country for months. Sometimes years."

I tense. "Are you considering—?"

"I would never consider a job away from you." He lifts his arm, inviting me to tuck in beneath it.

Curling up against his side, I rest my cheek on his shoulder and watch his eyes roam over the room, his gear, the guns, the pieces and parts of a life he was once so passionate about. He misses it more than he lets on.

He chose me, and I chose him. Yet we both still yearn for what we no longer have. It's profound. And depressing.

Let It Go plays again, saturating the atmosphere with bittersweet dread. The vocals croon about a relationship that will never succeed, no matter how much two people care. It hits too close to home.

"This song is so sad." I trace the line of his jaw, trying to smooth out the tension. "Why are you listening to it?"

"I know what you're doing."

I drop my hand, unsure.

"You're trying so hard to make this work." His voice cracks. "But the heart wants what the heart wants."

I jerk back. "No—"

"He's not physically here, but he's here nonetheless, always between us." His gaze drills into mine. "You're settling."

"Damn right, I'm settling." I ball my hands on my lap. "I'm settling into a beautiful life with a man who takes my breath away. I chose *you*, Cole. I'm *with* you."

"Someone told me once that love isn't a choice," he says softly.

I snap my mouth shut, and my legs tremble against

the floor.

"Why do you think I wanted you to wait six months?" He ghosts his fingers over my left hand, caressing the engagement band. "I didn't want you to choose. I wanted it to *happen*. I wanted it to rise inside you and become the beat of your heart." He lowers his voice, as if speaking to himself. "The most decisive actions are the ones with the least consideration."

"What are you saying?"

"The day you forced yourself to decide, I knew. When Trace walked out that door, I saw it in your eyes." Resolve sits on his face, sinking in his cheeks. "You voiced a decision your heart wasn't ready to make."

I want to shake him and tell him he's wrong. Except everything he said rings true.

"I've watched you fight an inner battle for seven months." He lifts my hand to his lips and kisses my knuckles. "You're fighting a war with your heart."

Smarting pain jolts through me. "If that's the case, why did I choose you?"

"I was your first. The logical choice." He strokes my hair, his breaths growing choppy. "But the heart isn't logical. Sometimes, we don't know what we want until it's gone."

"It doesn't matter." I climb onto his lap, desperate to hold him. "I love you.

"I know you do." He folds his arms around me, pulling my chest against his and tucking my head beneath his chin. "But you love him more."

I dig my nails into his shoulders, clutching tightly. Is that what the universe has been trying to tell me? Does it mean anything? I'm engaged to Cole. I love Cole. We have to work through this.

He goes still against me, like he's holding his breath. Like he's bracing for something that's going to harm us so deeply it'll change us on a molecular level.

I lean back and choke on a whimper. His expression is a canvas of suffering, twisted with the fall of ruptured dreams coursing down his cheeks. His tears. His quiet, broken defeat.

"Don't make that face." My throat closes, and a sob escapes as I frantically dry his cheeks with my hands. "Don't give up on me."

"I lost you, baby. I lost you the morning I got into that cab and left you crying on the porch." He pulls me against him, his embrace constricting and his mouth at my ear. "I'm not giving up. I'm letting you go."

I shatter in his arms, sucking jagged, throat-scraping gulps of air. I reach for him, his shoulders, his hands, clinging with desperation. He holds me through painful tears, crying with me, as I come to terms with the heartless truth.

As hard as we try and as much as we care, we've gone too far to go back to the morning we met. We began with a deep connection, a soul tie that made us comfortable, maybe even codependent, so much so neither of us could fathom ending it completely and not being in each other's life.

I have no doubt he's my soul mate, the friend who will always touch me the deepest. But that doesn't mean he's the partner I'm supposed to spend my life with. That realization leaves an emptiness inside me that I don't think will ever be filled by myself or anyone else.

Lifting my head from his shoulder, I cup his face and see his eyes in blurry shades of finality. He wipes

three is a war

away my tears as I dry his.

"No more crying tonight." He touches his mouth to mine, achingly tender and unhurried.

We sedate each other with a hopeless kiss, a kiss that carries us into the bedroom. No words are spoken as we undress. No tears are shed as he enters my body and moves slowly inside me.

We've done this before. Good-bye sex. But this time is different. This time there isn't a promise on his breath. There isn't a vow that he'll return. Through every long drugging stroke of his cock, he stares into my eyes and wordlessly says good-bye.

Good-bye forever.

After, I lie in his arms and memorize every feature on his face. Warm brown eyes, strong jaw, dark shadow of stubble—he's painfully handsome. Deeply passionate. And no longer mine.

"I'm grateful I had you to myself for seven months." He brushes my hair behind my ears.

"I'm grateful for every breath, every dance, every memory you gave me," I whisper back.

He led me to Trace. I won't remind him of that or ask about his phone call tonight. Whether or not Trace is single has no bearing on this moment. The fragile currents flowing between Cole and me are immediate and short on time. The future can wait.

We fall silent, joined by eye contact and separated by eventuality. I can already feel him pulling away. His gaze becomes duller, his body more rigid. I want to tell him again that I love him, but he knows. We said everything there is to say.

So I close my eyes and begin the grieving process.

The memory of his dimpled smile will be my secret indulgence when I'm sad. His deep breaths will be the soundtrack to the story of us. And his lips on my forehead will be the very last thing I feel before I fall asleep.

When I wake in the dark, I don't have to reach behind me to confirm what I already know.

He's gone.

twenty

I climb out of bed and plod through Cole's house, hollow, numb, lost. Down the hall, through the kitchen, I peek in the garage. The sight of the empty space where his motorcycle once sat is the trigger that brings me to the floor, sobbing on my knees.

He means so much to me. He's everything that's supposed to be, and that's what messes me up the most—letting go of the fantasy, starting over, without him.

I let myself grieve, let it all rush out in great heaves of sadness. It's over. Finished. He's gone, and I feel so utterly drained and empty. I'm falling down, but I refuse to shut down. I'm crying, but the tears are cleansing.

Our love came unannounced one fateful morning and maybe, a thousand mornings from now, it will fade. But even then, it will never slip away.

He was right. When I fall in love, I never fall out. And neither does he. I know with every anguished breath, he will always love me.

I sit in the doorway to the garage until the sun rises and spills light into the kitchen. Then I scrape myself off the floor and shove down the pain long enough to pack.

As I pass the kitchen island, a large white envelope catches my attention. *Danni* is scrawled across the front in Cole's handwriting. I lift it with trembling hands and empty the contents on the counter.

A house key.

Documents.

Legal forms.

My eyes blur, and my pulse races.

It's the deed to my house in St. Louis.

He bought my house.

The date of purchase is a month after I sold it to the young married couple. And the price… My jaw drops. He paid twice the market value.

More documents show the transfer of ownership to me. I only need to sign the pages and mail them to make it official.

Holy shit. I set down the papers and clutch my throat. Why did he do this and not tell me? Was it because he knew from the beginning it wouldn't work out between us? Or was it because he bought the house when he kidnapped me and didn't want to give me a reason to leave after that?

I guess I'll never know. Nevertheless, I'm thankful. He knew how much the house meant to me. The memories in those walls will smother me alive, but at least I have somewhere familiar to go, somewhere to call home, until I find my way again.

three is a war

After another perusal through the documents, I stack them with a shaky sigh. There's no note. No heartbreaking words to cling to. Maybe it's better this way.

I return the documents to the envelope and freeze. My hand. *No ring.* My right hand is ringless, too. He took the engagement band?

Just like he took the wedding gown.

I rub the ache in my chest as a sad smile bounces my lips. God, he's so sentimental. I'm going to miss that.

I already miss him so much.

The heartache surges anew, swelling my throat. I swallow it down and hurry back to the bedroom. I'll be leaving behind more than a ring and gown. The MG Midget doesn't have a backseat, and the trunk only holds two bags if they're small. The extravagant wardrobe, the dance costumes and supplies—all of it stays.

I pass the door to the dance studio and falter. My hands twitch at my sides, and I turn back, staring at the room with longing.

The room he built for me.

One more dance.

I move mindlessly to the stereo and select *What Is Love* by V Bozeman.

Then I dance slowly, tearfully, through the room, committing everything to memory—the give of the flooring, the glow of the sun through windows, the smoothness of the ballet bars, and the echo of the music through the high ceiling.

When the song ends, I dry my eyes and force myself to leave. To leave it all behind.

An hour later, I back the Midget out of the garage

and pull onto the dirt road, weeping. The moment I can't see the house anymore, I burst into ruthless, shoulder-shaking sobs. Then I grab my phone and call my sister.

Bree talks to me through most of the four-hour drive. She wants me to stay with her until I move my things out of storage. She wants to take care of me.

She's done that enough for one lifetime. Yeah, I'm sad. I'm fucking miserable. But I've got this. I can do it all by myself. Even if it means sleeping on the floor.

As my house comes into view, I'm hit with a poignant wave of nostalgia. It's been eleven months. I wonder how my neighbors are doing? God, I hope no one has died.

Someone's been keeping up with the landscaping. I pull into the driveway, squinting at the cut lawn and trimmed hedges. Did Cole hire a management company to take care of the property?

I park the car and enter through the back door, shivering against the cold December wind. It's not any warmer in the house. Shit, I didn't even consider the possibility that the utilities would be off.

As I race through the kitchen, I flip the light switch, and the ceiling bulb flickers on. Yes! In the hall, I push the thermostat to hell hot. Then I take a deep breath and step into the bedroom.

There's a bed and other furniture. At least, I think that's furniture beneath all the white cloth. With a burst of focus, I start yanking off the sheets, moving from room to room, revealing more furniture and scattering clouds of dust. Everything is mine. It's all the stuff I moved to storage.

Given the layers of dust, he did this a long time ago. Like he knew I'd come back to the house we shared.

three is a war

Our house.

If I inhale deep enough, I can smell him. I feel him in the air and hear him moving through the rooms. It's his spirit, like he's dead all over again. That's what it feels like.

The tears flood in, and I let them fall freely as I bring in my bags from the car and curl up in bed.

I need to give myself time to grieve Cole.

Then, when I'm ready, I'll take the next step.

If I'm brave enough, it'll be a step into The Regal Arch Casino.

twenty-one

I search through the crowd of restaurant patrons for a tall, scowling silhouette. My feet haven't even crossed the threshold to Bissara, and I'm already violently shaking in my high-heeled booties.

Around me, slot machines ding and clang. Cigarette smoke tinges the air, and servers bustle by carrying plates of Moroccan food.

I told myself to take it slow. I took it slow. I've been in St. Louis for a month. I survived the holidays with my sister, reconnected with Nikolai, my dance partner, and started volunteering at the homeless shelter again.

There's been no contact with Cole. No job hunting. No Trace.

If Cole and Trace still talk, Trace knows I'm back. Yet he hasn't called. Hasn't shown up.

He moved on.

I'm sweating, nauseous, wracked with ungodly nerves. But I have to do this. I have to know if there's a chance my heart will beat again.

Running a hand over my cute gray shirt dress, I tug on the mid-thigh hem and dry my palms on the soft fabric. *Where is he?*

"Danni?"

I turn toward the feminine voice and find the sweet face of a hostess I knew when I danced here.

"Crystal!" I hug her.

She was here the night Trace proposed to me. I can only imagine the rumors that circulated after our break up.

"You're back?" She returns the hug, grinning. "Are you dancing here again?"

"Just stopping by." I stare at the empty stage with an ache that burns in my bones. "Is the position open?"

"Mr. Savoy hasn't found the right dancer. I bet if you apply—"

"Is he here? I haven't seen…"

Then I see him. Sitting at a table in the far corner, cloaked in shadows, he's angled away from me. The dining room is so packed I can barely make out his profile behind the crowded tables of people.

"Excuse me." I leave Crystal standing there and float toward him, thoroughly hypnotized by his presence.

Black suit and tie, starched white shirt, arresting facial features, and not a sexy blond hair out of place, he's a paragon of masculine beauty.

I crane my neck, trying to make out his expression. Is he heartbroken? Reconciled? He's too far away. The lighting's too dim, and those ice blue eyes haven't shifted

three is a war

in my direction. Not once.

I pick up my pace, dodging servers, pushing through the crowd, growing more anxious with every step toward him.

Twenty paces away, his table comes into view. I stumble, breath hitching.

He's not alone.

My heart sinks to the floor.

An elegant woman sits across from him. Long black hair, lean muscle, long limbs, she wears a classy black dress, smiling and talking with beautiful red lips. Everything about her is beautiful. Especially the man she's with.

He's not looking at her and instead stares at the dark stage like he's watching a ghost dance to the soft background music. It gives me courage. Hope. He might be trying to move on, but he hasn't. Not yet.

I change course, veering toward the platform and stepping into his line of sight. My hands slick with sweat as he blinks, looks directly at me, and blinks again.

Time stands still. He doesn't move, doesn't react in any way. There isn't a hint of emotion etching his face. The man is a master at putting up a smoke screen.

If I found him gazing longingly at the woman across the table, maybe I'd turn heel and walk out. But he's not. If the roles were reversed… Scratch that. The roles *were* reversed. I loved two men, and Trace never gave up. He didn't leave me until I made a bullshit decision.

I need to know if he moved on, if he found happiness. If he hasn't, I don't care who this woman is. It's game on.

Pushing back my shoulders, I approach his table and fight like hell to keep my nerves out of my voice. "Sorry to interrupt your dinner." I turn toward his date. "Hi. I'm—"

"Where's Cole?" He scowls at me.

"I don't know." My entire body tries to curl in on itself.

"He hasn't answered his phone in over a month."

My pulse quickens. Cole hasn't called him? That means Trace didn't know I was back.

I straighten my spine and meet his cold, unwelcoming eyes. "It turns out I was right about one thing."

"Just one?"

I'm sure there are other things, but I don't recall them at the moment. "Yeah."

He releases a haughty huff. "What were you right about?"

"Love isn't a choice."

A twitch tugs at his mouth, there and gone so quickly I wonder if I imagined it.

Then something shifts in his demeanor. The stiffness in his spine leaks away, slightly dropping his shoulders. His expression slackens. His eyes grow distant, empty, and that's when I see it.

Deep sorrow.

My heart beats frantically, stabbing pain through my stomach. Maybe he's trying to find happiness with the quiet beauty at his table. Maybe he's too heartbroken to ever forgive me. But beneath his cool facade, he's not okay. Not even close.

I bend toward him, holding his gaze until my mouth reaches his ear. "I'm going to fight for you."

three is a war

His hand flexes on his lap, and the intoxicating scent of his skin threatens to bring me to my knees.

"Enjoy your dinner." I step back and force my feet to turn toward the door.

Then I go home.

twenty-two

Standing in my bathroom an hour later, I stare at my reflection in the mirror and cringe. *I'm going to fight for you?*

"Good one, Danni," I mumble around the toothbrush hanging from my mouth. "How are you going to do that exactly?"

Impulsive as usual, I jumped in without a plan. What I wanted to do was rip that woman away from the table by her *Pantene* hair and toss her out of the restaurant. But I won't win Trace by behaving like a psychotic, jealous bitch. He deserves better.

He deserves respect, sacrifice, and patience—all the things he's given me.

Maybe his dinner date is a worthy, ideal partner for him. If so, points for her. She's elegantly beautiful, and she's never broken his heart. More points in her favor.

But her greatest competition is a woman who has nothing to lose and everything to gain. There isn't a soul in the world who will fight as hard as I intend to fight for his happiness.

By tomorrow night, I'll have the dance position at Bissara. He's had seven months to hire someone. The job is still open because he wants *me* on that stage. After we negotiate a salary and schedule, I'll dance my way through his chilly exterior.

I don't have a strategy after that, but one thing I won't do is give up. I let him go twice, and both times destroyed me. I've fallen and lost and hit rock bottom, and through the deepest pain, I found strength, found myself, and found what makes my heart beat.

Dressed in fleece pajama pants and a long-sleeved shirt, I head to the kitchen and pour a glass of wine. Before the glass touches my lips, the doorbell rings.

Every muscle in my body tenses. It's after ten o'clock. My neighbors are asleep. Bree has school early in the morning. There's only one person who would show up at my door at this hour.

Trembling, twisting, nervousness rises and swells, months of separation threatening to spew my dinner across the kitchen floor. I swallow down the nausea and breathe. Another deep breath, and I concentrate on my lungs all the way to the door. But my tenuous grip on composure slips as I turn the lock.

I'm so nervous I don't remember to check the peep hole until I open the door to…someone I've never seen before.

Black suit, weathered face, and silver hair, a short

three is a war

man stares back at me, expressionless. Parked behind him on the curb is a black sedan.

Is he one of Trace's drivers? Is Trace inside that car? I squint at the tinted windows, unable to see the interior.

"I'm Oliver, a private chauffeur for The Regal Arch Casino and Hotel." He lifts his chin. "Mr. Savoy would like to meet with you."

His words invoke a profound sense of *déjà vu*, transporting me back to the night Trace and I met. A delicious shiver races through me, making me want to relive that moment, over and over. Maybe that's Trace's intent.

"Why does he want to meet with me?" I repeat the question I asked his assistant that night.

"He wants to discuss your services."

The same answer. This has to be rehearsed.

My heartbeat accelerates. "If he wants dance lessons, he can set up an appointment."

"He's waiting."

In the car? Instead of wasting words, I dart around him and sprint across the frozen grass, hunching against the cold. When I reach the sedan, I yank open the rear passenger door. My heart stops.

The back seat, the front seat, the entire fucking car is empty.

Shit. I close the door and back away, stomach clenching.

"Ma'am?" Oliver appears at my side. "I'm here to escort you to the casino."

What game is Trace playing? Should I go along with it? Or should I stick to the script from the night we

243

met? I bet he expects the latter, and I don't want to disappoint him. I've done that enough.

"He can make an appointment." I hug my chest and plod back inside. "I have plans tonight."

"He was quite adamant, Miss." Oliver trails behind me and pauses on the front porch. "The offer is now."

"Send my regrets to Mr. Savoy." I close the door partway, peering through the gap. "If he's interested in my services, he can call on me himself."

I close the door, twist the lock, and drop my forehead against the wood. "Fuck, fuck, fuck!"

Did I do the right thing? I want to fight for Trace, not piss him off.

He sent a driver to take me back to the casino. Does that mean he ended his date? Maybe not. He knows me well enough to predict I wouldn't have jumped into that car.

Dammit, I hate these fucking head games.

My insides shrivel as I pace through the sitting room. A year and a half ago, I sent Trace's assistant away only to find him sitting on my couch like he owned the place. The mystery, the sexual tension, everything about that night was thrilling. He loved me then, and I didn't know it. I didn't even know him.

That night marks a transitional point in my life. I was grieving Cole, wholly in love with him. Trace showed up and tipped my world upside down.

I still love Cole, but everything's different now.

My heart belongs to Trace, and I hurt him. Possibly irreparably.

Tomorrow, I'll go to the casino as planned and get my job back. Then I'll do whatever is needed to make him happy again.

three is a war

With a reinforcing breath, I stride through the empty dining room, into the hallway, and yelp.

Tall and imposing, Trace stands in the narrow walkway in the kitchen. Hands clasped behind him and shoulders back, he scowls at me with an intensity that lifts the hairs on my nape.

"How did you get in?" After seeing the photos of the dead body in my house, I always make sure the doors are locked. "You broke in."

"I have keys that will get me past every deadbolt."

He must've come in through the back before his driver knocked on the front door? I don't even care. He's in my house. *He came for me.*

My pulse goes wild, throbbing in my throat. He's so insanely good-looking I can't focus. It's not just the sexy suit, the alluring eyes, and strong jawline. It's the proud way he holds himself, the confidence he carries through every action. He radiates tenacity and strength without opening his mouth.

I clear my voice. "Was I supposed to get in the sedan?"

"You tell me."

"I think…" I scrunch my face, contemplating. "It doesn't matter. The point was you wanted me thinking about the night we met."

Stern and indifferent, he crooks a finger, commanding me closer.

I'm captivated by his eyes. They're things of beauty and power, made of magical ingredients that fuse with my eyes to create an unbreakable spell. I have to physically shake myself to look away and put one foot in front of the other.

Stepping into the kitchen, I pause just out of arm's reach. "How did you know I moved back into this house?"

"I had you followed when you left the casino."

"You didn't know I was in town?"

"No." He casts a clinical glance around the kitchen. "How did you get the house back?"

"Apparently, Cole bought it a month after I sold it. You haven't talked to him?"

He shakes his head, expression tensing. "Why isn't he here with you? He stopped answering his phone when—"

"I left. Or rather…he left. But it's not what you think."

I need a drink, and wine isn't going to cut it. Crouching, I dig through the bottom cabinet until I find the bottle of scotch I bought a couple weeks ago. Then I pour two glasses and slide one to him.

"When did you start drinking scotch?" He lifts the tumbler to his perfect lips and sips.

"Tonight. Can we…?" I point toward the sitting room. "Sit down?"

At his nod, I lead the way.

We settle on opposite ends of the couch, cradling our drinks. I take a second to steel my backbone. I'm not going to cry. I'm not going to fuck this up. I'm just going to lay it all out, honestly and maturely.

"I never got over you." I gulp down a swallow of scotch and launch into a fit of coughing.

Fuck that shit. I set the glass aside, wait for the burn in my throat to subside, and turn to Trace.

He watches me with disinterest, but I don't miss the twitch in his fingers. He wants to reach for me, and I desperately want to be worthy of his touch.

"I tried to make it work with Cole." I brush the hair from my face. "We had the connection, the commitment, it's just…it wasn't the same." I stare into his eyes, let him see the raw wounds in mine. Wounds that bleed for Cole. "When he came back from the grave, I wasn't the same person. I loved another man, and I still do."

"But you picked him." His hand balls against his thigh. "He's your first choice."

"He was a *choice*. Don't you get it? You were never a decision." I breathe in, recalling the words he said to me. "You're the realization clawing at my insides without coercion or doubt or the pressure of time. My heart beats for you and only you, not because you command it, but because we're meant to be."

He sets the glass on the coffee table and rises from the couch, staring at the front door.

"I'm sorry," I whisper, heart aching. "For everything, but mostly for making you so unhappy."

"I'm a grown man, Danni." His voice is harsh, snapping through the room. "I don't need your apologies or your coddling."

Sucking in a breath, I jump to my feet. "I'm not coddling, dammit. I'm fighting." I dart around the coffee table and stand before him, tilting my head back to see his face. "The day we went on the balloon ride, you told me I made you ridiculously happy, like you discovered a magical cure. You said you wanted to lock me away and protect me. Remember that?"

His jaw stiffens as he glares at me. Yeah, he remembers.

"I want to make you feel that way again. Lock me

away, Trace. Do whatever you want with me. Just let me in."

His unnatural stillness makes my scalp tingle. I search the shadows darkening his face, looking for hints that he's considering my words. I only see pain.

He reaches into the inside pocket of his suit jacket, removes a folded document, and offers it to me. I don't have to open it to know it's an employment contract. It's not a tearful reunion, but it's a lifeline, nonetheless. I grab on with both hands.

"Same terms we agreed on last time?" I unfold the pages.

"Read it."

His detached tone makes my skin crawl. *Be patient with him, Danni.*

From the drawer in the coffee table, I remove a pen. Then I quickly scan the document and make a few changes. Instead of working five days a week, I'll work seven. Instead of the obscene salary I proposed last time, I want a reasonable wage for a dancer.

"There." I hand it back to him. "Those are the new terms."

He glances at the modifications without emotion and returns the papers to his pocket. "You'll start tomorrow."

No argument. No reaction. I hate the distance between us. "Tell me about your dinner date."

Pinning his lips, he heads toward the exit.

Dammit, I said the wrong thing. "Don't go. We can—"

"Goodnight, Danni."

He opens the door and steps onto the porch.

When I came back to St. Louis, I didn't expect him

three is a war

to welcome me with open arms. But this…this is worse than a cold shoulder. It's a kick in the teeth. He's going out of his way to reject me without actually saying the words. If he didn't feel anything for me, he'd tell me to leave him the hell alone.

It's like he's trying to prove he can't and won't be affected by me, as if having feelings for me is a flaw.

"Trace?" I stand on the porch, hugging my waist and shivering against the chill.

He slows his strides along the sidewalk and stops, tilting his head without looking back.

I raise my voice. "If you still love me, even after I broke your heart, that's not a weakness. It's bravery."

His chest rises and falls. Then he climbs into the back of the sedan and leaves.

twenty-three

With a fluttery stomach and adrenaline-charged blood, I show up at the casino the next afternoon. An hour before my shift. I'm so excited to dance on that stage I can't sit still, can't breathe, can't think straight. More than that, I'm twisted inside out at the prospect of seeing Trace.

The dressing room is exactly how I left it. Other than the cleaning crew's routine vacuuming and dusting, it hasn't been disturbed in over a year. Costumes, makeup, glitter, hair products—everything is exactly where I left it.

Dressed to dance and buzzing with jitters, I walk into Bissara an hour later. The restaurant staff isn't surprised to see me. They must've been notified of my employment. Familiar faces. New faces. Everyone is eager to have a dancer on the stage again.

Trace isn't here, but cameras peer down from tiny black globes amid the mosaic art work on the ceiling. Maybe he's watching.

I cue up my set list on the sound system, flip on the stage lights, and climb atop the eight-foot-wide circular platform. Half the tables in the restaurant sit empty, but they'll fill up by dinnertime. Those who are already seated stare at me expectantly.

Standing at the center of the stage, I wait for the tempo of *Whenever, Wherever* by Shakira to build. Then I move. Abs, ribcage, hips—the energy gathers in my core and ripples outward to my head and limbs. God, I missed this.

A silver lace half-circle skirt hangs low on my hips, with extra draped panels attached to a mini underskirt. Crystals, beaded appliques, and fringe on the matching bra shimmy and sparkle with my movements.

I love all forms of dance, but belly dance is the core of my passion. I shake and sway for the next two hours, scanning the growing crowd for the one who holds my future captive.

When his towering shadow finally emerges in the entrance, my hips falter and my breath stutters. Those trance-inducing eyes narrow on me to the exclusion of all else, but his hand… His hand rests on the lower back of the black-haired woman from last night.

Jealousy hits me like a vicious slap across the face. I can't hear the music over the ringing in my ears.

This is what it feels like—the helplessness, the agony of watching someone I love with another person. To think he endured this every time he saw me with Cole.

He guides the woman to the table closest to the

three is a war

stage, and they settle in, side by side, watching me dance as the server takes their orders. His date doesn't even glance at the menu.

She must come here often.

With him.

Bringing her here while I'm dancing, putting her right in front of my face... He's punishing me. Except that's not his style. His discipline comes in the form of a red ass, not a cruel revenge game.

Something feels off, and dammit, it's hard to dance with the force of his cryptic gaze pressing against my senses. As the song ends, I steel my spine. I'm not backing down. As much as I want to run out of the restaurant, I'm going to continue to dance. If he wants to crush me, he'll have to try harder.

The next song begins, and I meet his compelling eyes.

He lifts a hand and curls a finger, beckoning me to the table.

I obey instantly, my windpipe caught in a stranglehold. Sliding off the stage, closing the distance, I don't look away from those eyes.

Beneath the stuffy suit and tie is a happily ever after. Behind the neat row of buttons is the heart that beats in sync with mine. The expensive threads hide my territory, where all my thoughts lie, where my future awaits.

Palms sweaty, I take the empty seat across from them.

"Hi, Danni." The woman gives me an easy smile and extends a hand across the table. "I'm Alexis."

I wipe my damp palm on my costume and clasp

her fingers. Strong grip, toned arms, intelligent green eyes… I hate her already.

Anger rises in a hot wave, but I keep my tone quiet. "Are you fucking him?"

Her eyes widen. "I beg your pardon?"

"Answer the question." Good lord, I sound like Trace.

"Danni." He leans toward me, his scowl threatening in its intensity. "Put the claws away." His gaze shifts to the woman at his side and softens. "Alexis is your boss."

Blood drains from my face, my voice a reedy whisper. "What?"

"I'm the new CEO of The Regal Arch Casino and Hotel." She folds her hands together on the table and tilts her head. "And no, I'm not fucking the owner."

"I'm sorry for assuming." Embarrassment trickles into relief as I lift my gaze to Trace. "You resigned as CEO?"

"I still own the company and a seat on the board, but I handed off the day to day operations about four months ago. It took me a while to find a good fit. She runs this place better than I did."

Is that the good news he and Cole were discussing on the phone that night? The timing is right.

"What are *you* going to do?" I ask him.

His expression transforms, the devil in his eyes. "Anything I want."

He doesn't glance down at my body, but he doesn't have to. His tone is pure sex, gliding over my skin and stoking a deep burn.

"I'm going to get my dinner order to go." Alexis rises from the table, her attention on me. "I've seen the

three is a war

financial statements. You used to bring a lot of revenue to the restaurant. I don't care what you do with him, just keep it behind closed doors and bring the money in again."

With that, she strides toward the kitchen.

I turn to Trace and find him watching me with a smirk on his lips.

"You're an asshole," I say without heat in my voice.

"I think we've established that."

"Why did you let me believe you two were an item?"

"You were so fired up to fight for me I wanted to give you an opportunity to do that. Until I saw your discomfort on the stage. I couldn't let it draw out another second. There's no reason for it." His timbre drops. "You already have me."

An overwhelming feeling of belonging and promise bursts inside me. I stand and circle the table, taking the seat Alexis abandoned. A foot of space separates us, but he feels closer the moment our eyes connect.

"It's been seven months." My throat tightens. "Don't go easy on me, Trace. I want to prove to you that you were never second choice. Or any kind of choice. It was always you. I just…I had to do a lot of growing up to figure that out."

His expression softens. "What would you have done if I was fucking her?"

"If it was just sex, I would've sabotaged the relationship."

"You don't have the ruthlessness or skill to do

that." He stares at my mouth.

"I've been taking notes, learning from the best. How many men have you chased from my house?"

"Touché."

No part of him touches me, but the warmth of his brilliant blue gaze is enough to make my heart thunder out of control.

He turns his chair, angling his body to face me. "You've already proven your feelings, Danni. The day I left, the devastation on your face, it nearly destroyed me. I don't have to imagine how hard it was for you to go through that again with Cole. Just knowing you did it, *because* you love me, is enough."

"I made it so much harder than it—"

"Shut up and listen." His jaw flexes. "You needed the journey to discover who you are and what you want." He straightens. "You've suffered enough. I love you, and I will not put you through hell for another minute."

"You haven't put me through hell."

"Haven't I?" He pulls in a breath and slowly releases it. "I proposed to you knowing Cole might return. He and I manipulated and deceived you while you were being pulled in two directions." He lowers his voice. "When you gathered the courage to leave, we dragged you back illegally, against your will. Have you forgotten this?"

I shake my head. "I made mistakes, too."

"Mistakes? No, Danni. You love with everything you have. Christ, how many times have you forgiven me? The least I can do is forgive you for the last seven months. But that's the thing. You've done nothing wrong. Cole and I went into this knowing how it would end. We put you in a horrible position, and you're sitting here

three is a war

telling me *not* to go easy on you?"

He's so damn mature and logical I don't know why I expected anything less. His levelheadedness is one of the countless things I depend on.

"We're putting this behind us," he says firmly. "No more fighting about the past. No more regrets. We're moving forward."

My mind races as everything sinks in.

"You're single." Saying the words aloud feels like a newborn breath.

"I gave my heart away a long time ago." Months of regret retreat under the raw affection in his voice. "I'm *taken* in every way."

My chest squeezes. "I have things to say."

"Say them." He leans in, a hand on the back of my chair, the other on the table, surrounding me in the strength of his presence.

"I'm not perfect. I'm messy. I'll scatter shit all over the floor and jumble up your self-control. I'll irritate you, do impulsive things, piss you off, and beg for forgiveness." I swallow hard, fighting tears. "I'll always love Cole."

His silence is so deep the whispers of restaurant patrons envelope us in an airless bubble, where we're a universe of two holding its breath.

When he finally speaks, his voice is rough. "I'll always love him, too."

My face crumples, and I grab his hand on his lap. "I'm *yours*. You'll never find a woman who loves you as much as I do."

"I talked to Cole this morning, and he told me the same thing."

"You did?" My stomach churns as I search his face for answers. "Why wasn't he answering his phone? Is he…?" *Okay? Will he ever be okay?*

"I sent him a text mentioning your appearance last night. That was the trigger for his call this morning. He didn't want to talk to me until you made contact. Didn't want to be the one to tell me what happened." He bends closer and trails a finger along my jaw, sending shivers down my spine. "At his request, I won't give you updates on him. It's the same request I made seven months ago, and I trust that he honored it."

I nod, trembling against a surge of tears.

"Shake it off," he says sternly. "He told me you've been back for a month. I assume you spent that month crying for him."

I nod again. "I needed the time."

"Good. Now it ends."

He reaches into the pocket of his pants. My pulse detonates as he slides a silver band on the ring finger of my left hand. The same infinity band he gave me a year ago.

"We'll marry on Valentine's Day." It's an order, not a question.

My lungs pant with confusion and excitement. "That's only—"

"Thirty days away." He lifts my hand and touches his lips against the inside of my wrist. "You have a month to choreograph the dance. I'm in charge of everything else, including the dress."

Shaken by the turn of events and the inflexible demand in his voice, I let my mouth hang open until he shuts it with a finger beneath my chin.

"I informed the restaurant you would only be

three is a war

dancing for two hours." He stands, pulling me with him. "Your shift is over."

I follow him in stunned silence out of Bissara and down the hall toward his private elevator. I've been so worried about winning him back I hadn't let myself even think about the feel of his mouth against mine, let alone a night in his penthouse.

He doesn't touch me, doesn't look at me until we step inside the lift. Pressing the button for the 31st floor, he steps back, hands behind him with the width of the elevator between us. Then he gives me the full force of his gaze.

"I haven't had sex in seven months, and that was..." His jaw sets. "Cole was with us. Before that, it had been—"

"Seven weeks." I remember that night, the angry sex, with agonizing shame. "You didn't come inside me." I peer at him from across the elevator, begging for forgiveness. "We haven't been together, *really* been together, in over a year."

He nods, eyes hard and unblinking as he glares at the painful-looking erection pressing behind his zipper. "I'm...excited."

It's a strange, wonderfully endearing thing to hear from such a self-restrained man.

"I want to..." I step toward him hesitantly. "I need to kiss you."

The elevator dings. The doors open, and I wait, caught in the heat of his eyes.

"Go in." His hoarse growl shivers through me.

The moment I step into the penthouse, he spins me to face him and lifts me from the floor.

His tall frame crushes me against the wall, vibrating with strength and power. His hands tangle in my hair, and his mouth devours my gasp. Despite the urgent tension in his body, his kiss is tender. He licks across my lips, parting them with his tongue, and sinks slowly inside.

We share a thousand unspoken whispers, tasting and savoring each one. Beneath the kisses, however, lurks something more primitive, carnal. His cock presses hard against my hip, and I slide a hand around the warmth of his neck, bracing for it, anticipating it.

"On your knees." He lowers my feet, panting. "I'm going to use your mouth to take the edge off." The hot warning caresses my ear. "Then I'll fuck you properly."

With a shiver, I slide down the wall, roaming my hands across his shirt and tracing the ridged muscle beneath. When my knees meet the floor, I stroke the flexing strength in his thighs, front to back, glorying in the hard shape of his ass.

"Don't toy with me." He flattens his palms on the wall, head lowered between his arms, watching me with hooded eyes.

With trembling hands, I unfasten his belt, lower the zipper, and free his swollen length. He's so aroused there's a damp spot on his briefs.

"You're beautiful." I pull his clothes down his thighs, exposing every thick inch of him.

"Suck me, Danni."

His legs shake as I touch my lips to the broad crown and sip gently. He groans, low and rough, and his breaths grow louder, shorter. I expect him to slam into my mouth, but he doesn't.

He's giving me control. His hands remain on the

wall. He doesn't thrust, doesn't grab my head and force my mouth on him. He just stands before me, hungry and coiled with desire, and allows me to enjoy him.

Stretching my jaw, I take him fully into my mouth, sucking him to the back of my throat.

"Fuck." He grunts, chest heaving, and adjusts his feet on the floor.

His reactions turn me on like nothing else. Thighs clenching, I grip the base of his cock and stroke as I suck. My other hand takes care of his balls, kneading and rubbing and sending him into a groaning fit of primal need. He explodes within seconds, shooting streams of come down my throat while shouting my name.

I lick and nuzzle his spent cock as his body slackens and his breathing returns to normal.

"Thank you." He cups my face, eyes sleepy, looking for all the world like a happy man.

"Better?"

"Ask me in a few days. I have a lot more of that to work out of my system. It might take years."

"Just keep me hydrated." I slide up his body, pulling off his suit jacket. "I'm all yours."

"You think I'm kidding." Gripping my backside, he runs his hands upward and shapes my hips, my waist, my breasts. A hard squeeze makes me whimper and wriggle closer.

"Remove your clothes." His breath kisses my throat, his mouth wet as he nibbles and bites.

Shivering, I step back. Then I turn and walk slowly toward the bedroom, putting a sway in my hips.

The sound of his footsteps trails me down the hall. I unclasp the beaded bra and let it dangle from an outstretched finger before dropping it and glancing over my shoulder.

He prowls behind me, expression smoldering as he slowly unbuttons the cuffs on his sleeves. His trousers are back in place, unzipped and hanging precariously on his hips. Heavy-lidded eyes, lips swollen from our kisses, he's so potently, seductively good-looking my brain stops working whenever I look at him.

I veer into his bedroom and tackle my skirt. As I start to shove it down, I remind myself to go slow, to tease and seduce, to make this as perfect for him as I can.

Rolling my hips, I slide the lacy material downward and take the panties with it. As each inch of my nudity is revealed, his breathing grows louder behind me. I don't give into the temptation to look back until I'm completely bare. Then I turn my head.

His shirt lies on the floor at his feet, his upper body ripped with lean muscle from throat to groin.

"Don't move." He closes the distance in three slow strides, making my blood burn hot with nervous desire.

His mouth brushes my shoulder, and my skin sizzles. His tongue curls around my earlobe, and I moan.

"So delicate yet so strong." He feathers his fingertips down my back.

"So handsome yet so cruel." I reach back and grip his hard thigh. "Stop teasing and take off your pants."

To my surprise, he obeys, stripping quickly before lifting me up and dumping me on the bed. I roll to my back, and he climbs up my body, kissing and licking his way to my mouth. Then he straddles my waist and thrusts his tongue past my lips.

He's hard again, the heavy weight of his cock jerking against my abs as he kisses me with deep, greedy

three is a war

tastes. Just when I think I can't bear another teasing second, he moves back down my body, his hands and tongue worshiping every dip and curve.

"Come back," I groan, pulling on his arm and squirming beneath his tickling lips. "I want to breathe in your sexiness."

"Hold still." He nips at my hipbone and wedges his shoulders between my legs, spreading me wide.

When his gaze lowers to my pussy, he sucks in a breath.

"No piercing?" His eyes narrow on mine.

"I removed it. I thought…" I got the piercing with Cole, and reminders of him hurt my heart.

"It's okay." He runs a hand up my chest and pinches a nipple. "There are plenty of other places to wear jewelry."

"I love you." I stroke my fingers through the soft texture of his blond hair.

"I love you, too." He presses a kiss to my navel.

Then he returns to my pussy and uses his finger and tongue to send me into a writhing, moaning, mindless blob of liquid bones. One orgasm isn't good enough. He spends another ten minutes pushing me over the edge again.

Smiling an intoxicating rare smile, he moves up my body and frames my face in his warm hands. I'm so wet there's no need to work himself in.

A shift of his hips aligns us, and he imprisons me in the bright fervency of his eyes. Then he sinks inside, fitting our bodies together with agonizing slowness. Languidly, heavily, he strokes along my inner walls. We groan together, lips seeking and colliding. My nerve-endings stir and my chest tingles as our tongues dance and mate, licking and rubbing before going wild.

When he breaks the kiss, it's to stare into my eyes. Then he kisses me again, going back and forth, looking at me, kissing me, like he can't get close enough, deep enough. All the while, the roll of his hips maintains a tortuously slow pace.

He's never made love to me like this before. I feel everything. Not just the physical connection, but the soul-deep attachment. He's inside me, in my heart, exactly where he's supposed to be.

I sense the moment he climbs toward the pinnacle. His rhythm accelerates, and he hooks an arm beneath my knee, shoving my leg up and out, stretching me wider.

"With me," he gasps against my lips and thrusts more aggressively, urgently.

"I'm with you." I buck against his driving hips, chasing the pleasure and trembling against the swelling surge. "Fuck me. Hard. Harder."

He rides me like a damn devil, grinding, ramming in and out. It's so good, so impossibly perfect. But it's his unwavering eye contact that sends me over. I come with his name ripping from my throat, and he explodes with me, his gaze naked and feral as he grunts and thrusts to completion.

I sag, limp and breathless, against the mattress with the thrum of his heart as my only anchor. This isn't a dream. It's really happening.

Despite his orgasm, he continues to move inside me. Then he takes my mouth, gifting me with a kiss as raw and satisfying as the sex.

"I'm not finished with you." He bites at my lips.

"Promise?" I kiss him back.

three is a war

"I promise those will be the last words you hear before you fall asleep."

"Every night?"

"For the rest of my life."

twenty-four

"I can't believe he's taking you to the French Riviera for your honeymoon." My sister releases a dreamy sigh and props an elbow on the table in her kitchen.

"I can't believe he gave up control of his casino operations to do philanthropy work." My chest swells for the thousandth time in three weeks.

Three weeks of utter bliss in Trace's bed, on his stage, and in his arms. He nourishes me physically and soulfully. All forms of happiness are insubstantial beside him.

"He what?" Bree's jaw drops, her voice shrilling against my ears.

"Shh." I shoot her a glare.

We both turn our heads toward the doorway and stare at the far corner of the living room. My five-year-old niece, Angel, perches on a tiny chair at a kid's activity table. Beside her, Trace sits on the floor with his legs stretched out beneath the table. He's such a big man it looks like a plastic tray on his lap.

With their backs to the kitchen, their heads bow in concentration as they color with crayons. They connect on some enigmatic level I don't understand. It's irresistibly charming.

I shift back to Bree and speak quietly. "He launched a private foundation to help homeless people secure jobs, but it's not just about finding employment. Through donations, he's funding training programs that teach job skills. Skills that will increase their earnings as they transition out of homelessness."

She reaches across the table and grips my hand. "You're so excited your voice actually rises an octave when you talk about it."

"I *am* excited. We're talking huge donations, Bree. With his network of business partners, he'll be able to pull in high-profile sponsors for events like charity dinners and galas."

"The kind of dinners and galas you used to perform at? Will you dance at them?"

"That's the plan." Happiness doesn't begin to describe the huge feeling in my chest. "I have no doubt he'll run this like he runs everything else."

"Like a boss." Bree smiles.

I was going to say meticulous, overbearing controller, but yeah… "Like a boss."

"He made this career change for you?"

I shake my head. "He started pursuing it six months ago. When I was with Cole."

"He definitely did it for you." She gives me a

three is a war

knowing look. "Whether you would be part of it or not, you inspired him."

We fall silent, our attentions returning to the quiet, imposing man and his tiny demonic sidekick in the living room.

In one week, I'm going to marry Trace Savoy. I didn't choose a ballroom dance or a song, and there won't be any choreography. Just like love, our first dance isn't a choice. I won't control it. It's just going to happen, and I'll hold onto every second of it for dear life.

When I told him this, I ended up naked and thoroughly pleasured on the counter in his kitchen.

Our kitchen.

I moved in with him immediately, and we spend most of our time together in bed. I wake every morning tucked into his body, his muscular arm clamped around my back and his thigh bent between my mine. The best part of my day is watching those sleepy blue eyes whisper good morning to me.

When I'm not working, we run errands, go to dinner, watch movies. Really, we don't need to do anything to pass the time. We just need each other.

I haven't sold my house. I won't. As much progress as I've made on healing the jagged hole Cole left behind, I can't give up the home he bought for me, the dance room he built for me, or the memories that cling to the walls. So I'm renting it to Nikolai. It's twice the size of the crappy apartment he lived in, and he no longer has to borrow space at another school to teach his dance students.

I don't have any plans to reopen my dance company. Teaching was a means to pay the bills and never my passion. That said, I haven't worked much over the past three weeks. When I negotiated the employment contract that night in my house, I failed to look at the fine print. Trace sneaked in a restriction that states I can work a maximum of two hours per night. No wonder he didn't argue when I changed the schedule to seven days a week.

His deviousness is irritating in the best way possible. He challenges me constantly, dominates me to no end, and keeps me coming back for more.

"I need to use the bathroom." Bree rises from the table and vanishes around the corner.

I stand, too, and make my way to the living room.

Crouching behind Trace, I rub my hands over the crisp fabric of his t-shirt. "Did you starch this?"

"Maybe." He looks at me over his shoulder.

I immediately forget what we're talking about because that devastating grin, it ravages my senses and catches at my heart.

Resting my cheek on his shoulder, I hug him from behind and breathe in his masculine heat. He returns to his crayons, letting me caress his chest and pepper kisses across his nape. There's so much sexual energy contained within his powerful body it's bone-melting when he unleashes it. And he *will* unleash it the moment we get home.

I lean between him and Angel, studying the drawing beneath his crayon. The cartoon-ish lines were etched by a child — a rather artistic child — but why did she draw a picture of a horned, dog-like beast with blazing red eyes? I can only imagine what Trace is thinking as he colors it in.

"Trace drew this one. See?" Angel holds up a stick-figure woman dancing on tiptoes. "It's sexy Aunt Danni."

Sexy? How does she know that word? I glance at

three is a war

Trace and find his smoky eyes fixated on my mouth.

"You can't teach her that." I bite down on my smile.

"I just did." His voice, bedroom gruff and pure naughtiness, steals my breath.

"I don't think it looks like you." Angel examines the picture. "Your face looks more like a dog."

"What kind of dog?" *Please don't say a horned beast with red eyes.*

"A dead dog."

I don't even know what to say to that.

"Angel." Trace drops his tone in warning. "We talked about this. If you want to persuade and intimidate, do it with your attitude, not your words."

"I want to be like you." She lifts her chin, staring at him with adoration.

"I'll teach you." He pats her head, making her pigtails bounce.

"Oh, dear God," I mutter under my breath.

"There is no God. Only Zuul." She smiles, but it doesn't touch her huge, brown demonic eyes.

My mouth falls open. She's been all about God for as long as I can remember. What changed?

"I'm afraid to ask who Zuul is," I say just as Bree walks into the room.

My sister looks over the drawing of the horned dog and makes a pained face. "Her obsession with Christianity has moved on to...*Ghostbusters*." She lifts Angel from the chair and gives her a nudge toward the hall. "It's bath time, young lady."

"I like him better." Angel points at Trace as she struts by. "The other one had holes in his cheeks."

Dimples.

Cole.

My heart freezes in my chest, my entire body paralyzed beneath a wave of torment.

As Bree and Angel disappear down the hall, Trace wraps a hand around my neck and uses his grip to guide me onto his lap.

"Talk to me." He pushes the coloring table to the side and leans back against the side of the couch.

"I'm fine." I curl up against his chest and wrap my arms around him. "It's just… Sometimes, she's painfully honest."

"She's five." He strokes his thumb across my throat, the touch possessive and comforting. "And logical. Of course, she likes me better. I don't have holes in my cheeks." At my ragged sigh, he brushes a lock of hair behind my ear. "Keep talking."

"When he died, it left a permanent wound inside me. I think I've been subconsciously moving on from him for years, but the tiniest thing can reopen the wound, and once it's open, it takes a while to stop the bleeding." I straighten and meet his eyes. "I don't regret, but I think about him often and feel heavy with sadness. I miss him."

"I know." His expression softens. "I miss him, too."

"But you talk to him."

"Yes."

"I need to know." I shift on his lap, putting my face in his and clutching his shoulders. "You have to tell how he's doing."

"He's okay, Danni." His thick lashes lower, lift again, revealing eyes warm with compassion. "He's going back to work."

three is a war

"The job offers..." My breath stammers, and my stomach turns to ice. "He said it was dangerous."

"His job has always been dangerous. He's good at it. Good enough that I don't worry about his safety." He runs his fingers through my hair, soothing me.

"Did he let me go because—?"

"I'm the one who talked him into working again. That conversation began *after* you came back to me." His hand tightens against my neck, punctuating his words. "I know him. He needs the distraction. Understand?"

"Yeah." I don't like it, but I gave up all rights to have a say in Cole's life. "Thank you for telling me. And for being there for him."

"He was there for me. Funny how that worked out, huh? Despite it all, we salvaged our friendship."

It's more than I could've ever asked for, and I'm so fucking grateful.

"Go tell your sister good-bye." He lifts me off his lap. "We're leaving."

And just like that, the conversation is over. I love that I can count on him to listen when I need him and to shut it down before it becomes repetitive and unproductive.

On the ride home, I sit beside him in the Maserati, thoughtfully silent and focused on the future. I'm getting married in a week. Trace is spearheading a foundation for the homeless—a cause that's near and dear to my heart. And I'm sitting beside a man who sets my skin afire with merely a look. Like now.

"You should probably keep your eyes on the road." Just the thought of having him inside me again, all swollen heat and hunger, makes my thighs clench.

"Then I'll have to use my hand." Deliberately lowering his voice to the pitch of sex, he roams a hand up my thigh and teases the fly on my jeans. "I told you to wear a skirt."

"And I told you it was too cold."

He slides his touch away to shift through the gears, and I'm momentarily distracted by how strikingly attractive he looks driving this sporty piece of hot metal. His hand drapes over the steering wheel, the leather seat molding around all that powerful muscle, as he zips through traffic with a wildness that magnifies his confident male beauty.

The night sparkles around us, shining brighter up ahead where the casino towers over the horizon. He veers onto the next street and heads in the opposite direction of the penthouse.

"Where are you going?" My lower body melts as the hand returns between my legs.

"It's a surprise."

"What kind of surprise?"

"The kind I won't tell you about, so don't ask again."

He crosses the bridge into Illinois and drives twenty minutes to the town of Belleville. There's not a lot in this area, but the moment he pulls up to the huge *Skyview Drive-In* sign, I bounce in the seat.

"Is it open?" I only see a couple cars in the parking lot.

"365 days a year." He pays the attendant at the drive-through window and parks at the far end of the lot, away from the other two cars.

Movie trailers flicker across the massive screen, revving my excitement. I've never been to a drive-in, especially not in January. I suspect it's a lot busier in the summer months, when movie watchers can sit atop their cars and enjoy this uniquely American experience beneath the stars.

"Where are the speaker poles?" I scan the empty parking lot, wondering how we'll listen to the movie. "I thought there were little boxes that hang on the car windows."

"They were replaced with an FM broadcasting system." He leaves the engine running and cranks up the heat.

As he tunes the radio to the right FM station, the screen lights up with a movie intro that hitches my breath.

"*Dirty Dancing.*" I shake my head, grinning. "How did you—?"

"I made a request a couple weeks ago." He hits a button that reverses his seat as far back as it will go. Then he bores his gaze into mine. "Remove your clothes."

Deep and gravelly, his command tightens my nipples against the satin of my bra. The man is raw, hard, biteable perfection, and the pleasure he ignites in my body is ruthless.

Even if the tinted windows didn't conceal my nudity, I would obey simply because it pleases him. Jeans, sweater, boots, undergarments—I remove it all and kneel on the seat, facing him.

His lashes hood over eyes glowing with male approval. "Come here."

Fragile tremors tiptoe across my skin as I crawl over the console. The space is so tight I don't know how we'll fit behind the steering wheel.

Hands on his shoulders for balance, I place a knee on the seat between his thighs. With my lips so close to his, he kisses me, his mouth hot and moist, his tongue rubbing against mine and the hand on my bare butt possessive as always.

The heat of his body heightens the kiss, stirring and warming the deepest parts of me. He caresses my backside and licks lazily inside my mouth. No tension. No time lines. Nothing but the contentment of togetherness humming between us.

The movie soundtrack streams through the car speakers, drowning out the panting sounds of our breaths. He pulls me closer, breaking the kiss to position my body on his lap with my back to his chest.

"I want your mouth." I twist toward him.

"Watch the movie." He clasps my waist and turns me back.

Gritting my teeth, I rein in the compulsion to steal another kiss. He intends to torment me, his hands already wandering over my nude skin. The best movie of all time fills the windshield, but I can't concentrate on it. Not with his grip on my thighs, spreading me open and hooking my legs around the outsides of his.

He has full access to my body and takes advantage. Cradling my back with his chest, he nibbles at my throat and swirls his fingers through my wet heat until pleasure weighs down my bones.

The lips on my neck are relentless as he presses his wicked touch inside me. Sinking to the deepest knuckle, he grinds in and rubs the spot behind my pelvic bone as his thumb plays with my clit.

The first orgasm hits hard and fast, priming me for another. I squirm on his lap, and he pins me tight against

three is a war

him, thrusting his hand and holding me on the precipice.

"I love to feel you come." The thickness of his voice makes my body ache, but deeper and longer lasting is the grip he has on my heart.

He continues to finger me and buries his face against my neck, sliding his cheek against mine, his hips moving just enough to let me feel how badly he wants me.

Desire hot in my veins, I come again, this one harder, tighter, robbing my breath.

"Trace!" I writhe on his hand, my nipples pointing skyward, which he doesn't hesitate to torture with a brutal pinch.

When he finally removes his fingers, he wraps a hand around my throat, angling my head back to attack my mouth.

His kiss is raw and aggressive as he releases himself from his pants. "Sit on my cock."

Breathless and shivering, I reach beneath me, curl my fingers around the hot length of his erection, and stroke. He could easily haul me down and slam himself to the root, but he seems utterly lost in the kiss. Lips raw and tongue deep, he focuses all his attention on my mouth.

I caress his cock through the kiss, but eventually I can't wait any longer. Dropping my head back on his muscled shoulder, I position him against me and slide down on his hardness. We both moan, and his hands sweep over my chest, my hips, and my pussy.

He widens my thighs and pushes deep, rocking into me, his body tightening and shaking around me. I reach between our legs and play with his balls as he thrusts deeper, faster. With a groan, he returns his lips to my neck, biting and licking and pushing me closer to oblivion.

I moan in the back of my throat with every grinding flex of his hips. Blissful fulfillment waits at the peak, luring me, demanding my surrender. But it's his fingers wrapping around my throat, the perfect pressure of his iron fist, that unravels me.

My legs fall open to the thick, relentless slide of his cock, and I scream, shuddering in ecstasy. As he joins me, it's with my name on his breath, his muscles clenching and releasing and fingers pressing against my skin with unbridled passion.

After, I lift off him, twisting to straddle his lap. Then I kiss him the way I want to, with playfulness and affection, sliding my hands beneath his t-shirt to molest all that hot skin over steely muscle. His lips taste like untamed love and his breaths fill my lungs with the strength of his happiness.

"It's always going to be like this, isn't it?" I trail a path of kisses across his bottom lip.

"Yes." Dauntless and inviolable, his confidence is my sanctity.

"I will always, always love you." I kiss him again. "Down to the very depths of you. Thank you for showing me how to smile again."

twenty-five

The restaurant erupts in rowdy cheers as Trace kisses me long and hard on the stage at the center of the dining room. *You may kiss the bride* reverberates through the chambers of my heart, expanding my chest to accommodate the overwhelming swell of emotion.

We did it.

We're married.

It's so surreal I continue to stand in place after he jumps down and holds up his hand. The hard, shiny band of platinum on his finger is made of elegant, unbending strength like the man I chose it for.

He's wearing a wedding ring.

This obscenely gorgeous man in a tailored black tuxedo with arresting blue eyes is my husband.

I pinch myself to make sure it's real.

He transformed Bissara into an opulent seating room for the wedding ceremony and stood beside me on the stage encased in the beam of light as we made our vows. There's no place in the world I would've rather married. He fell in love with me when he first saw me at the restaurant. I fell in love with him while I danced on this stage. He proposed to me right here in this dining room.

This is our home.

"Mrs. Savoy." He grips my hand and pulls me to the edge. "You owe me a dance before I take you upstairs and rip that dress from your hot little body."

There's no way I'm letting him destroy this dress. The sleeveless sweetheart neckline and heavily embellished bodice hugs my frame like a dream. Ruffles of white lace tumble from my waist in a romantic *A*-line. The layering of the skirt gives it a bohemian feel with the illusion of a back chapel train. It flows around my legs without tangling, making it ideal for dancing. He did good. Better than good. I couldn't have picked a more perfect dress.

I lean toward him, and he clutches my waist, swinging me off the stage. Then we're moving, caught up in a chaotic whirlwind as two-hundred wedding guests make their way to the ballroom.

He didn't close the gaming area, so there are unfamiliar smiles everywhere, people crowding around to check out the excitement.

We wind through the maze of clinking, flashing slot machines, stopping every few feet for handshakes, hugs, and tearful congratulations from wedding guests and casino patrons. It takes forever to walk such a short distance, but Trace holds tight to my hand the entire

three is a war

time.

Until he doesn't.

He jerks away from me, his attention on something in the crowd.

"Trace?" I grip his arm, following his gaze, unable to see whatever it is he's looking for.

"I need to…" He sprints away, pushing through the throngs of people in his hurry.

My stomach hardens, and a chill skates down my spine. What the hell is happening?

I crane my neck, holding my breath. That's when I see it.

The back of a black leather jacket.

The military-style cut of familiar brown hair.

Trace is chasing Cole.

My heart falls with an agonizing thud. I scoop it up, along with layers of ruffled lace, and chase them.

Evidently, the sight of a runaway bride makes people scatter, because the crowd parts as I barrel forward, hugging the skirts around my thighs. I spot Trace at the entrance twenty feet away. He shoves his way through the doors and vanishes into the night.

I pick up my pace, pulse racing and lungs burning. I have no idea what I'll find when I get there, but my eyes are already aching with tears.

Just inside the lobby, I reach the exterior glass door and slam to a stop, spotting them instantly. My hand flies to my mouth, stifling a whimper.

Cole's motorcycle is parked on the curb of the circle drive. He and Trace stand beside it, locked in an embrace. Trace's head is lowered, his mouth moving at Cole's ear as Cole nods and hugs him tighter.

Silent tears stream down my face. I press my palm to the glass, dying to go to them. But I won't. I never want to come between them again.

Cole's hair is shorter, his brawn impossibly more defined. He looks harder, older, but healthy. I wouldn't dare say he's happy, but the set of his shoulders shows purpose, his posture radiating determination. His eyes… I can't see…

He lifts his head and stares directly at me. I stop breathing, and my hand slides off the window, falling to my side.

Trace releases him, and they step back. Cole rests his fingers in his jean pockets, scans my wedding gown from chest to toes, and returns to my eyes.

"Be happy," he mouths and gives me a soft dimpled smile.

My lips curve upward, despite the terrible tremble in my chin. "Be safe."

He stares at me as I stare at him, suspended in a moment as defining as the day we met. Our story began and ended with a smile, every second in between marked with love.

He looks away first, and my insides pull painfully. He and Trace exchange more words, their postures relaxed and eyes bright.

Without another glance in my direction, Cole straddles the motorcycle and rumbles out of my life the same way he rumbled into it.

I feel the loss all over again, but it's swaddled in an unexplainable sense of peace. I watch the fade of his taillight long after the darkness swallows it, and so does Trace.

Eventually, Trace turns to me and shakes his head

three is a war

with a concerned look on his face. He strides in my direction and steps inside.

"Sorry I left you standing there." He pulls a tissue from his pocket and wipes my cheeks. "You messed up your makeup."

"I don't care about the makeup." I grip his wrist, stalling his hand. "You invited him?"

"Yes. I thought you both might need closure."

"I know you told me you're still friends, but witnessing with my own eyes…" My chest hitches with a ragged breath. "It's the best wedding gift you could've given me. Thank you."

"You're welcome." He pockets the tissue, studying me closely. "You can ask me what we talked about."

"If I need to know, I trust you'll tell me."

He cradles my face in his hands and leans his forehead against mine. "I love you, Danni Savoy."

"I love y—"

He kisses the words from my mouth with a passion that choreographs the dance of my heart.

Hours later, after dinner and speeches and cake, we stand at the center of the dance floor, surrounded by friends and family. Bree and my parents, colleagues and old neighbors—everyone is here.

"This is it, my tiny dancer." He trails his fingertips across my cheek. "Your one and only chance to put a dance in the history books of best-ever first dances. No pressure."

"I'm not sweating it." I might be sweating it.

A few minutes ago, I gave the DJ a song title, one I didn't have to think about. I meet the DJ's eyes, letting him know I'm ready. Then I turn back to Trace and smile.

The piano harmony of *Yours* by Ella Henderson spirals around us, pulling us closer, chest to chest, hand and hand, hearts beating.

"You're my waltz." I kiss his neck, whisper in his ear, "I'm yours."

His chest rises and falls on a deep inhale. Then we move together, our love leading the steps, guiding our breaths, carrying us elegantly, fluidly across the floor with sweeping turns.

I cling to him, all wide shoulders and arctic eyes, lost in his depths. This is the dance, the one I'll always remember. To everyone watching, it's a waltz—the controlled, pronounced, wave-like rise and fall. But to us, it's the beginning of forever, the swelling and contracting of passion, with our hearts thundering at the center of the turns.

"I'll never be finished with you." He yanks me close, his breath at my ear.

"Good thing this is a forever thing."

The moments, the memories, the pain, and the happiness—I'm grateful for it all.

Everything led me to him.

books by pam godwin

DARK ROMANCE
DELIVER SERIES
Deliver #1
Vanquish #2
Disclaim #3

DARK PARANORMAL ROMANCE
TRILOGY OF EVE
Heart of Eve (FREE)
Dead of Eve #1
Blood of Eve #2
Dawn of Eve #3

STUDENT-TEACHER ROMANCE
Dark Notes

ROCK-STAR DARK ROMANCE
Beneath the Burn

ROMANTIC SUSPENSE
Dirty Ties

EROTIC ROMANCE
An Infidelity World book
Incentive

playlist

Go To War by Nothing More
This Is What You Came For by Calvin Harris
Talking Body by Tove Lo
Lovesong by Adele
Back to Black by Amy Winehouse
Wait (The Whisper Song) by Ying Yang Twins
Yeah by Usher
Lose My Breath by Destiny's Child
Booty by Jennifer Lopez
You Don't Know by Katelyn Tarver
Where's My Love by SYML
Honest by The Chainsmokers
XO by Beyoncé
Let It Go by James Bay
What Is Love by V Bozeman
Whenever, Wherever by Shakira
Yours by Ella Henderson

thank you

First and foremost, a huge thank you to my beta readers — Ellie, Helene, E.M, Angela, Ketty, Shabby, LittleKitten, Shea, Brooke, Jillian, and Ann — for giving me the best feedback ever. Not only did you read this under the pressure of a deadline, your suggestions were beyond perfect. I can't tell you how much I appreciate your endless help.

To bloggers, readers, authors, friends, and family — you support me in so many ways I'm forever in your debt. This is a challenging business to be in — the ungodly hours, pressure, and demands. Your continued encouragement doesn't just make it easier to publish. You make this adventure exciting in every way. I can't imagine doing this without you. Thank you so much for everything you do.

pam godwin

New York Times and USA Today Bestselling author, Pam Godwin, lives in the Midwest with her husband, their two children, and a foulmouthed parrot. When she ran away, she traveled fourteen countries across five continents, attended three universities, and married the vocalist of her favorite rock band.

Java, tobacco, and dark romance novels are her favorite indulgences, and might be considered more unhealthy than her aversion to sleeping, eating meat, and dolls with blinking eyes.

EMAIL: pamgodwinauthor@gmail.com
www.pamgodwin.com

Printed in Great Britain
by Amazon